The Philadelphia Matriarch

Beth Brubaker

Published by Beth Brubaker, 2025.

This is a work of fiction. Similarities to real people, places, or events are entirely coincidental.

THE PHILADELPHIA MATRIARCH

First edition. August 21, 2025.

ISBN: 979-8999136206

Written by Beth Brubaker.

Table of Contents

Dedication

This book began as a whisper from the past—a family story half-told, half-lost—and grew into a journey I never could have imagined. I owe its very heartbeat to the real women who inspired it: my grandmother, Florence, and her mother, Estella. Though time and circumstances separated them, their bond, strength, and stories found their way to me. This is for them.

To my best friend and husband, Scott—thank you for your steady support, your endless patience, and for believing in this dream even when I was buried in drafts, doubts, and far too many moods. And to my children, who endured plot rants at dinner and emotional whiplash during edits—thank you for letting me chase this calling. You've lived with these characters almost as long as I have, and I couldn't have done this without you.

To the beta readers, and mentors who guided this manuscript into its final form—you made me a better writer. Your insight, honesty, and encouragement helped me find the soul of the story.

To my savvy marketing friend—thank you for your unwavering patience with my marketing-challenged brain. You nudged (okay, shoved) me into arenas I never thought I belonged in—and somehow made it all feel possible. I'm endlessly grateful for your vision, your generosity, and your good humor.

To my readers—thank you for opening this book. Whether you came for the history, the heartache, or the hope, I'm honored to share this journey with you.

And finally, to every woman who's ever been underestimated, silenced, or left to start over alone—this is for you. May your story be told.

Happy Heavenly Birthday, Mom (21 August).

The Fidler Family of Philadelphia

Aaron J. Fidler Virginia Estella Fox

(1882-1946) (1883-1966)

Frances Fidler John Fidler Florence Fitler*

(1902-1989) (1903-1969) (1905-1989)

Florence m. William S. Adams (1924)

(Children: William Adams, Jr., Dean Adams, Gerald
Adams, Ronald Adams, Dale Adams, Sylvia Adams**,
Donna Adams, Robert Adams)

*Florence's last name was changed to Fitler when she
returned to Philadelphia and applied for a Marriage License.

** Author Beth Brubaker's mother

THE AMISH FARM
Florence, Age 8 | Lancaster County | Spring 1913

The light patter of rain against the roof gently stirred Florence from her deep slumber. Morning had come, soft and gray, and before long the day's work would call her into full motion.

She sat up slowly, blinking sleep from her eyes, and began to dress in the quiet dimness of her room. From below, the familiar clatter of pots and pans told her Mamm was already busy in the kitchen.

Crossing to the window, Florence peered through the misted glass. The lights in the barn cast a soft glow in the rain, and through the haze she saw the silhouette of her Daed finishing the morning milking. It wouldn't be long before he came in for breakfast. She knew she'd best be downstairs quickly to help.

Her bare feet padded down the hallway, then scurried across the top of the stairs. She descended quietly, her head slightly bowed.

"Gude mornin', Mamm," she said softly, her eyes lifting to meet her mother's briefly before she turned to set the table.

Mamm Sara responded without turning from the stove. "Mornin', girl. You'd best hurry, your Daed will be in soon for breakfast. He's headin' into town for the sale barn, and he mustn't be late."

Florence nodded and moved with quiet purpose. She sliced the fresh bread and buttered it while it was still warm, watching the butter melt into the soft crevices. The scent of sausage and eggs filled the kitchen, mingling with the earthy aroma of rain-soaked wood outside. It was a simple morning, like so many before, but for Florence, it was one of quiet belongings.

The long plain table was set with plates of dippy eggs, sausages, and fried potatoes. The bread was set in the middle to be passed around after prayer. A jar of homemade raspberry preserves was set beside it. Sara had already begun to pack a sack lunch for Amos to bring along to the sale barn.

The screech of the back kitchen door hinge told them that Amos had returned from the barn. He carefully removed his shoes before walking across the clean floors. He quietly whispered in his soft, low voice, "Gude mornin', wife and girl. Let us sit together".

Amos took his place at the head of the table while Sara and Florence sat across from one another on either side of him. They bowed their heads while Amos led them in prayer, "Dear God, bless this food and sanctify it. Use it for the enrichment of my body. Bless the hands that have provided this food and bless those who need food and shelter. Bless this day and make it a productive one. In Jesus' name, Amen".

They ate heartily, knowing the day would be demanding and that another family meal wouldn't come until nightfall. They sopped up the dippy eggs with buttery bread, leaving the plates nearly spotless. Afterward, Amos shared his hopes for the sale barn—he was looking to add a new horse to the farm. With the spring rains nourishing the fields, the workload was growing, and an extra four-legged helper would ease the burden. On the way, he planned to stop at Jacob Weaver's farm to drop off the morning milk. The two men had arranged to ride to the sale together.

Sara and Florence had a full day of chores ahead that would be long and laborious since the gentle rains had let up. The sun was just beginning to peak through the clouds and a light fog began to lift off the fields. Before any outdoor chores, the kitchen needed to be tidied and cleaned. There were other meal preps and bread to be started. Amos softly spoke and all bowed their heads again while he gave a brief prayer of thanks for the meal, "Lord, thank thee for this meal together". The Blank family set about the day.

While Sara began clearing the breakfast dishes, Florence headed out back to the woodpile, gathering splits for the stove. On her return, she slipped on the wet step and nearly dropped the bundle of wood. The stove was the home's only source of heat. Though spring had arrived, a damp chill still hung in the air, and the kitchen remained the warmest room in the house. That was a comfort in the cooler months—but in the summer, when bread, pies, and other hot meals were still being baked, it made for stifling days.

"Come here and finish the breakfast dishes once you put up the wood," Sara said firmly.

She dried her hands, then turned to the side table to begin preparing the bread dough. Measuring out the flour with practiced ease, she added a sprinkle of salt and made a well in the center for the liquid. Slowly, she brought the mixture together into a wet dough, kneading it with steady, purposeful movements. Once it reached the right consistency, she shaped it into a firm round and covered it with a damp towel. She set it near the oven, where the gentle heat would help it rise just right.

Sara and Florence finished up the morning kitchen tasks together, moving in quiet rhythm as they wiped down the table and rinsed the last of the bowls. Outside, the spring garden—planted from seed several weeks earlier—was beginning to take shape. So too were the weeds, sprouting eagerly alongside the tender shoots. Much of the morning would be spent tending the rows and pulling stubborn roots from the earth.

Florence was especially eager to plant her marigold seeds that day, scattering them along the garden's perimeter. She adored the golden blooms, watching with wonder as something so bright and fragrant could come from such a small, hard seed. For her, the marigolds were the garden's reward—a touch of beauty earned by early mornings and dirt under the fingernails.

Sara, ever practical, reminded her they served a purpose: to help keep pests away from the vegetables. Florence didn't mind that they weren't always effective. Truthfully, they didn't keep much away, and she often found herself tasked with soaping the leaves to deter insects anyway. Still, she loved them. To her, they made the garden feel complete.

While Mamm Sara and Florence toiled away in the garden they talked aloud about the upcoming barn raising and the food they would prepare and bring for the big gathering. Sara was known for her incredible pies. Florence smiled and asked, "Can you please make the shoofly pie—and the peach, too?"

Sara thought for a moment before speaking and said, "I'll check the canned goods and may have some peaches that we put up last year." It was still too early for some of the berry pies so that was settled for now.

The chatter continued until Sara approached Florence and pressed a small brown bag into her hands. Florence looked up at her Mamm with wide eyes, her face lighting up with quiet gratitude. Scrawled in pencil on the front of the bag was a single word: "ZINNIAS". It was the first time Sara saw a flicker of joy return to her daughter's eyes.

"Girl," Mamm said, her tone brisk but not unkind, "get those seeds into the wet ground quick—and fetch the eggs on your way back in. I need to finish the bread and get us a light meal."

Each one knew the morning routine by heart, and off they went in their separate directions. Florence hummed a tune from the hymns they sang at church. She didn't know the words—they were all in German, a language she'd only heard spoken around her—but she liked how the melody made her feel. There was joy in it, just as there was joy now in the thought of the zinnias her Mamm had given her.

It didn't take long for her to tuck the seeds into the damp earth, scattering them among the marigolds. As she worked, she thought of the bright, cheerful flowers that had bloomed the year before at the Weavers' farm, where they often visited on Sundays after church.

She got closer to the hen house and could hear the final late laying hen squawking proudly at her accomplishment. She knew she had to be quick to grab the egg from this protective, broody hen that would no doubt fly up and try to peck at her hand and make a fuss for the taking. The other hens had already laid and gone about the day foraging for bugs and insects and little morsels in the grassy area next to the barn. As anticipated, the last egg was the most difficult to collect and without haste the hen flew up and out of her laying box, but Florence was prepared and snatched the egg without incident.

Returning with the basket of eggs, she got them sorted, then brushed them off and placed them in the back storage area. Her Mamm would be using them for many meals and the pies they discussed earlier in the garden. She got a rumble in her tummy reminding her she was a bit hungry after all the hard work in the garden. She knew it wouldn't be a huge meal since her father was at the sale barn today, but it would be enough to hush her rumbles until supper.

Sara had returned to punch down her bread dough, setting it aside for its second rise so it would be ready to bake just before her husband came home—hopefully with a new horse in tow. Turning her attention to lunch, she set about preparing a simple meal for herself and Florence. A jar of pickled eggs sat at one end of the long rectangular table where the family shared their meals. She added a bowl of warmed potatoes left from breakfast, then asked Florence to fetch a jar of green beans from the storage room. Sara quickly heated them on the wood stovetop, where the water was already hot and waiting.

Finally, Mamm cut thick slices of warm bread and slathered them with creamy butter for each of them to enjoy alongside their meal. They sat in the same seats they had used at breakfast and ate together in quiet companionship.

It was a satisfying, quiet time of reflection—a morning well spent, with much to look forward to in the season ahead. The promise of a garden soon in full bloom, yielding bounty for the months to come, brought a quiet sense of purpose. Sara ended the meal with a brief prayer of thanks, and the girls rose to tend to their afternoon tasks.

Mamm placed a large roast into the deep oven, seasoning it simply with salt and pepper. Florence cleared the lunch dishes and moved on to light cleaning, humming her favorite tunes under her breath as she worked.

Once the day's tasks were finished, the girls gathered their sewing materials and settled around the large, plain kitchen table. The warmth from the oven was welcome—clouds had gathered overhead, dimming the sun and bringing a chill to the air. Sara spread out the large quilt she'd been working on with the other women and began stitching the squares with practiced precision. Florence focused on a smaller section of the quilt, carefully learning the skills her Mamm was passing down.

They chatted softly as the afternoon passed, with Sara occasionally rising to check Florence's progress, guiding her hands and offering tips on technique and stitchwork.

From the oven, the scent of roasting meat mingled with the yeasty aroma of risen bread—an almost miraculous fragrance that filled the kitchen with warmth and anticipation. It wouldn't be long now before Amos returned from the sale barn. There would be plenty to hear about the day spent with Jacob Weaver and, perhaps, the excitement of bringing home a new horse—an extra set of hooves to help work the land. Supper promised not only good food, but lively conversation, rich with the stories of the day.

***

Amos and Jacob rode quietly in the cart together to New Holland. The air was wet and misty from the gentle soaking rains overnight and the smell of the wet soil was strong with fertilizer. The sun was slowly burning away the layer of fog paving the way for a nice day ahead, but there was still a chill in the air.

The silence was broken when Jacob asked, "Would you consider purchasing two horses if the price is good? It would be a big help on the land, and some of our people are lending out workhorses to neighboring farms."

Amos tilted his head in silent consideration of the question and was slow to reply. "I've been thinking of this possibility since we talked about it at our gathering," he said. "We shall have to see what comes of the day ahead. It would be a valuable resource for many while also providing more for my family." It wasn't much longer until they turned the corner and saw the buggies lined up to the far right of the long sale barn. There were large groups of Amish men mixed with a few English, standing about chatting.

Amos Blank and Jacob Weaver stepped up to the sale window to register for the bidding—a familiar ritual they'd known since boyhood, whenever the farm called for fresh stock. The atmosphere buzzed with anticipation. Noisy chatter filled the air, and a sea of straw hats bobbed atop men dressed in plain black clothes. A few English buyers stood out starkly in their more modern attire.

When the doors opened, the mostly male crowd surged into the area where the horses were held in rows of stalls. Amos didn't have to look long before his eyes landed on a pair of Belgian draft horses—strong, well-muscled animals that looked more than capable of handling the heavy fieldwork. A pair wasn't what he'd set out to find, but the idea took root quickly.

He also noticed a lone Percheron—sturdy, but aged, his best seasons likely behind him. Still, there was something dignified in the way he stood. There were plenty of possibilities, and Amos' practiced eye and steady instinct gave him confidence. He was already beginning to weigh his options as the bidding hour approached.

The two men walked through the barn area and got themselves a spot standing by the arena where the animals would be paraded through for sale. There was a buzz in the air that was stirring before the noise of the auction began. There was a tension building that was palpable until the slam of the small wooden mallet started the process.

Horse after horse was led through and run back and forth until a number was agreed upon, then led out the opposite gate. Meanwhile, another sale would begin and end in the same way. The rhythmic chant of the auctioneer was like a song—blended words slurred together into tongue twisters. It seemed to intensify the urgency, hurrying things along in an almost impulsive manner.

"Whatiwannagive, nowadollar!" shouted the man with the gavel.

Amos found himself bidding on the pair of Belgian draft horses parading back and forth. One other man was trying to outbid him, clearly just as interested in the team, and the price climbed higher and higher. Back and forth they went, until the sharp crack of the gavel finally ended the chaos. Amos was left wondering if he had made the right choice, feeling a twinge of buyer's remorse at that very moment.

It was well past noon when Amos and Jacob finally stepped outside, the bidding behind them. After settling payment for the pair of Belgian draft horses, they took their packed lunches and found a spot to sit in the fresh air. The sun had broken through the clouds, and they welcomed its warmth as they unwrapped their food, letting the weight of the morning settle. The noise of the sale faded into the background, replaced by the quiet satisfaction of a decision well-made and the steady promise of hard work ahead.

A quiet sense of satisfaction settled over both men. The Belgians would ease the strain on Amos' other two draft horses during the demanding season ahead. The cost had been more than he'd intended, but the value they would bring to the farm—and the family—would more than repay itself in time.

Before eating, Amos bowed his head and offered a brief prayer of thanks. Then the men dug into their hearty sandwiches, thick with meat and layered between slices of buttered bread. The food took the edge off the hunger that had crept in during the long morning.

Tucked beside the sandwiches were fresh-baked berry muffins, wrapped in cloth and still faintly warm. Jacob's wife, Rebecca, had added a generous crumbly streusel topping—a sweet finish to the meal and just the fuel they needed before preparing the horses for the journey home.

The men returned to the cart to gather the horse tack they'd need for transporting the newly acquired Belgian team. They decided it would be best to have the two drafts pull the cart, with the other horse tethered behind to follow. It was not an uncommon sight, especially on sale barn days, and they expected a slower ride home.

They went about making the preparations, and soon they were on their way. It was agreed that Amos would head directly to his farm, where, with Jacob's help, they'd ready a space in the barn to quarantine the new horses. The drafts would be kept apart for a couple of weeks as a precaution, with food, water, and a grassy pasture of their own to graze.

Jacob's sons, Isaac and David, were just finishing the milking with Florence when the cart and horses turned into the long driveway of the homestead. They knew the day might stretch late for their father and his friend, so they'd been sent ahead to help with the evening chores.

The boys lit up at the sight of the new horses, and Florence, too, stood in awe of the gentle giants pulling the small cart, the other horse following behind. Their size was impressive, but even more striking was their calm demeanor as they were led into an unfamiliar place that would soon become home.

Florence felt a deep connection to them. She knew what it was like to be somewhere new, surrounded by unknowns. Watching them, she saw herself—quiet, alert, uncertain, and hopeful.

Jacob and his boys rode home together as the sun began to sink below the horizon.

Florence followed her father up the three steps and into the house, where they slipped off their shoes and washed up in the basin of water Sara had thoughtfully left out. Eager for supper and to share the day's events, they joined the others at the long kitchen table.

Sara had prepared another hearty meal, filling the room with comforting aromas. As they ate, Amos shared the big news—the purchase of the Belgian draft horses—and spoke of the return he hoped this investment would bring for the family. Sara listened with quiet relief, glad to hear the conviction in his voice and to know the day had gone well. He had spoken of this need often, and now that it was done, a long-held concern could finally rest.

Darkness set over the farm and while Sara and Florence washed the supper dishes and cleaned the kitchen, Amos caught up with some of his bookkeeping and notes in the corner of the large room aglow in the light of the hanging lantern.

He added more wood to the stove as the nights were still cool. The heat would rise above and warm the bedrooms enough to take the chill off, making a change to night clothes a little more bearable. Soon the oil lamps would be turned out and they would drift off to sleep and begin the day anew.

Florence lay on her bed, gazing out the window toward the new horse pasture beyond the barn. In the moonlight, she could just make out the outline of the two massive horses. The sight stirred a memory—the day she first arrived at the Blank farm several years ago. It had been a time of deep sadness and despair. She'd been so overwhelmed by the loss, she'd nearly crumbled under the weight of it. Her entire world—though only five years long—had been torn away, and this family had taken her in as their own. Yet she was loved and well cared for, an emptiness lingered. A quiet void nestled deep within, unresolved. Lost in these thoughts, she slowly drifted into sleep.

WORKSHOP OF THE WORLD
Estella, 3 Years Earlier | Philadelphia | Summer 1910

Estella sat at the kitchen table, cradling a mug of hot coffee, grateful for a rare moment of quiet contemplation. The children were still asleep, and her husband, Aaron, had just stormed out to work in one of his foul moods. For now, she allowed herself the small luxury of silence, letting it calm her frayed nerves.

Soon enough, her three children would be awake, hungry for breakfast and needing something to fill their day now that school was out. The shift in routine made it harder for Estella to be at Aaron's beck and call, especially when he barged in at lunchtime, expecting her full attention. Lately, she had made a point to read a story to little Florence before her nap—ensuring the child would be resting by the time her father came through the door.

This certainly wasn't the life Estella had imagined when she'd run off from her well-to-do family to marry Aaron Fidler. She had been barely eighteen then, headstrong and heartsick, craving a life of passion and independence beyond the manicured lawns and expectations of her Eastern Shore upbringing.

The Fox family estate in Easton, Maryland, stood proud along the Miles River, its white columns and rose-covered trellises a far cry from the soot-stained rowhouses she now called home. Her father served as a respected circuit judge on Maryland's Eastern Shore, known for his commanding voice and unwavering standards. The law was his gospel, and reputation was everything. Her mother had raised Estella to be a devoted wife and hostess—trained in music and conversation, and well-practiced in the art of creating a gracious home.

But when Aaron came—sharp-jawed and silver-tongued, full of grand dreams and charm—she had abandoned it all. Her family warned her, of course. Her father thundered about disgrace; her mother wept for weeks. But Estella had chosen love—or what she thought was love—over inheritance, over reputation, over comfort.

Estella knew she could never return. Pride kept her from writing. Pain kept her from hoping. And if she was honest, she knew her family too well: the Foxes had likely written her off long ago, sealing her memory behind the same heavy parlor doors where her portrait once hung.

And yet... there were days she could still hear the soft clink of china, smell lilac perfume, or recall the way her mother whispered her name like a hymn.

Aaron, also from a well-known Maryland family, had abandoned his former life to work as a weaver in a Philadelphia mill—a job that came with a modest house and a decent wage to support his growing family. His father, an English immigrant, had started as a mill worker and eventually bought and operated the very mills where he once labored. Aaron had been fortunate to learn both the trade and the business side under his father's guidance.

But he had his own ideas about how things should be run. He'd lived a privileged life until he defied his parents' wishes and married Estella, choosing love—or perhaps rebellion—over expectation. That impulsive nature defined him. He was quick to make decisions without weighing the consequences, and the fallout often felt like a cyclone that never stopped spinning.

Estella's son, John, seven years old and the middle child, was the first to come into the kitchen and sit down beside his mother. "Good morning, mom, what are we doing today?"

She hadn't even given it any thought, but blurted out, "A walk to the park with your sisters shall be nice."

He was pleased with that outcome and sat quietly studying his mother's face. He could see the worry in her far-off gaze. She pushed away from the table, as she knew it wouldn't be long for the other two children to come into the kitchen quite hungry after a good night's rest.

She scrambled the last three eggs, thinning them with a bit of milk to stretch the meal. Two slices of bread were set aside for Aaron's lunch; the children were given the scrap ends to eat with their eggs. She fried a single piece of ham and divided it among the three small plates.

Lately, it had grown harder to get grocery money from Aaron. Still, packing his lunch sometimes softened him enough to leave her with a few spare coins. He resented the time and money she spent on the children, as if their needs were a burden rather than a shared responsibility.

Her daughter Frances, now eight years old, came into the kitchen with her sister Florence, hungry as expected. Both girls went over and hugged their mother and joyfully wished her a good morning while she was preparing breakfast for all of them.

Florence, who was only five years old, ran over to her big brother, John, and leaped into his lap. He wrapped his arms around her and she asked him to tell her a story. She adored her big brother and he loved to give her the attention she craved. Frances helped her mother with plating the food and bringing it to the table.

They all sat together and dove into the hot, delicious breakfast. Estella just nibbled on a piece of toasted bread with butter, watching her children satisfy their hunger. She sipped on the last of her coffee which had gotten cold.

She told the children while they ate, "John had a wonderful idea to take a walk to the park today and see what treasures there are along the way."

That possibility seemed to put a spark of delight in them. They finished their meal rapidly and without much chatter.

They descended the steps of the company rowhouse and Mrs. Murphy called after them, "Have a good swing and slide for me old bones!"

She was a lively soul, always kind to the children and to Estella. Her husband worked long hours at the weaving mill, and her grown children had families of their own. Some lived nearby, working at the same mill, and would occasionally drop off a youngster for her to watch.

On baking days, she never failed to share an extra loaf of crusty Irish soda bread, knowing just how hard it was to keep little tummies full.

The rich green hues had unfurled across the big deciduous trees that shaded the park grounds. Faint yellow daffodils, now past their prime, lined the gentle grassy knolls leading to the children's playground. Just over the hill, a bank of azaleas had begun to burst into flashy pink and white blossoms, though few paused to notice.

With shrieks of delight, the children ran down the hill. Florence glanced back at her mother, who gave a nod of approval. That was all she needed—she took off in full pursuit of the merry-go-round. John and Frances clambered onto the seesaw, their laughter echoing. A few other children joined in, and soon they were all swept up in the carefree joy of a warm afternoon.

Estella was joined on the park bench by Margaret, another company wife whose husband worked under Aaron at the weaving mill. Margaret always brought along her sewing—mending trousers or stitching shirts as she chatted with the other women. It never failed to amaze Estella how much Margaret could complete in the span of a single conversation while the children played nearby. Every bit of extra income mattered.

If it wasn't sewing, the women found other ways to stretch their earnings—taking in laundry, or, when desperation called, working shifts at the mill themselves. The mill provided housing for its workers' families, but the hours were long, the conditions dangerous, and the pay barely enough to keep food on the table.

Too often, children were pulled into the same grueling labor, their futures swallowed by the roar of the looms. Estella was determined that her children would not follow that path. It had become a constant source of tension between her and Aaron—one more point of conflict in a home already strained.

The children laughed and played together in the warm afternoon air while the mothers lingered nearby, chatting and swapping stories.

Margaret waited for the right moment before handing Estella a folded newspaper from the week before. Turned to the fifth page and creased neatly over, the headline read: *"Children's Aid Society of Pennsylvania (CAS) to Ease Family Crisis."*

She knew Estella had been struggling—stretching every meal, enduring Aaron's stinginess, and too often left alone for days without word. Margaret hoped this would be a small step towards something better. What she didn't know was that this quiet gesture would be the first nudge in a whirlwind of change for the entire family.

When Estella and the children returned home from the park, she was surprised to find Aaron sitting on the steps of the rowhouse, waiting with visible impatience. He rarely came home for lunch, especially when the children were out of school. They all gathered around the small kitchen table as Estella warmed a large pot of stew on the stove. Without much preamble, Aaron turned to John and said, "We could sure use your hands at the mill. School's out now, and a wage from you would help keep food on the table."

Estella, hearing that request, froze in place and her heart sank. He had been pressing for months now for John to get a job at the mill. Many arguments and discussions about this did not make a difference to Aaron and now he had crossed a line too far. Estella kept quiet and served the hot stew to her family, then she came around and took a seat with them. The children nervously ate their stew while they picked up on the tensions between their parents.

Aaron pushed back and away from the table, proud of his timing, knowing Estella would not argue back with the children all together in the same room.

She got up from the table, having hardly touched her stew, and followed behind Aaron as he descended the rowhouse stairs on his way back to work. She begged him for food money that he had been withholding from her, to which he tossed coins at her feet, flatly stating, "This is all you get until our boy comes to the mill to work and help the family."

She took a deep breath and without a second thought blurted out, "My children will not become mill workers like their father and have a fate sealed into indentured servitude and poverty."

Aaron stormed off and returned to the mill.

Estella bent down and picked up the scattered coins at her feet. It wasn't much, but it was enough to visit the nearby market and gather a few essentials—just enough to feed her children for another couple of days. The joy that had begun her morning on these very steps had vanished as quickly as the blue skies turned to gray, storm clouds brewing both above and within.

She drew a steady breath and mustered the strength to go back inside. To her surprise, John and Frances had cleared the table and washed the dishes, leaving her bowl of stew waiting, still warm. In the quiet of the back room, Frances had taken Florence to lie down and had fallen asleep beside her, the book she'd been reading still open on the bed.

Estella sat down to her bowl of stew. She had no appetite, but she forced herself to eat. She needed strength, if not for herself, then for the children.

John entered quietly and took a seat at the table. Before he could speak, she held up a hand to stop him.

"You will not work at the mill," she said firmly. "No matter how much pressure he puts on you. Do you understand?"

John nodded, but then added softly, "I just want to help the family."

Estella's heart ached. She had seen it too many times—children who started working at the mill during the summer months, drawn in by the promise of wages, only to become maimed, injured, or worse. The fast-moving machinery demanded small hands and long hours in stifling heat. Many never returned to school. The mill swallowed them whole, and the work became their life.

She refused to let that happen to her children. And she knew, it was only a matter of time before Aaron turned his sights on Frances.

***

Philadelphia had rapidly earned its title as "The Workshop of the World." The surge in industry drew waves of immigrants, causing the population to soar beyond previous records. To meet growing demand, niche markets and factories sprang up across the city, transforming neighborhoods almost overnight.

Family rowhouses and crowded boarding houses rose in migrant enclaves, while markets and taverns pulsed with constant activity. Philadelphia, once a major player in trade, had lost ground to its rival, New York. In response, it shifted its focus to manufacturing—and thrived. Goods produced in the city were now sought by buyers across the nation and around the world.

But the booming industrial system came at a steep cost. The labor force couldn't meet the mounting demand, and so sweatshops, factories, and mills turned to an all-too-readily available solution: the children of mill workers and the city's most vulnerable. These young laborers were exploited to fill the gaps—cheaper, smaller, and more easily discarded than their adult counterparts. Their well-being was rarely, if ever, a consideration.

Estella knew that the mass industry was bigger than any of them could imagine. Philadelphia had fast become known for the fine textiles and garments, boots and shoes, hats, iron and steel, metal trinkets, machine tools, locomotives, rugs, furniture, shipbuilding, chemicals, pharmaceuticals, glass, cutlery, jewelry, varnishes, printing and publishing, medical instruments, and continued to develop and manufacture the dreams of inventive citizens. They came from far and wide with their familial skill sets and work ethic to gain a better life. If not for themselves, then for their families to come. One could be consumed by all the energy and promises of return and the reality of those indentured was far from the glamour of its production.

When Aaron and Estella arrived in Philadelphia from Maryland, a newly wedded and happy couple, he quickly found employment in a familiar setting at the weaving mill. He understood the industry and quickly worked himself from a weaver into a supervisory position. He was astute at recognizing the demands and needs of the quickly shifting setting that required flexibility and awareness of the overall production. He was a natural in leading others to keep up with the demands. He kept long hours and was rewarded with a decent hourly wage, although he had little to show for it.

The mill offered decent company housing to attract the best workers and that came with a big price tag of consuming work that left little family time.

The mill relied on a variety of specialized processes and raw materials to produce its woolen rugs and customized tapestries. Mass production was rare; instead, the focus remained on craftsmanship, attention to detail, and quality. Aaron was often pulled from his usual duties to track down skilled weavers in niche markets—artisans who worked with rare fibers and fine cloth. From there, he would follow the materials through the complex journey to specialty dye houses, ensuring that every step met the high standards expected.

The growing demand and constant stream of special requests kept him under pressure, always needing to stay several steps ahead of fulfillment at the mill. His resourcefulness and eye for quality earned him a reputation in the industry, and his name became known among those who valued precision and artistry. With that respect came confidence—though in Aaron, it often tipped into arrogance.

That inflated sense of self followed him home. Most evenings ended not with his family, but at the local tavern just blocks away, where he spent freely and talked too much. Coins slipped through his fingers as easily as the liquor flowed, fueling his need to boast and be admired. His pride and vanity—traits Estella's family had long distrusted—had been part of the reason they disapproved of their marriage in the first place.

***

Estella returned from the nearby grocer, grateful for the few coins Aaron had tossed at her feet earlier that morning. It wasn't much, but it was enough to piece together a meal. She set to work, washing and preparing the ingredients with practiced efficiency. Stews had become her staple—hearty, humble, and able to stretch over several meals to fill her children's bellies.

As she climbed the steps of the rowhouse, the warm scent of yeast and fresh bread drifted through the air from Mrs. Murphy's kitchen. Estella closed her eyes for a moment, letting it soothe her frayed nerves. The bread would be especially welcome today.

The lunchtime visit with Aaron still weighed heavily on her. His words echoed in her mind, sharp and humiliating. She was used to his pressure—but to speak that way in front of the children? That was new. That was cruel.

He had changed. Somewhere along the way, he had grown cold, distant—hardened by the long hours and unrelenting demands of the mill. In chasing a livelihood, he had lost something vital.

It felt to Estella as if he had sold out his family for the sake of pride and machinery.

The stew simmered gently atop the small iron stove, its slow bubbling a steady, comforting sound. Estella sat for a moment at the worn kitchen table, a chipped cup of hot tea warming her hands. This was the quiet sliver of the day she clung to—when the chores slowed, the house settled, and she could think.

She reached for the folded newspaper Margaret had discreetly handed her earlier at the park. It had been tucked beneath her shawl ever since. Opening it carefully, she found the article Margaret had marked—a piece about a newly organized society dedicated to helping women and children.

The story spoke of the growing crisis: homelessness, abuse, and abandonment rampant in neighborhoods just like hers, where the weight of immigration and relentless labor demands bore down hardest on the most vulnerable.

Estella read slowly, uncertain why Margaret had shared this with her. Was it a mistake? Had Margaret meant for her to read something else entirely? But as her eyes scanned the paragraphs, a truth began to settle over her like a heavy shawl—there was no use pretending. No matter how tidy she kept her home or how brave a face she wore in public, the cracks in her life were visible. Aaron's absence, his sharp words, the near-empty cupboards, the children's thinning shoes, these things spoke louder than she ever could.

A wave of sadness crept over her. She let the paper fall softly into her lap and took a final sip of her tea. Her gaze drifted out the small window, eyes unfocused. In her mind, she was no longer in the cramped kitchen but somewhere else entirely—a memory of light, laughter, and a time when joy had been simple and abundant.

She had tried to create that place for her children, to offer them a sanctuary amidst the hardness of life. They counted on her for everything.

And so, despite the ache in her chest and the weariness in her bones, Estella would go on.

The pounding sound was abruptly interrupted by the shrill voice of Mrs. Murphy coming through the door. "Estella, you in there, you okay?" she asked.

Startling her back to both her reality and confusion she snapped up and replied, "Just fine, Mrs. Murphy, and you?"

The ladies chatted for a moment and Mrs. Murphy, with a look of concern, handed Estella the loaf of warm bread. Living this close to one another it was hard not to know about someone's life and happenings. Mrs. Murphy made it her business to be the mother hen of the mill village and stepped in to be a helping hand when she saw a need arise. She too was on her own most often with the busy mill always in high demand of her hard-working yet kind husband. Estella invited her to stay for a cup of tea, but she declined as she usually did on her bread baking day and a few of her grown children would be coming by shortly for a visit and loaf.

Estella heard the children shuffling about and quietly interacting with each other. It wouldn't be long until they were in the kitchen asking when they would have supper. In anticipation she pulled out her stool so that she could put the newspaper up high on top of the cupboard where it would be concealed alongside her small tin that she kept coins in. She did this as Aaron had a habit of scavenging any loose change that was lying around. It was these spare coins that often made the difference between his stingy offerings for food and the necessities for the family.

Tomorrow was her laundry and pay day as she often found spare change in Aaron's work pants. His late nights at the tavern often found him reckless and in a hurry to undress, leaving behind the pocket contents. She doubted he would ever leave it behind for her use.

The days were growing longer and Estella with her children decided to step outside their rowhome for some fresh air together. John was thrilled to see some other neighborhood boys coming together to play their favorite, stick ball. They used a broken broom handle and small rubber ball and dreamed of the chance to be like the players they heard so much about at Shibe Park, the huge, brand-new baseball stadium.

One of the boys, Billy, had recently gone to a game with his dad and couldn't stop talking about it. He described every detail as if he'd stepped into a palace, with the biggest grandstands you ever did see. And seeing the Phillies play? That was better than Christmas morning. It became the talk of the boys from the moment they woke up until they drifted off to sleep again—no doubt dreaming of the crack of the bat and the roar of the crowd.

While John ran off to play ball with his friends, Estella strolled to the corner with Frances and Florence, hoping to catch sight of the first mill workers returning home. Maybe, just maybe, Aaron would be among them, and they could all sit down to a hot meal together.

As usual, it was Florence who broke the silence. Always full of questions, she pointed to a lantern and asked, "Why do the lanterns stay on even in the daylight?"

Estella smiled. "They have a constant gas supply, so they don't need to be turned off and re-lit each day," she explained. That answer seemed to satisfy her for the moment.

But the question stirred a memory in Estella. She'd recently read a charming article about Robert Louis Stevenson's boyhood in Edinburgh, his fascination with the old gas streetlights, and the lamplighter who made his rounds at dusk. The story struck her especially because she had been reading *Treasure Island* to the children at bedtime—a thrilling tale they all adored.

She turned to Florence with a gleam in her eye. "Remember the story of the boy who saw the lamplighter poking holes in the darkness?" she asked. Florence's eyes widened with delight.

Estella cherished moments like this—when a child's curiosity sparked connection, and the world, just for a moment, felt full of wonder and light.

Most of the mill workers had returned home and the children were beginning to fall away to go back indoors. It was unusual for Aaron to be this late returning home. The streetlights began to illuminate the short walk home when Estella decided they had waited long enough. The children needed to have supper and wash up and be tucked in for the night.

The four of them climbed up the front steps and Estella turned once more to look for her husband before stepping indoors. Coming into the kitchen she was pleased to see John serving up the hot bowls of stew. Frances had already taken the fresh loaf of rustic bread that Mrs. Murphy had delivered earlier to the table on the wood board. They were all seated at the long table.

Estella sliced into the loaf of bread and smeared a little dab of soft butter on each piece and passed it to the children. They ate their meal in silence. They typically would listen to their father sharing the news of the mill while they had supper together. His absence was emphasized by the silence.

Estella rose from the table and asked the children to get ready for their bedtime reading. She'd be upstairs shortly, just as soon as the kitchen was cleaned and everything put away. She was grateful for their self-sufficiency—how they quietly stepped in to help with Florence and supported one another without needing to be asked.

Still, she had sensed their unease when Aaron hadn't come home for supper. Estella tried to push the worry aside as she finished tidying up the kitchen. Her time was rarely her own, yet this—this part of the day—was something she cherished.

She climbed the stairs, book in hand, ready to join her children in their nightly escape. The thrilling adventure story transported them all, offering a brief and welcome journey far from their worries—into a world of courage, treasure, and imagined shores.

Frances and Florence shared a bedroom, and John had a connecting room. When he heard his mother coming up the stairs, he raced across the doorway threshold and leaped onto one of the beds for story time. She picked up the borrowed library book and started where they left off from the night before. The children listened intently as the adventure on the high seas continued and transported them elsewhere. It was a sweet distraction for all of them.

Estella finally stopped reading and said a prayer with the children and asked especially to watch over Aaron and return him safely home. She wished the children a restful night, then kissed each child on the cheek and turned to descend the stairs.

She stepped into the kitchen and set a kettle on the stove, warming water for a cup of tea. Perhaps Aaron would walk through the door and solve the mystery of his absence. This was usually their time—after the children were tucked into bed—when they might share a few quiet moments together. But lately, those evenings had unraveled into quarrels over money and the children.

He had grown more irritable since school was now out on break, the constant presence of the children wearing on his patience. Often arguments ended with him storming out and heading to the tavern just down the street. What angered Estella most was his hypocrisy—he claimed he had no money to spare for food, yet somehow always found enough to spend on drink.

Hours later, he would stumble into bed while she feigned sleep. The stale scent of cigar smoke clung to his clothes, laced with the unmistakable bite of liquor. He would pass out quickly, snoring like a freight train, while she lay awake beside him, thoughts churning.

Now, she stared at the door, wondering if this would be the night he sauntered in once again.

The bright moonlight shone like a lamp streaming through the upstairs window. Estella turned and felt the empty space beside her and immediately sat up with concern. The room was lit up and Aaron was still not home. She decided in the morning she would ask Mrs. Murphy to keep a watch on the children after breakfast while she looked in at the mill after Aaron. Surely if he had been injured the mill would send a messenger to notify her.

Decidedly, she lay back down to try and get her rest for the uncertainties that lay ahead. She was deeply saddened with the emptiness as she gazed over the illuminated space that he typically would've been sprawled out on. She reached her hand over to his side of the bed and rubbed it, perhaps grasping for answers, but none came.

She awakened to the dawn light gently nudging her into the reality of her day.

She descended the stairs and silently slipped into the kitchen to start the water kettle. She had a small bit of coffee she rationed off for herself, a boost for her day ahead. This was typically her laundry day. She would get it started early now and leave instructions for John and Frances to finish it while she went to the mill to inquire about Aaron.

She sipped her hot coffee, feeling the warmth spread through her limbs and the energy slowly returning to her body. Tearing off a piece of crusty bread, she nibbled thoughtfully, then rose with purpose and made her way to the backroom, where a daunting pile of laundry waited to be sorted before she could even begin washing.

As she rifled through the clothing, she checked the pockets of Aaron's trousers—more out of habit now than hope—and smiled faintly when her fingers found a few stray coins. She slipped them into her pocket, later to be tucked away in the tin she kept hidden high above the cupboard.

She uncoiled a long hose from the kitchen sink, feeding it into the washtub that held a well-worn washboard. As the tub filled, she prepared herself for the work ahead. She plunged her hands into the water and began scrubbing the garments against the ridged board, working the dirt and wear from the fabric. The repetitive, physical motion let her mind drift elsewhere—a kind of temporary escape from the world.

Several times she drained the tub using another hose that ran out to the small backyard, then refilled and rinsed the clothes, wringing them out by hand. Once she finished, she draped the damp laundry over the porch railing to wait. After breakfast, she'd have the children hang it all on the clothesline to dry under the morning sun.

Estella prepared a hot breakfast of oatmeal. She cut up a small apple and sprinkled a bit of cinnamon atop for the children and left it on the stove. She quietly dashed out the front door and over to Mrs. Murphy's as, surely by now, Ed would've been off to the mill.

She lightly tapped on the door and was greeted by Mrs. Murphy who insisted she come in and sit down.

Mrs. Murphy moved her portly figure past Estella's chair and asked, "Would you like coffee or tea?"

Estella without thinking about it blurted out, "Coffee, black, please."

Mrs. Murphy returned with two cups in hand and a small plate of biscuit style cookies. She had a big heart and shared with the other ladies and families in the mill house neighborhood.

Before Estella could even ask for her help with the children this morning, Mrs. Murphy asked, "What has happened with Aaron and how can I help you?"

Estella clearly was puzzled with that question and returned that with her own query: "Do you know something I do not because

Aaron didn't return home last night. I was coming to ask if you could possibly watch the children this morning while I inquired at the mill."

Mrs. Murphy leaned in with a furrowed brow. "Ed came home from the mill yesterday and asked about Aaron—said he hadn't shown up all day. We figured he was ill and staying home to rest. But look here, I'll watch the children while you go to the police and report him missing. My nephew's a sergeant—just tell him Auntie Nora sent you. He'll know what to do. Anyway, I'm sure Aaron's fine and will wander on home soon."

Estella felt as if she'd been struck. Her mind spun, the world suddenly tilting with uncertainty. She forced herself to sip the coffee and take a small bite of the biscuit, grateful for the comfort and Mrs. Murphy's steady presence.

"Thank you," she said softly, her voice thick with worry. She knew the children would be safe with Nora, but the thought of not being there when they awoke—of not hearing their hungry morning cries—unsettled her. Still, she had no choice. Everything in her clung to the hope that all would be well, because the alternative was too vast, too terrifying to grasp. Where would she go? What would she do with the children?

They both rose from the table, bracing themselves for the day ahead. With silent resolve, they stepped through the front door and descended the stoop of the mill rowhouse—two women with separate tasks, both steeped in quiet emotion, moving forward into the unknown.

Mrs. Murphy was no stranger to hardship. Life had handed her more than her share, but she had learned to take it all in stride. Worry never solved a thing, she often said. The only way forward was one foot after the other—and with steady faith in her Maker, she trusted that, in time, God would right the course.

She carried with her a burlap sack stuffed with small treasures—goodies for the children, bits of kindness she'd managed to squirrel away. She didn't make a fuss about it; she simply brought what she could, when she could.

She knew Estella was struggling. It wasn't Estella who said as much—it was the gossiping hens who nested outside the community market each morning, their tongues sharper than their knitting needles. Mrs. Murphy had no patience for them.

She recalled the Parish Priest's homily from just a few days earlier—a fiery message drawn from 1 Timothy 5. He'd leaned into the words with intention: "Besides, they get into the habit of being idle and going about from house to house. And not only do they become idlers, but also busybodies who talk nonsense, saying things they ought not to."

She had nearly said amen out loud, thinking of those very women. They spoke nothing but poison, never offering help, only whispers. Mrs. Murphy believed in grace over gossip. And she knew that what Estella needed wasn't pity or judgment, but a neighbor's quiet support. That, and perhaps a few sweet rolls and a hunk of cheese to lighten the day.

***

Estella walked quickly, her steps fueled by determination and anxiety. By the time she reached the police department and stepped through the heavy door, her cheeks were flushed pink from the brisk pace and rising emotion. The officer behind the front desk looked up, immediately noting her no-nonsense posture. He straightened in his chair and asked, "What can I do for you, ma'am?"

"I'd like to speak with Sergeant Murphy," she replied, her voice firm despite the weight she carried.

He nodded politely and gestured toward a row of wooden chairs. "Have a seat. I'll fetch him for you."

Estella sat down, smoothing her skirt and willing her hands to stay still in her lap. The room was dim and smelled faintly of stale tobacco and dust. It could've used a good scrubbing, she thought—though it was hardly the worst thing on her mind. She sat upright, carefully holding her composure, knowing she had to be taken seriously. Still, her thoughts were racing. Where do I even begin?

The door to a back room creaked open, and out stepped a tall man with a ruddy complexion and a shock of red hair beneath his cap. He scanned the room until his eyes landed on her.

"Ma'am," he said with a polite nod, "I understand you've come to pay me a visit."

"Yes, your Auntie Nora thought it would be wise if I came to report a missing person to you," exclaimed Estella.

His demeanor softened with the mention of his auntie, and he knew immediately he needed to bring her to the back for more details to see how he could assist her.

Grateful for this lead in the department, she followed closely behind him to a small room with a table and chairs. It was dark and cold with only a dim light. He motioned her to sit down and asked if she wanted something to drink. She shook her head and politely declined his offer.

The sergeant asked her, "So tell me, who is it that's missing," although he already knew the words that were coming next.

Estella flatly stated, "It is my husband. He never returned from the mill last night. We, the children and I, were out with all the others playing and waiting for his return and when it got dark, and he was not home, we decided to have our supper and thought perhaps he would come home. We just thought he got busy at the mill or stopped off at the tavern and got involved in a conversation. When I awoke and discovered he still had not returned home was when I planned to come make a report here. At a more decent hour

I went to see your Auntie Nora next door to ask her to help with the children. She has been so kind to us."

Seargent Murphy was not surprised at the last remark. His Auntie Nora was the strength of his family and was always there for all of them.

He asked her more detailed questions, starting with, "What tavern does he visit and is this something he has done before?"

They went back and forth with these questions and answers until Sergeant Murphy was convinced he had all he needed to know to locate Aaron. He had a few good ideas about what may have happened and would get busy filing the report and exploring his suspicions.

Meanwhile, Estella graciously thanked him for his time and attention to the matter as she and the children were very concerned now about Aaron's safety and well-being. He reassured her that he would turn up home or that they would find him and get to the bottom of this mystery. She was hopeful when he led her out through the lobby. She exited the building onto the sidewalk.

Many years would pass before the good sergeant would finally track Aaron down—and when he did, the truth would be harder to bear than his absence. For all the time Estella had spent fearing for his safety, it would be the betrayal, not the mystery, that cut the deepest.

By the time Estella stepped back onto the street, the city had fully come alive. There was far more activity than when she'd first arrived—automobiles rumbled by, horses and carriages clattered over the dusty roadway, and voices rose in the noise of midday bustle. The ragman trotted from building to building, delivering large, wrapped bundles and disappearing behind shops to collect the soiled lots. The Wawa dairy wagon, its big wheels creaking, passed by slowly, pulled by a lone horse on its morning route.

Men in suits and hats hurried into banks and office buildings that lined the street, the rhythm of city life pulsing forward with purpose.

But for Estella, there was nothing normal about this day.

She paused at the edge of the curb, glanced both ways, then lifted the hem of her long skirt to keep it clear of the dusty road. With a determined breath, she made a quick dash across the street, weaving through the traffic and commotion, eager to be home.

All the while, a single thought clung to her—Maybe he'll be there. Maybe he'll have an explanation waiting.

DAY OF REST

The Weaver Family | Lancaster County | Spring 1913

Florence stepped out onto the backsteps, carrying two loaves of freshly baked bread wrapped in cloth. Her Mamm followed close behind, balancing two shoofly pies with practiced care. Amos waited patiently in the horse and buggy, the reins loose in his hands.

A chill hung in the early Sunday air, and a light mist draped itself over the young spring crops, softening the landscape in a gentle hush. Once they were settled on the hard, flat bench of the carriage, Amos gave the reins a light flick, and the horse moved forward at a steady pace. They were headed to the Weaver farm for church—a day of rest, reflection, and community fellowship.

Florence, however, felt somewhat apart from it all. The service was long and delivered mostly in High German, a language she couldn't understand. She sat quietly through the half-day ritual, her mind drifting elsewhere. But afterward, when the families mingled and the children were free to run and play, her spirits lifted. That part of the day—laughter, games, and time spent with friends—felt like a world all her own.

The clip-clop of the horse's hooves on the packed earth was almost melodic, a gentle rhythm that matched the stillness of the early morning. The family rode together in quiet harmony, their gazes sweeping across the misty valley below, where fertile farmland stretched out in a patchwork of greens. It was a moment to take in the fruit of their recent labors—hard work slowly transforming the land into abundance.

Up ahead, other buggies approached from the opposite direction, black silhouettes drifting like shadows through the fog. Soon they would turn onto Weaver's drive, the narrow lane that led to today's service. Church was held every other Sunday, rotating from one home to another. It was nothing like what Florence had once known—no pews, no altar, no stained glass. Yet there was a reverence in its simplicity that moved her, even if she didn't fully understand it yet.

She felt a small sense of relief that today's service was close by, just the next farm over.

Amos guided the buggy off the main road and turned down the Weaver's long dirt drive. One of the Weaver boys stood waiting near a makeshift hitching area, waving them over. Amos nodded, brought the horse to a gentle stop, and stepped down to tie it securely. Nearby, a large water trough stood ready, its surface rippling in the breeze—an offering of care for the horses that had brought them here.

The long black church wagon was parked beside the Weaver's barn, a clear signal to the community that today's service would be held there. The wagon carried everything needed to transform a family farm into a place of worship: benches for the congregation, folding chairs for the elderly or less mobile, crates of dishes and utensils, and other simple supplies to accommodate up to seventy-five people.

Like many Amish families, the Weavers—Jacob, Rebecca and their ten children—were responsible for setting up the portable church. Mrs. Weaver and several of her daughters had been cleaning and baking for days in preparation. It was their turn, one of two each year, and with the largest family in the district, they were often the most practical hosts.

Other families brought food to share, usually coordinating the dishes in advance. After the service and fellowship meal, everything would be carefully packed back into the wagon, just as it had arrived. Later, it would be delivered to the next host family, ready to be set up again for the next Sunday gathering.

It was a practical and orderly tradition—no need for a separate church building, nor the upkeep that would come with it. Faith, after all, lived in the people and their homes.

After Sara and Florence delivered the pies and bread to Mamm Weaver, they crossed the drive toward the barn. Florence walked close to her Mamm, her small hand brushing the edge of the long skirt, her eyes lowered to the ground.

As they stepped over the threshold of the barn, Florence glanced up and took in the orderly rows of benches set out for worship, a narrow aisle dividing them down the center. The space was simple, reverent, and prepared with care.

They made their way toward a group of women seated with young children and infants and quietly joined them. The women sat together on one side, as was custom, each one facing forward in anticipation of the service's start.

Florence settled beside her mother, clutching a small hand-sewn doll in her lap. She played with it silently throughout the long hours that followed. Around her, other children held small toys of their own—simple, cherished comforts to help them sit still through the solemnity of the morning.

Once all the women and children had settled into their seats, the men began to enter. The order was always the same—first, the eldest men, walking with quiet dignity to the folding chairs with backs. Then came the married men, followed by the unbaptized boys and youth who brought up the rear.

Florence watched quietly, her eyes scanning the line of familiar faces. She spotted Isaac and David, the Weaver boys who had helped her with chores when her Daed had gone to auction. Though the two were quite different in temperament—Isaac more serious, David quicker to smile—they both reminded her of her brother John. She missed him terribly.

Caught in her gaze, she lingered too long. A gentle but firm tap on her leg from her Mamm brought her back to herself. It was a silent reminder—staring was not considered proper.

Florence quickly looked down at the doll resting in her lap. Its stitched face was expressionless, but in that moment, she imagined it was John. She held it close, letting her mind drift to memories of his laughter and the way he used to tease, gently and protectively, as older brothers do.

Worship began with an opening hymn. At the end of each bench sat a stack of *Ausbunds*, the Amish hymnbooks, though few needed to open them. The old tunes were sung from memory, passed down through generations. Many of the hymns had been written centuries earlier by Anabaptist prisoners, voices of faith rising from the depths of suffering. They were sung slowly, in unison, without rhythm or instruments. The sound—a low, droning chant—seemed to stretch endlessly, wrapping itself around the beams of the barn and into the rafters above.

Florence felt the hum and buzz of it settle into her chest, soothing her despite the strangeness. It transported her somewhere else, somewhere quieter and still. The words were in German, and she didn't understand them. That difference always set her apart in ways that made her feel quietly lonely.

After the hymn, the deacon stood and read a passage of scripture, followed by two prayers—one silent, the other read aloud from the prayer book. Florence only knew it was prayer time when everyone shifted to their knees in reverent stillness.

Then came the sermon, delivered in Pennsylvania Dutch. The cadence was unfamiliar; the meaning lost to her ears. Mamm Sara had reminded her, many times, that understanding the words wasn't the point. "We gather here in humility," she would say, "to yield to God's will and reflect with thankful hearts."

Her mind wandered. She turned her attention to her plain cloth doll and began to trace its seams, letting her thoughts drift to faces she hadn't seen for years—her mother, her brother John, her older sister. She tried to remember their voices, their laughter, the feel of her mother's hand on her cheek.

Several men stood to speak throughout the service, and finally the man who seemed to be in charge led them into the final hymn.

Florence felt a wave of quiet relief, and she wasn't alone. The other children stirred on the benches, eyes drifting toward the open barn doors, already anticipating fresh air, food, and space to run.

As the last low note faded, the group rose in unison. With quiet steps and solemn hearts, they filed out into the soft light of late morning.

After the service, a few of the young men remained behind to convert the benches into tables. The women followed, laying out table covers and smoothing the creases with practiced hands. In the kitchen and main room, Rebecca and the other ladies busied themselves setting out the prepared dishes, uncovering platters and bowls that had been carefully arranged ahead of time.

The long wooden table quickly filled with baskets of warm bread, creamy peanut butter and cheese spreads, pickled beets and eggs, pretzels, an assortment of sliced cheeses and meats, and a hearty pot of beans with ham. Nearby, another table stood dedicated entirely to dessert—shoofly pies, fruit tarts, cookies, and other sweet treats awaited eager hands.

Soon a steady line of hungry congregants formed, each one filling a plate with the lovingly prepared food. A few young mothers slipped into a quiet sitting room to nurse their babies before rejoining the gathering. Many made their way back to the barn, where the transformed benches now welcomed them for the meal. After a brief blessing, the room hummed with quiet conversation and the sounds of contented eating.

Outside, the younger adults, teens, and children gathered in small groups, standing as they ate, chatting and laughing under the soft spring sky. Rebecca's eldest daughters—Sara, Eliza, and Hanna—moved through the crowd with pitchers of water and hot coffee, refilling mugs and glasses with care and grace.

Once the meal was served and enjoyed by all, a bunch of the ladies got busy cleaning up the dishes. Together with so many others helping, it didn't take long to get it all finished in an assembly line of order.

Florence sat on the back porch with a few of the other girls, quietly playing with their dolls. They were always kind to her, gentle in their manner, but she still felt different. She wasn't immune to the soft whispers—questions spoken just out of earshot but never quite out of reach. Was she a Jew? they wondered, eyes lingering on her darker skin and the soft, textured curls of her brown hair.

Even Florence wasn't sure of the truth. Her earliest memories were hazy, like scenes from a dream, and this—this Amish farm, this porch, these people—was the only world she had truly come to know as home.

Her Mamm, Sara, and Daed, Amos, were kind and steady souls. She had learned over time that they had not been able to have children of their own—something that brought them both great heartache. Years ago, they had approached the Bishop with heavy hearts and open arms, seeking permission to foster a child. He had given them his blessing, and Florence had entered their lives, and their world.

Within the community, her presence was seen as a generous and faithful act. It gave Sara the chance to become a mother, something she had long prayed for. In the Amish way of life, children were considered the greatest earthly treasure—souls to be nurtured and guided, the only ones a parent might hope to take with them to heaven. Large families were the norm, and children were received not just with joy, but as divine blessings.

Florence, too, was a blessing—though sometimes she still wondered if she truly belonged.

Around the side of the house, a group of young boys were tossing a ball back and forth, their laughter rising into the afternoon air. Florence watched them for a moment, their energy and ease a sharp contrast to how she often felt—tentative, watchful. One boy in particular caught her attention: Samuel. He had been cruel to her at school, though she didn't understand why. He would pull her hair and then run off, never saying a word. She hadn't done anything to provoke him. At least, she didn't think so. Perhaps it was because she was different—an outsider. That thought lingered often in her mind, quiet and heavy. She knew his behavior was wrong, but she was too afraid to say anything. Stirring up trouble wasn't something she dared do.

Instead, she kept her distance. She made sure never to be alone when Samuel was nearby and always watched him carefully out of the corner of her eye. Still, aside from those uneasy moments, she found comfort in the warmth of the day. The families and friends gathered together in a way that felt safe and familiar. The conversations flowed easily, children played freely, and the hours passed with the quiet rhythm of a community at peace.

And for the most part, Florence was learning to enjoy it.

A few of the men had gathered to discuss the upcoming barn raising and the preparations that had been underway to support the newly married Millers and their farm. The land had been a wedding gift, with a small humble home built by the senior Eli Miller who was recently deceased. His death had caused a brief delay in the barn raising, but it was back on track and soon the community would come together to make this barn a reality for the couple who were just starting out in life with a small dairy.

The sun was beginning to shine from the westerly sky as the day peacefully wound down. The elderly members climbed into their wagons that had been made ready for them, and they headed down the dirt lane toward home.

The young men quickly set to work dismantling the tables, stacking them neatly for return to the long black church wagon. The women had already gathered the table covers to be washed and brought to the next service in two weeks, hosted by the Yoders. Dishes, utensils, and other essentials had been washed, dried, and packed away—ready for the men to load. It was a well-rehearsed rhythm, orderly and efficient, with every hand contributing.

The fully loaded wagon would be delivered to the Yoder homestead on a separate day, in keeping with the Amish observance of rest on Sundays. A steady line of horses and buggies began to file out from the Weavers' yard, each one carrying families homeward across the farmland roads.

For the Blanks, the ride was short—their property adjoined the Weavers'. But even a Sabbath day held its share of responsibilities. Farm life never fully paused; animals needed tending, no matter the day.

Amos brought the buggy to a stop, and Sara and Florence stepped down, carrying their empty pie plates and bread baskets. They climbed the back steps and entered the small mudroom. Without a word, Florence turned and darted back outside with an empty egg basket, ready to gather the evening's collection.

Inside, Sara added fresh wood to the oven and checked the risen dough, preparing to bake another batch of bread. Soon, Florence would return to help Amos with the evening chores—feeding, milking, and tending to the animals who, like the land, paid no mind to the calendar.

Once the chores were done, the three of them gathered around the long wooden table. The scent of Sara's bread baking filled the room, warming the space and taking the edge off the evening chill. The rich, yeasty aroma mingled with something sweeter, shoofly pie.

Sara sliced generous pieces of the gooey, molasses-filled dessert—its soft "wet bottom" and crumble top still warm from the oven—and served them with steaming cups of hot tea. They quietly enjoyed the simple pleasure of pie and tea, the warmth of the kitchen wrapping around them like a quilt. After a few bites, Amos shared news of the upcoming barn raising—a much-anticipated event that Sara and the other women had been planning for weeks, carefully coordinating the meal preparations.

Florence remembered the last barn raising, faintly. It had taken place not long after she'd first arrived. This time would be different. She would help prepare, not just attend. There was a sense of importance in that shift, a sign that she had been folded more fully into the life of the community. Everyone had a role to play when neighbors needed help.

After the pie was finished, Amos rose and took a seat by the window, opening his worn copy of *Martyrs Mirror* beneath the soft glow of an oil lamp. Florence and Sara cleared the dishes and washed them together, preparing the kitchen for the next morning. The loaves of bread, now golden and perfectly baked, were set out to cool on the stones along the counter.

Later, the two joined Amos in the sitting room. Florence brought out the sewing basket, and together she and Sara worked on piecing a quilt. The flickering light of the oil lamps cast soft shadows across the fabric as they stitched. It was in these quiet, shared moments that Florence felt truly cared for—loved, even. She was learning not just to quilt, but to see herself as part of something larger. Mamm Sara guided her in matching patterns, working the needle in steady rhythm. Florence found the motion soothing, far more comforting than the noise and activity of larger gatherings. She preferred this—home, heart, and hands busy with purpose.

From behind his book, Amos glanced at the hour. He closed it gently and leaned forward to extinguish the flame of the oil lamp. Florence and Sara folded their fabric, tidied the basket, and blew out the smaller lamp on the side table. The house slipped into stillness, warm from the day's work, and ready for the next.

They climbed the stairs to the bedrooms where the heat had risen from the oven below. It had taken the chill out of the air, making it a touch easier to prepare for bed. Florence crawled beneath the sheet of her quilted bed. She said her prayers for her family, long gone and her current one, asking God to bless them all and most especially giving thanks for all the blessings He showered over her life. Sleep came fast for all of them.

***

The days grew longer as the early summer settled in, and the fields, now fully planted, promised a bountiful harvest ahead. With the crops in the ground, it was the perfect time to take on bigger projects. For weeks, supplies had been gathered and delivered to the Miller farm in preparation for a long-awaited barn raising—affectionately known as a "frolic."

One by one, horses and buggies pulled into the open field, forming a great, dark grey cluster on the green landscape. Teams of draft horses arrived pulling wagons heavy with lumber, tools, and helping hands. The air buzzed with the energy of purposeful activity, and the early morning start was welcome before the heat of the midday sun took hold.

Everyone who was able-bodied and well came to take part in the endeavor. Each person had a skill to offer and a task to fulfill, all lending their time, strength, and hearts to build something lasting—for a neighbor, and for the good of the whole.

"Many hands make light work" was a well-known saying among the Anabaptists, and nowhere was it more clearly lived out than at a barn raising. This frolic was no exception. The older, more experienced men took the lead, organizing crews and assigning tasks with efficiency born of practice. These were the crew chiefs—respected for their knowledge and trusted to guide the day's efforts.

Younger men, many of them participating for the first time, had grown up watching barn raisings and knew what was expected. The most critical tasks—especially the post-and-beam construction—were reserved for the seasoned carpenters. These jobs required deep knowledge of joinery and the precise doweling of beams, and only the most skilled were entrusted with them.

Older boys dashed back and forth, gathering tools and parts, while the youngest did what they could—eager to join the steady rhythm and shared purpose of the day. Women and girls prepared food and water, cared for the littlest ones, and made sure no one went without.

Florence had never seen such a flurry of activity. It reminded her of a hive of bees—everyone working in harmony, each with a role, moving with cheerful urgency toward a common goal.

She helped her Mamm unload their contributions: warm loaves of bread and rolls, glass jars filled with pickled eggs, and several berry pies. Everything was arranged on long folding tables brought in by the church wagon. Around her, other women and children did the same, laying out baskets and dishes with practiced grace. This too was part of the work—part service, part celebration. And for Florence, it was another chance to feel the comforting rhythm of togetherness, to help and to belong.

The men teamed up and began work in earnest. The pounding of hammers and swoosh of saws signaled the beginning of the building project. The teams of young men lifted heavy timbers, guiding them into place while others secured them. The walls were carefully lifted and positioned using ropes and levers and secured with temporary bracing. The roof trusses, rafters and ridge beam would soon be painstakingly secured. All the preparations leading up to this day were coming together and the barn was forming.

Florence, along with her friends, poured water continuously for the young boys who were the runners. The day was warming up with the hot sun and keeping hydrated was critical. Her Mamm Sara spent time with the other mothers. It wouldn't be long before they would be working hard to keep the crew fed.

When much of the framework was complete, it was a cue for the women to organize the assembly line of food that had been brought earlier and spread out on the tables. It looked a lot like the Sunday church meal, only this one served out in the field in the fresh air.

The men got to a good stopping point and descended from the barn building. As they made their way to the food tables they stopped and turned around to take in the sight of the structure for the first time. Removing their hats and in silent prayer they bowed their heads, giving thanks to the Lord.

The women and children assisted with serving the food and making sure everyone had something to drink. They all sat about the field, some finding a nearby grove of trees with shade and stretching out their legs, taking a moment to pause and enjoy the delicious, prepared foods. It was a good and humbling feeling to experience the satisfaction of this collaborative effort.

After a good meal and rest it was time to get back to the task. The barn would be far from finished, but the bulk of it and the most important parts would come to completion by day's end. The other details would be seen throughout the rest of the week, but not with the same number of people. The men scaled the barn with ease to the roof to cover it with sheathing and roofing material. Again, it was all team-organized and from the ground they sent supplies to the top via rope and lever while the crew leaders labored away on the rooftop finishing up this vital phase. Another crew was beginning to install the walls while the roof was being finished up.

While this second wave of activity unfolded, the women prepared picnic-style packages of food, wrapping leftovers in cotton flour sacks for families to take home and enjoy after the day's labor. This allowed them to pack their baskets and ready their buggies for the return journey.

Some of the young men, having finished their duties as tool runners, began dismantling the long wooden tables and carefully stacking them into the black church wagon. Meanwhile, the women and children washed plates and utensils, placing them into their designated boxes to be loaded alongside the tables. Every task had its rhythm; no time was wasted.

As the sun dipped lower in the sky, casting golden light across the fields, it signaled the end of the day's work. One by one, the men climbed down from the framework of the barn. Tools and supplies were gathered and stored neatly within the shelter of the new structure.

Though there was still more to do—flooring to lay, doors to hang, finishing cuts to be made—the barn stood upright, sturdy and sound. It had been humbly raised by the many hands of a willing community, each one offering strength, skill, or service to bring it to life.

EVICTION
Estella | Philadelphia | Summer 1910

Estella was cleaning up the breakfast dishes when a light tap on the door startled her back to reality. She dried her hands on the nearby tea towel and went to the front door.

There stood, a stocky little man, wearing a suit and hat, standing on her front steps.

She asked, "May I help you?"

He introduced himself, stammering, "Ah, ma'am, my name is Norman Fitch from the mill office. Your husband, Aaron, well, hasn't shown up for work now for two weeks and we have been instructed to let him go of his position. We will need you to vacate the house by the end of two weeks. His last month's wages have been deducted up until that time."

Estella stood frozen in place as though she had been run over by a streetcar. She kindly inquired, "Where will my children and I go to live. We don't have family nearby. I'm sure that Aaron will return soon. This is not like him to vanish, and he's been a loyal worker."

"Ma'am, I'm sorry to inform you, but we have no accommodations for non-mill workers, and you'll need to vacate this home in two weeks," Mr. Fitch firmly stated. He wished her a good day, turned abruptly and scurried down the front steps and across the street to another rowhouse, leaving Estella staring in disbelief.

So many thoughts swirled in her head, but she needed to remain calm and focus on the task ahead. She had taken in laundry for two families nearby for the extra money to buy food for the children.

Grateful that the children had gone to the nearby park to play with friends, Estella dug into the laundry. The task was repetitive and mindless, but it gave her space to think. Though her hands were busy, her mind was wholly present—turning over the urgent question of how to find work and, more pressingly, how to secure a roof over their heads.

The thoughts that had been swirling in panic earlier now settled into sharp clarity with each scrub against the washboard, each dunk into the soapy water. She moved through the task with quiet purpose, determined to stay ahead of what was coming. Once the hired laundry was washed and hung to dry out back, she grabbed her shawl and dashed out the door toward Mrs. Murphy's. The children would be returning from the park soon, hungry from play, and she needed to be quick.

Mrs. Murphy opened the door before Estella even had a chance to knock. Without hesitation, she waved her in and pointed to the kitchen chair. "Sit yerself down," she said firmly.

News traveled fast in their neighborhood. Estella didn't have to explain a thing.

"I heard about that Mr. Fitch fellow from the mill comin' to kick ya to the curb," Mrs. Murphy said, her voice thick with indignation. "And here's what we're gonna do."

Before she could get another word out, Estella cut her off.

"I read something in the paper about a service for women and children—some place that helps in situations like this. I was wondering if you could keep an eye on the children while I go inquire."

Mrs. Murphy's brow furrowed. She nodded but leaned closer, her voice lower and edged with warning.

"Those places don't always help much, Estella. Sometimes they take more than they give. You might be invitin' trouble in, not knowin' the kind you'll find there. But go on if ya must. I'll mind the children and see they get lunch. You're welcome to stay here with us until you find a job and a roof of your own. That sort o' place don't move fast, and two weeks'll be gone in the blink of an eye."

Mrs. Murphy's warning about the Children's Aid Society lingered like an unwelcome draft. Estella hoped it was just bitterness talking, but in time, she'd come to understand exactly what she meant.

She had just given Estella the greatest gift one person could offer another—and with it came a wave of relief Estella hadn't felt in days. Buoyed by hope, she hurried back home, climbed up onto the kitchen stool, and reached for the tin tucked high in the cupboard. Inside was her small stash of spare coins. She grabbed the newspaper clipping with the Children's Aid Society address and tucked both into her bag.

She smoothed back her hair, straightened her long skirt, and took a steadying breath.

Moments later, as expected, the door flew open and the children burst in—cheeks flushed pink, eyes bright, and stomachs growling from their play at the park. Estella's heart lifted at the sight of them, joyful and full of life.

She smiled and knelt to meet their energy. "Mom has to visit an office across town," she said gently, "and you'll be staying with Mrs. Murphy for lunch."

She turned to Frances. "After lunch, I'd like you to bring Florence back here and settle her down for a nap."

Then to John: "Check on the laundry for me. If it's dry, take it down carefully and fold it the way I showed you."

She paused, taking them all in with a look of love and quiet pride. "All of this will be a great help while I'm out. I love you all."

The children in unison said, "We love you, mom".

Estella knew she needed to get to the end of the street to catch the electric streetcar that passed by several times a day. The Children's Aid Society was far too distant to reach on foot and still return home in good time. Riding the streetcar was a rare indulgence—one she could scarcely afford—but this visit might be her best chance at securing a future for her family.

Clutching her coin tightly in one hand, she gripped the railing with the other and stepped up into the car.

"Excuse me," she asked the driver, "can you tell me where I should get off?"

He didn't answer, only gave a quick jerk of his chin and motioned toward the rows of seats behind him.

She took her place near the front, settling onto the wooden bench and wrapping her fingers around the brass pole beside her as the car lurched forward.

The ride began smoothly, but as it rounded a sharp corner, the streetcar tipped first to one side, then the other, rocking her roughly. Estella tightened her grip and steadied herself. Only a few passengers dotted the car at this quiet hour of the day, their faces blank or buried in papers.

Suddenly, with a jolt, the streetcar came to a stop.

"Offa here-a, ma'am," the driver boomed.

Startled, Estella stood and stepped toward the front, reaching into her purse for the fare. But when she tried to hand him the coin, he raised a calloused hand and waved her toward the sidewalk without a word. Only then did she understand his silence—the thick accent, the clipped speech. His broken Italian-English, foreign yet familiar in a city built on labor and hope, was just another thread in the tapestry of Philadelphia. A melting pot, they called it. A city of industry and immigrants, dreams and hardship. No wonder it was called a workshop. Estella tucked the unused coin into her pocket and stepped onto the pavement. Ahead of her loomed the building that might hold the answers she was looking for.

Estella stood before the huge doors of the Children's Aid Society and took a deep breath before walking in to seek assistance. Nervous and with no idea of how to approach this big undertaking she pushed through the wide doorway into a very large lobby filled with women and children. The street she walked in from seemed much quieter than the hollow echoes of fussy children inside. She saw a desk in the distance and made her way through the maze of people. An older woman sat behind the desk and without much expression asked how she could help Estella, obviously without children, and assumed her presence was for something altogether different.

Estella started to explain, "My husband went to work many weeks ago and hasn't returned home. My children and..." But was unable to finish her words.

The stern-faced woman handed her a folder with papers, flatly stating, "Fill it out and bring them back to me."

There was unkindness in the woman's voice, sharp enough to sour the air, and it seemed to seep into every corner of the building. Estella crossed the large, echoing room once more and took a seat to complete the paperwork. She focused intently on each question, pouring her hope into every answer, praying this effort might offer some measure of security for herself and the children.

When she finished, she rose and joined the line at the desk. When it was finally her turn, she handed the folder to the woman, who gave it a cursory glance before lifting a heavy rubber stamp. Without pause, she slammed it down on the top page: *ABANDONED.*

The sound echoed louder than any voice. Estella flinched as if struck, her face flushing with shame. It was as though the word itself had been hurled at her, branding her not just on paper—but in spirit.

The expressionless woman looked up at Estella and said, "We'll send a case worker to your home soon to interview you." With that she empathetically closed the folder and tossed it on a heap behind her.

Not feeling all too well about the experience, Estella stepped out onto the sidewalk and decided she needed to walk a little way before she found the streetcar to return home. There were many more people out and about, walking as if in a hurry, crossing the streets haphazardly, dashing between horse and wagon, automobiles and trolleys. The businessmen, most likely bankers, were all dressed alike in dark suits, while wearing hats. The ladies all wore long skirts topped with a fashionable hat. Estella took notice of what she didn't have and how things had changed while she was raising her children. Dressed rather plainly compared to all the others around her, the men still tipped their hats to her, and she thought she caught a glimpse of a few staring at her with interest. She certainly hadn't seen that look in ages nor did she encourage it, most especially from strangers.

Estella's mind reeled from her visit to the Children's Aid Society. The building's echoing halls, the clipped voices, the stream of faces—it had all left her overwhelmed. Lost in thought, she barely registered the commotion on the street until it was nearly too late. A Ford Model T, wobbling wildly, suddenly veered from the roadway. One of its wheels shot off, rolling ahead like a rogue cannonball. Before she could move, a tall gentleman stepped swiftly from the bank's doorway and seized her arm, pulling her back just as the automobile careened to a stop against the short curb.

Estella gasped, stumbling in his grip. She bit her lip hard—so hard she tasted blood. A shudder ran through her as she realized how close she had come to being struck. The thought chilled her: if she had been hit... who would care for the children?

It took a moment before the man's quick actions registered fully in her mind.

"Kind sir," she said breathlessly, "I am most grateful for your protection—for pulling me from danger."

The man tipped his hat slightly, his voice steady but warm. "My name is Stephen Masters," he said. "Are you all right?"

She nodded, though her hands trembled slightly. She felt so indebted to him, so startled, that she barely thought before speaking.

"Kind sir," she blurted, "I must find a way to repay your kindness."

He gave a small smile. "Do you have a name?"

She met his eyes, steadying herself. "My name is Estella Fidler," she replied. "I'm not familiar with this part of town—all these people, automobiles, and wagons. It's a bit overwhelming."

He nodded, understanding. "It can be," he said. "But you're safe now."

Curiously, Stephen inquired about what had brought her here. It was very apparent to him with her attire that she wasn't the ordinary wife or secretary of a businessman. She did not know what to say and paused for a moment in thought.

He immediately recognized her discomfort and reached into his pocket retrieving a contact card with his name and business information, "Please, take this and if ever you come to this part of town again, I'd like for you to come visit."

Estella took the contact card Stephen had offered, thanked him once more, and tucked it carefully into her bag. "Good afternoon to you, Mr. Masters," she said with a small, respectful nod before turning away.

As she hurried down the bustling sidewalk, her thoughts shifted from the day's close call to something more pressing—the time. It was growing late, and the children would be expecting her home before supper. At the corner, a small grocery market caught her eye. Drawn by the display of produce in the window and the scent of freshly turned soil clinging to the root vegetables, she stepped inside. She scrounged in her bag for the remaining coins, mindful to save enough for her streetcar fare. Her fingers closed around just enough to buy a few modest items: a handful of decent potatoes, a firm onion, and a small hunk of shoulder meat—surprisingly cheaper than what her neighborhood market would've charged.

Pleased with her bargain, she stepped out just in time to see the electric streetcar slowing to a stop at the corner. Without hesitation, she clutched her parcel and ran, leaping aboard as the driver waited just long enough for her to catch the step.

She didn't look back. Down the street, half veiled by the crowd and fading light, Stephen Masters stood at a quiet distance. He hadn't followed with the intention to intrude—but something about the determined woman had held his attention. He watched as she boarded the streetcar, noting the direction it took. Then, without a word, he turned and walked away, slipping her name and face into the corners of his memory.

The streetcar made more stops along the route home, and it seemed to take longer now. Perhaps because Estella wanted to be as far away from the experience she'd had at the Children's Aid office as well as nearly being run over by a rogue automobile.

Then Stephen Masters' image took hold of her thoughts. What were the chances of that encounter? She recalled him handing his contact card to her and removed it from her bag to glance at his name and an address that he had obviously walked out of when they met. The streetcar came to a stop and Estella recognized the corner very well. She tucked the card away, grabbed up her bag of food from the market and stepped off the streetcar.

***

A week had passed since Estella's visit downtown to inquire at the Children's Aid Society. She nervously wondered when she would hear from them and receive help, if at all. She had taken in more laundry, thanks to Mrs. Murphy putting in a word for her at church. That, for the moment at least, kept food on their table. She would have to find more suitable work soon. It had never occurred to her that this would be the life she ran toward happily against her family's wishes. It all felt like a lifetime ago.

Between washing and hanging laundry and shuffling personal belongings over to Mrs. Murphy's next door, there was very little time for rest. The constant activity kept her mind occupied and made the days pass quickly. The children happily slept later and played longer at the park with friends during these summer months.

Little Florence spent more time at home than her older siblings, but she enjoyed the crayon she was given as a gift by her teacher at the end of the school year. It was a pretty sky blue. John and Frances had also been given a crayon and they shared them with her, adding a bright red and green to her collection. She would take the old newspapers and draw frilly flowers and vines that swirled around the news of the day. Estella would peek in on Florence between washing and hanging clothes and admire her cute artwork. And on this particular day she heard a gentle knock on the front door.

A smartly dressed older man stood on the top step of the rowhouse, a brown folder tucked under his arm. It was the folder that jolted Estella back to reality—reminding her instantly of her recent visit to the Children's Aid Society downtown.

She pulled her sleeves down over her red, aching hands, raw from hours of scrubbing laundry, and quickly smoothed her hair back from her forehead, hoping to make a decent first impression.

He introduced himself as an interviewer from the Division of Aid, following up on her application, and asked if he might come in for a brief discussion.

"Of course," she said, her voice even, though her heart was already pounding. She led him into the front room, modest and worn, with just enough furnishings to make it livable.

He began with formal questions about the head of the household.

Estella's cheeks flushed as she spoke. Her husband, Aaron, the father of her three children, had not returned home from the mill weeks ago. She explained that she had filed a missing person's report but had heard nothing since.

Unwittingly, as she went on, offering honest details of her struggle—the irregular meals, the absence of support, the constant worry—she had no idea that her words were setting into motion a shift that would alter the course of their lives.

The man nodded as she spoke, offering little in the way of response, just the occasional scratch of pen to paper. He asked where she and the children lived, and if the housing had been provided by the mill.

Estella assumed he meant to determine what help she might qualify for—whether the children had a roof over their heads and whether she could realistically keep them fed and clothed.

He jotted a few final notes, then slowly closed the folder and capped his pen. Resting the folder on his lap and folding his hands atop it, he looked at her with practiced gentleness.

"Our agency would be pleased to assist with the children," he said carefully. "We'll arrange for them to be brought to our downtown site for further interviews."

Estella felt the room tilt ever so slightly. The word "arrange" lodged in her chest like a stone.

She had come seeking help. She hadn't realized she might be opening the door to something else entirely.

Estella nodded her head in approval with an audible sigh and he handed her a slip of paper with a time scribbled onto it for having the children ready to be taken downtown. It had specific instructions for sending along a comforting familiar item from home such as a doll, ball or toy for each child. Estella had mixed feelings about this interview, but didn't want to stand in the way of receiving help and agreed to send the children with one of the division team members the next day. She wanted to discuss this with them over supper, preparing them for the interview. The man was finished with his work, thanked her for her time and she walked him to the door, watching him descend the steps onto the sidewalk.

Estella returned to the kitchen and sliced a small apple for Florence, handing her the pieces one by one while nibbling on a bit herself. The child chewed contentedly at the table, her small fingers sticky with juice.

Estella turned her focus to the evening meal, preparing a large pot of stew, her go-to supper, hearty and forgiving, able to stretch across a few meals if needed. She stirred it thoughtfully, letting the gentle simmer fill the quiet room.

With the stew underway, she moved on to the day's laundry, sorting and folding as the scent of broth and vegetables warmed the air. Her thoughts wandered, as they often did, to Aaron. She wondered if they would ever hear from him again.

The children rarely asked about their father. Even young as they were, they had sensed his absence long before he had physically left. When he was home, not at the mill, he had been distant, withdrawn. The mood in the house would shift, growing tense and silent. It wasn't lost on the older children that he often slipped out after they went to bed. The sound of the door, the creak of footsteps down the front steps—they knew. He never said where he went. But his actions spoke volumes. He had made it clear, in his own silent way, where he preferred to spend his time.

Estella sighed and wrung out the last damp garment, hanging it to dry with practiced hands. She tucked a lock of hair behind her ear and glanced toward the stew pot.

Whatever came next, she would be ready.

The children were up early and dressed in their finest clothes. Estella made them a delicious porridge breakfast with the last sliced apple and a dash of cinnamon. A splash of cream cooled it down enough for them to eat. She wanted them well fed and to look their best for the day ahead. Instead of cleaning up the breakfast dishes she ushered the children into the front sitting room to encourage them about the day ahead. Trying to make it out to be a fun adventure she asked them to remember it all so they could share it at suppertime together. Florence had her soft little rag doll that always comforted her to sleep. Frances took along the book they enjoyed reading together and said she would continue their next chapter. John had his favorite baseball card that came in a package of gum his father gave to him. They rarely got dressed in their finest clothes unless they were going to church for a special occasion.

A large woman tapped at the door. She introduced herself to Estella as the case worker, Martha Maddison, who would escort and take in the children. She handed Estella a folder with instructions that she advised her to read later to understand the process better. Florence did not want to go along and put up a fuss, but her brother John stepped in to distract her for a moment and got her to think of this as a game.

Estella hugged and kissed each of them goodbye, holding on just a moment longer than usual. She reminded them gently, "Remember all the details so you can tell me everything later," then paused, her voice softening. "I love you."

They nodded, wide-eyed and solemn, and climbed into the waiting vehicle—a first for all of them. Estella stood rooted in place as the automobile pulled away slowly, then disappeared down the road and out of sight.

That image—their small faces framed in the window, the gentle wave, the sound of the engine fading—would be forever seared into her memory.

She had been tricked and nearly fell over with disbelief. The folder she held in her hands fell to the floor and she let out a loud, painful shriek, "No, how could you have let this happen?" Her entire body began to convulse as she sobbed after reading the contents of the folder, "For the safety and welfare of the children it has been determined by our agency that they must be removed from your care until such a time as they can be given a stable home for the following reasons."

There were remarks handwritten below by the interviewer the previous day, "Abandoned by husband, mill worker community, mill housing and furniture denied, children need immediate shelter and care, recommend orphanage home until housing can be secured, no immediate family of record."

The anguish was so great that she collapsed into a heap on the front room sofa and wept for what seemed like hours. She could barely breathe and with her mouth agape for air she turned and with big swollen eyes glanced up to see a very worried Mrs. Murphy standing over her.

"Lordy, I thought me was goin' to have to call on the sergeant, ya had me worried yee was dead. What eva happened, where are the children?" Mrs. Murphy blurted out.

"It happened all so fast and before I knew it the children were gone." Estella said.

"What are ya talkin' about, what happened?" Mrs. Murphy pressed.

Estella sadly relayed to her the horrific events that took place.

Mrs. Murphy quietly listened and rubbed her hand up and down Estella's back for comfort. "Let's get ya up and go sit at the kitchen table."

The two ladies moved to the kitchen and Mrs. Murphy motioned for Estella to sit at the table. She busied herself getting the hot water kettle started and looked into Estella's nearly bare cupboards, pulling together a few things for the two of them to nibble on with tea.

Estella looked dazed and felt numb. Mrs. Murphy smeared the soft butter onto the stale bread, put it on the dish next to the teacup and returned to the table with both plates. She sat down across from Estella and looked her straight in the eyes and said, "Drink up cause we've got work to do."

Mrs. Murphy flat out told Estella that the priority now was getting her to move out of the mill house to her home next door. The mill would most likely refund part of the money they withheld at the beginning of the month for the house. That would be a start. It shouldn't take too long for the two of them to gather up the family's personal effects.

The furnishings, including the washing machine, all stayed with the mill home. Mrs. Murphy instructed Estella to work on the hired laundry and to get that finished while she took the stairs to the children's rooms. She couldn't imagine Estella would be very productive in that endeavor.

There were books and little paper dolls in the girl's room that she carefully folded up into the clothes. Empty flour sacks once used for laundry were now stuffed with all their belongings. Once she finished, she went across the hall to John's room and gathered his clothing in the same way along with his little collection of pebbles and a marble or two. Sadly, Mrs. Murphy had helped other families in similar straits before. She was something of an old pro.

Estella finished up folding all the clothes and orderly stacking them for the two households she had taken in for extra income. Mrs. Murphy came down the stairs with the children's belongings to take next door. She leaned them in the doorway. She told Estella she would pack her kitchen dishes and pans using her bedding and towels and gently put them into the milk crates to easily store them for her. "Yer gonna need 'em at your new home someday soon," she smiled, trying to keep positive.

The ladies worked hard all day long, cleaning as they went until all the mundane packing and wrapping of personal effects was accomplished. They stopped for nothing, and the work kept Estella from breaking down, although the thought of the children in a strange place made her tear up.

Once the hired laundry was picked up, Mrs. Murphy and Estella began to take all of the packed belongings over to the Murphy's home. She made it easy for Estella and gave her the entire front room in her home. They only used it for holidays with family. This made it a little easier for them to eliminate a set of stairs to navigate while moving her belongings. Mrs. Murphy had already made up the couch in the room as a bed for Estella. Both ladies were exhausted, but they had finished and were relieved to lock the door behind them.

Descending the stairs to the sidewalk below, Estella paused and turned to look back at what had once been her home. In the span of a heartbeat, it was all gone—her husband, her children, the life she had clung to. She drew in a sharp breath and forced the ache down deep, refusing to let self-pity take hold.

Straightening her shoulders, she made herself a silent promise: she would find steady, respectable work, and she would create a home for her children once more. Holding fast to that resolve, she followed her companion, and together the two women stepped into Mrs. Murphy's house, carrying with them the quiet weight of determination.

***

Estella had fallen into a deep, dreamless sleep from sheer exhaustion. But when she stirred in the early morning light, disoriented and unsure of where she was, the weight of the previous day came rushing back. The memories struck her like a wave, and she bolted upright, heart pounding. The shock had been dulled by fatigue the night before, but now, fully awake, the reality was sharp and unavoidable.

She stayed silent, still tucked away in the front room, not wanting to intrude. From beyond the doorway, she could hear Mr. Murphy coming down the stairs—his heavy footsteps and the faint creak of the worn floorboards.

He moved quietly about the kitchen, opening drawers and cupboards, fumbling for his tin lunch pail. Moments later, Mrs. Murphy joined him, her presence light and efficient as she fixed breakfast and packed his meal for the long shift ahead. Mr. Murphy didn't speak much. He never had, really. He was a quiet man, worn from the years and the endless hours at the mill.

Mrs. Murphy had already assured Estella he wouldn't mind her staying—that he was hardly home except to eat and sleep. But still, Estella felt awkward, like a guest out of place.

She remained in the front room, waiting for the moment he would leave. Soon, she heard the scrape of his chair being pushed back, followed by his steady footsteps. He walked over to his wife, bent slightly, and pressed a kiss to her cheek.

"Sweetie, I love ya," he murmured before heading out the door.

Estella blinked, unexpectedly touched by the small tenderness in his voice. She had almost forgotten what that sounded like.

"Good morning, Mrs. Murphy," Estella whispered so not to be too disruptive to the mood of the day.

"Good mornin', Estella, ya can at least call me Nora by now. Ya be wantin' some coffee"?

Estella nodded and came over to Nora and took the cup from her. She did not want to be waited on and wanted to be more of a help than a burden while she was kindly given a place to live. Nora told her to go have a seat and sip on the hot, bold liquid energy.

"There's only room for one of us at this ol' stove and it rather knows me workin' it so you best sit yerself down. What'll it be, one or two eggs?" Nora asked.

The ladies both ate their eggs and toasted bread in silence. When they finished the last bite, Estella rose and said the least she could do was wash the dishes. She was more than happy to do this chore. Once the dishes were cleared and washed the ladies shared another cup of coffee together and Estella told her about the incident the other day with the runaway automobile and the fateful meeting with a banker, Stephen Masters, who pulled her to safety while also giving her his contact card.

Nora listened, keenly aware of that name from the papers. He was not just a banker, but a well-known and respected businessman in Philadelphia.

Estella had made up her mind—she would return and pay him a visit today. She knew the only way to get her children back was to find work. With steady income, she could begin the search for a place to rent, a home where they could all be together again.

She still had a few spare coins from the laundry she delivered the day before, just enough to take the streetcar back to the spot where everything had shifted the week before. She didn't know what skills were required to work in a bank, but she was quick, willing, and eager to learn. It had to be better than spending half her life in a hot, grimy mill, breathing in dust and risking injury with every shift.

Her thoughts turned sharply to the children and their current situation. The ache in her chest gave way to resolve. She pushed back from the table, thanked Nora for the meal, and quietly cleared the dishes.

"I've got to go," she said, her voice low but steady. And with that, she stepped out, propelled by the one thing that always gave her courage: the thought of bringing her children home.

Wearing her finest clothes, Estella walked to the end of the mill housing along the sidewalk of rowhomes and turned onto the main street to hop on a streetcar that would take her downtown. She was familiar with it from her last experience. She would pay a visit to the kind gentleman and inquire about a job. She hoped such a well-known person would be available.

The streetcar made more stops, and the ride seemed to take a lot longer than she recalled. When she recognized the tall buildings coming into sight, she knew her stop was getting closer.

As she descended the steps of the streetcar, she took a deep breath and set out to find the address on the calling card. She noticed numbers to the right side of the doorways on the buildings. She quickly found the doorway listed on Stephen Masters' calling card, but it was two buildings further from the one he had walked out the day that they stumbled upon one another.

As Estella reached for the door it was opened by a well-dressed man who invited her to enter the foyer area and take a seat. "Madam, someone will be with you shortly," he formally stated.

A smartly dressed woman came out into the foyer sitting area and asked Estella how she could help her.

Without hesitation she spoke up and said, "I've come to see Stephen Masters. We met one another and he gave me this calling card," she confidently stated.

With that the woman knew it was not a news agent or other prying organization and offered, "Of course, come with me. He's expected to return shortly and wouldn't want to miss your visit. Please tell me your name so that I can let him know who's calling."

"Estella Fidler," she stated, wondering if she should have used her maiden name instead.

Estella was led into a sumptuous, grand seating room, far beyond anything she had ever known. The overstuffed furnishings were richly upholstered, and large oil paintings adorned the paneled walls, their gilded frames catching the light. Ornate rugs covered the polished floors, and crystal accents gleamed from every corner.

It was the kind of wealth she had only ever read about in books. Even her childhood home, prosperous by working-class standards, had never approached such splendor.

The well-dressed woman asked gently if she would care for tea or anything else while she waited for Mr. Masters.

"No, thank you," Estella replied politely, offering a small, practiced smile.

She took a seat and, with a nervous breath, brushed down her long skirt, smoothing a wrinkle at her knee. She adjusted her posture, sitting tall, composed, careful to make herself neat and proper.

Though she felt somewhat out of place amid such opulence, she refused to let it rattle her.

What mattered most, the only thing that mattered, was her purpose for being there.

Her children.

She repeated it quietly in her mind like a steady drumbeat: *For the children.*

The woman reappeared and said, "Mr. Masters will see you now, come along with me."

Estella paused for a moment, wondering—Had he been here all along? She hadn't seen Stephen enter through the front, but then again, perhaps the other door she'd seen him use the day of the accident led to another part of the building.

The woman gestured for her to follow, and Estella did so, her steps careful on the richly carpeted floor. They entered a spacious office, elegant and sun-drenched, with tall windows stretching from floor to ceiling. The light poured in, casting a warm glow over the large, polished desk that sat squarely in the center of the room.

Behind it was the man she remembered, the one who had pulled her from the path of the careening automobile and rogue wheel on that hectic Philadelphia street.

Stephen Masters stood as she entered, offering her a gracious smile.

"Please, have a seat," he said warmly.

Estella nodded and sat with quiet poise. The assistant gave her a polite nod before gently closing the door behind her.

Stephen leaned forward slightly, folding his hands on the desk.

"Thank you for coming," he said, his tone genuine. "I must admit, I'm quite surprised you returned, but I'm very glad you did. I've wondered whether you made it home safely. You seemed in such a rush that day."

He paused briefly, then asked, "What brings you into town again?"

Estella took a deep breath nervously and shared with him her reason for calling on him. "I am here to inquire if there is a job you might have for hire."

It wasn't exactly the answer he'd hoped for, but she was here now, and that was something. Stephen offered a thoughtful nod, keeping his expression open. He leaned back slightly in his chair, studying her with quiet interest.

"And what type of work would you say you're qualified for?" he asked, his tone even, encouraging. "I assume you've had to manage quite a bit on your own." He didn't want to press, not yet, but something in her eyes told him there was more behind her visit than polite thanks.

Not wanting to be dismissed for a lower-paying position, Estella straightened slightly in her chair and met his gaze. "My experience has been mostly in caretaking," she said with quiet confidence. "But I was a very good student in school, especially in mathematics and English. I'm also very willing to train."

She hesitated just a moment, then added firmly, "I can learn anything I set my mind to."

Stephen smiled and said, "I can see that determination in you. Is that what brought you into town the other time?"

"No, sir, I was here for another reason when our worlds collided that day. It was not until recently that I decided to search for a job and immediately thought of our meeting and the calling card you gave to me," she replied.

Easing her mind a bit, he said, "Well, I'm glad that you came to see me because we are opening a new bank branch in the Overbrook area, outside of the city, and we are looking for trainees in all areas of that location. The training will take place downtown and it will require afterwards reporting for work in Overbrook permanently. There will be a wage paid during your training and uniforms will be provided. Would this be something that interests you?"

"Yes! When may I begin this training?" Estella eagerly leaped at the opportunity.

Stephen hadn't expected such a direct and composed response. Her clarity and conviction caught him off guard in the best way.

He paused, collecting his thoughts before replying. "You can begin as early as tomorrow," he said carefully. "I'll have Ruth, the woman who brought you in, take you to be fitted for your uniforms nearby." Then, with a slight smile and the hint of something more in his tone, he added, "And perhaps, once that's finished, you might care to join me for lunch."

It was phrased as a statement more than a question.

Estella parted her lips to respond, but before she could speak, the door opened with perfect timing. Ruth stepped in, almost as if summoned by intuition.

Stephen turned to her. "Ruth, please assist Miss Fidler with everything she needs to report for training in the morning."

Ruth nodded briskly, already reaching for her gloves and bag, ready to carry out her instructions.

Estella stood, still absorbing the pace of it all, surprised, grateful, and unsure of what she had just stepped into. But her purpose remained clear.

Stephen looked directly at Estella and said, "I shall await her at The Club for lunch at one o'clock."

Ruth gave a slight nod, then turned and led Estella out of the office.

She didn't say much as they walked, but her thoughts churned. In all her time working alongside Mr. Masters, she had not seen him this engaged, this animated, since before his wife had passed the year prior. Since then, he had moved through his days with a quiet, haunted air, completing meetings, overseeing operations, and fulfilling obligations with a kind of subdued efficiency. He wasn't cold—just distant. He hadn't only lost a wife. He had lost the child they had longed for together. The child they had prepared for, dreamed about, built a future around.

All of it was taken in a single, shattering moment. And though Stephen had never spoken of it aloud, Ruth knew that part of him remained frozen in that loss. The moment he had watched his world collapse was one he couldn't undo.

He had told her only once how it had happened. She'd heard him say the words as if through fog: "If only I was there... if I'd only gotten help sooner..."

And now, he'd spoken of Estella, not just with interest, but with something like hope. Ruth had seen it in his eyes when he pulled her into his office. He had stepped out that day and seen Estella in danger, just as he had once seen his wife, but this time, he had been in time. He had pulled Estella to safety. And perhaps, in some unspoken place inside him, that moment had stirred something deeper. A sense of redemption. Or a fragile second chance.

THE ORPHANAGE

Frances, John & Florence | Philadelphia | Summer 1910

The children sat quietly in the back of the automobile, their wide eyes taking in every unfamiliar sight. The plump older woman who had only just come to visit them now rode in the front passenger seat, speaking little. It was the first time any of them had ridden in an automobile, and seeing the world pass by through moving windows felt like the beginning of the adventure their mother had once promised them.

Florence clung to John's arm, resting her head gently against him for comfort. Frances sat still and quiet, her hands folded in her lap, her gaze fixed on the tall buildings and steady stream of people along the city sidewalks. She looked thoughtful, perhaps even brave, though her silence spoke volumes.

The ride seemed to stretch on endlessly, each street a new world flashing past. Finally, the automobile began to slow, turning off the main road and onto Milnor Street. As they rounded the corner, the children caught their first glimpse of the Delaware River. Wide, glittering, and impossibly real—it felt like stepping into a story.

They drove a short way along the river and came to a stop outside of a large iron gate. A short man, dressed plainly, came from behind a stone wall area and greeted the driver who showed him a handful of paperwork. He peered into the rear of the car and again back down at the papers as he thumbed through carefully. Not sure where they were, the children looked at one another questioningly. The man returned to the imposing gates and pulled one aside, waving the driver to come through.

Within the gated property sat a tall brick three story house and several other buildings. The automobile came to a complete stop and a person in a long black robe and hood descended the steps and conversed with the Maddison woman. The driver opened the door, and had the children step outside of the automobile.

John, Frances, and Florence stood at the base of the wide stone steps of St. Vincent's Orphan Asylum, uncertain and afraid. None of them understood what was happening.

Sister Henrietta, her black habit fluttering slightly in the breeze, motioned for them to follow.

They climbed slowly, hand in hand, the stone steps stretching upward like a threshold to a world unknown. At the top, two towering white pillars framed the entrance. The large wooden doors with thick glass panes etched in a worn crosshatch creaked open into a cavernous lobby.

Sister Henrietta led them across the tiled floor, the echo of their footsteps bouncing off the high ceiling. A long hallway stretched out ahead, dimly lit and cool.

When they reached a set of doors, Sister Henrietta turned to John and gently took his arm. "You'll just go into this room here," she said, her tone kind but firm. John hesitated, glancing at his sisters.

Sensing their fear, Sister Henrietta added quickly, "Don't worry, we'll all come back together soon."

Florence clung tightly to Frances' arm, her small fingers gripping the fabric with quiet desperation. Her wide eyes darted around the unfamiliar hallway, scanning every corner, as if searching for a way back home—back to something known, something safe.

Inside the girls' room, a folded set of plain clothing was handed to each of them.

"These are your new uniforms," Sister Henrietta explained.

The girls looked at one another, then slowly began to undress.

Sister Henrietta remained nearby, carefully examining their slight frames for signs of neglect—lesions, swelling, infection, or anything in need of attention. Across the hall, John was undergoing the same quiet examination.

Once dressed in their matching uniforms, gray and modest, with stiff collars and tightly stitched seams, the children were brought together again and led into a large office. The room was dark and solemn; the walls clad in heavy wood paneling. The furniture loomed large, the kind meant to dwarf its visitors.

Seated at the great desk was an older woman in a long black robe and stiff white habit. Her expression was unreadable, her face pale and pinched.

"This is Sister Theresa," Sister Henrietta announced.

Sister Theresa gave a slight nod but did not smile. "Please, children," she said, her voice flat and measured, "have a seat."

The three of them obeyed quietly, side by side on the hard wooden bench. Florence's legs swung just above the floor. Frances took her hand without looking at her. Everything felt colder now. Smaller. And none of them knew what would come next.

She asked Frances for the book she was holding. She advised her that it was not permitted in the orphanage, and that other appropriate reading would be provided. She then went over a long list of rules for the orphanage.

What was only supposed to be an outing had turned into the children's nightmare. John spoke up and asked when the driver would return for them to take them home.

Sister Theresa looked at him coldly and said, "this is your home."

A silent fear and darkness fell over all three of them.

Once Sister Theresa had explained to the children about the situation and conditions of living while in the asylum, she called for Sister Henrietta to take the children to their stations.

Florence clung to her doll while they were led down a long hallway to a set of stairs which they climbed to the next floor. When they reached the top of the steps, a man wearing all black met them and ushered John away to another area, causing great panic and fear in Florence.

The girls were led in a different direction from the boys, following the nun down a dim hallway into a large room filled with a sea of beds arranged in neat, rigid rows. The Sister stopped beside two narrow beds placed side by side—one for Florence, the other for Frances. There was barely any space between them. They were instructed to set down the blankets and pillows they had been given, along with the stiffly folded uniforms issued when they first arrived.

Afterward, the children were led down a staircase to the basement dining hall. The air buzzed faintly with the sounds of movement—footsteps, the clatter of trays—but not voices. The silence among the children already seated or moving through the line was striking. They all wore the same matching uniforms, their faces blurred by sameness.

Sister Henrietta quickly formed them into a line and instructed them to take a tray. They followed closely behind the others, watching carefully, mimicking each step. One by one, they received the same rationed meal: a scoop of stringy meat, a helping of green beans, a dry potato patty, and a glass of milk.

The dining room mirrored the dormitory—long rows of tables, everything lined up with precision. Florence, John, and Frances found three seats together and sat quietly. They had already been told: no talking during meals, no eating until every child was seated and a communal prayer had been said.

When the prayer was finally spoken, the children picked up their utensils and began to eat. The food was plain, barely warm, and far from appetizing, but the day had been long and their hunger deep.

Florence mostly picked at her plate, unable to stomach more than a few bites. John and Frances quietly ate from her tray, remembering the Sister's warning about not wasting food. The silence at the table remained—each child lost in their own thoughts, their new reality settling in.

After finishing their meal, the children lined up in silence, marching in rhythm to stack their trays at the end of the dining hall. A few of the older boys and girls assigned to cleanup duty disappeared through a swinging door into the back kitchen. The rest were ushered outside, where a large grassy field opened behind the building, sloping gently toward the river in the distance.

There, at last, came a sense of breath. Of freedom. Though rules still loomed, strict instructions forbade anyone from venturing past a certain line of trees and thick shrubs near the riverbank, the fresh air and space offered a rare reprieve. Children ran in clusters, their voices rising in laughter and chatter. Some clambered onto the swings, taking turns pushing each other.

Florence held tightly to Frances' hand as they walked along the edge of the play area, eyes scanning the crowd for their brother. It didn't last long. The loud, insistent clang of the bell echoed across the field, drawing every head toward the looming, three-story building. Time to go back in.

The children lined up again, boys to the left, girls to the right. They were led down to the chapel on the lower level, where rows of simple pews faced a modest altar. The boys filed in first, taking their seats on one side of the aisle. The girls followed, settling into the opposite pews.

A priest stood at the front, his robe dark against the pale stone wall behind him. Without much preamble, he began the evening prayer.

Up. Down. Kneel. Sit. Stand again. The movements were unfamiliar, and Florence simply followed the rhythm of the others, watching for cues, trying not to stand out. She didn't understand the words. It all felt foreign, strange, like stepping into someone else's dream.

But then, as she tilted her head and glanced across the aisle, her eyes found John.

He was seated a few rows up, back straight, expression still. Relief bloomed quietly in her chest.

He was near. And for the moment, that was enough.

The children were led back up the stairs to their sleeping areas. Sister Henrietta pulled the two girls aside as the others who knew the routine walked by. She instructed them to dress for bed. There was to be no talking or play of any sort.

Once lights were out and all the children were lying in their beds a final prayer was recited. Florence was scared and quietly slipped over to Frances' bed. There had been so much shuffling that this was the first time the two of them had stopped to even question where they were and what had happened. None of it made sense.

Florence whispered to her big sister, "Do you think mom knows where we are?"

Frances didn't know what to say and whispered back reassuringly, "I'm sure she will come get us soon." The two girls lay there silently just clinging to one another. It was so comforting that they were next to each other. They both gazed out at the tall windows across the aisle and other beds. The night sky was lit up by the moon.

Frances whispered quietly, "Look, mom can see the same moon and stars so she can't be too far away. Remember when we read about that in the lost swan book? I think John will see that same sky and be with us right here and right now."

They both lay there gazing out the window at the night sky. Frances was keenly aware that she must stir Florence to slip back into her bed so they wouldn't get into trouble for breaking the rules.

Sleep came fast for both of them. What had begun as an adventure had turned into a worrisome journey of unknowns. They at least had one another aside from being separated from John. Knowing he was nearby reassured them.

Neither could imagine how that single night would mark the end of life as they knew it. The months ahead would stretch into years, and the distance between their worlds would only grow wider with time.

PALACE OF CONSUMPTION
Estella | Philadelphia | Summer 1910

The automobile was packed to the brim with shopping bags and boxes, leaving little room for Estella in the rear seat. She had been encouraged to wear one of the new outfits for her luncheon with Mr. Masters, though calling it a uniform felt like a stretch.

Ruth had taken her to the grand department store just a few blocks away, a place Estella had only glimpsed in newspaper advertisements and window displays. John Wanamaker's.

They called it the "Palace of Consumption", and Estella could see why. The soaring ceilings, gleaming counters, and attentive clerks gave the impression of something just shy of royalty. She had never stepped inside a store like it.

Ruth, however, moved through it with ease. She had once escorted Stephen's late wife on shopping trips just like this and knew the store well—where to find the finest ready-made dresses, which fabrics were best suited to modest refinement, and how to select pieces that blended practicality with quiet elegance.

With Ruth's guidance, the entire experience passed in a blur—hemlines were measured, gloves selected, hats tilted just so. It was all done in far less time than Estella expected.

As the hour neared for her luncheon with Stephen at "The Club", it seemed the entire city had taken to the streets. Philadelphia bustled with its usual midday chaos. A blend of pedestrians, clattering delivery wagons, honking automobiles, streetcars sparking along their tracks, and the steady clip-clop of horse-drawn carriages weaving between it all.

The driver eased the car to the curb, and Estella stepped out with quiet confidence. She had chosen a tailored coat suit for the occasion; the jacket neatly fitted over a high-necked lace gilet blouse.

The cut emphasized the gentle curve of her waist and fell gracefully over her hips. Her skirt, solid and pleated, reached to the tops of her ankles, just enough to reveal the polished tips of her shoes. Beneath it all, a silk petticoat moved with a subtle whisper. She wore a smart, structured hat adorned with a single bow—simple, elegant, and just daring enough to feel modern. For a brief moment, Estella felt as though she had stepped straight from the pages of a fashion advertisement in the *Ladies' Home Journal.*

Carefully, she climbed the steps leading to the grand entrance, steadying herself with the composure she had learned over years of necessity. A doorman, upright in his classic coat and tails, stood at attention. With a dignified nod, he opened the tall brass-handled doors and gestured her inside. Estella crossed the threshold, aware of every sound—her heels against the polished floor, the soft rustle of silk, the hush that seemed to follow her into this new chapter.

Estella came across the large gallery and was greeted by the maître' d. He escorted her to the table where Stephen was awaiting her arrival. He stood delighted and admired her transformation as she was seated. He took his place and they began to chat. He was quite taken by her plain beauty and the uncomplicated air of confidence she seemed to exude. However, their conversation seemed to leave him with more questions than answers.

A waiter came to the table with glasses of water and menus. Estella had not been out to dine, especially not to a place as grand as this, and was nervous about what to order. The server mentioned the fish and soup du jour and walked away for a moment to give them time to peruse the selection.

Stephen smiled at Estella. "Everything on the menu is delicious—I hope you'll try as many as you like." Once they placed their order, the conversation flowed on.

Estella shared most of her growing up in nearby Maryland and kept the conversation strictly about the time before she was married and had children. She would not lie to Stephen, but there was no good reason now to bring that part of her life up to him. She was keenly aware that he was very much smitten with her, and she was likewise attracted to him. Those details could wait. Her focus was having a job that paid her well enough so that she could afford her own home and retrieve her children from the Children's Aid Society. Clearly, she didn't want to complicate things with a relationship.

Over lunch, Stephen spoke thoughtfully of his younger years—growing up as the son and protégé of a respected banker, learning the trade under the firm yet watchful eye of his father. Recently, his father passed the baton fully to him, entrusting him with the legacy of their institution.

He recounted stories of early missteps and small victories, of ledger books and long days at the desk, offered with a quiet humility that softened his otherwise composed demeanor. Notably, he made no mention of his late wife or the child they had lost. That chapter, too painful and too personal, remained tucked away in silence. Estella did not press. She sensed it in his pauses, in the faint shadow that passed through his eyes when conversation veered too close. Instead, he shifted the topic to something forward-looking.

"There's a new position I've been planning," he said, leaning forward slightly. "A new bank just outside the city is underway. What we'd like to introduce is a new concept, a department run by and for women." He paused to gauge her reaction.

"We've seen growing interest among women—especially widows, working women, and wives managing household accounts wanting more direct involvement with their finances. And frankly, most banking halls don't offer them much welcome." I believe you'd be the perfect woman to lead this new Ladies' Department. It's a fresh space, one that could become a model for others. What do you think?"

Estella set her teacup gently onto its saucer, the soft clink filling the momentary hush between them. She met Stephen's gaze, composed but thoughtful.

"It's a generous offer, Mr. Masters," she began, her voice calm but layered with quiet emotion. "And it sounds like a remarkable opportunity—especially for someone like me."

Her fingers smoothed the edge of her napkin as she continued.

"I've never pictured myself behind a bank desk," she admitted with the faintest smile. "Most of my experience has been... less formal. But I've always taken pride in being dependable, quick to learn, and unafraid of hard work."

She hesitated, choosing her next words carefully.

"If this is truly something new, uncharted, then I suppose I'd be new to it too. But I'd want to understand what's expected of me. What kind of guidance or support would be in place."

She paused, lifting her chin just slightly. "I wouldn't want to take on a position only to discover it was never meant to succeed."

There was no bitterness in her tone, only quiet conviction, not from entitlement, but from experience, hard-earned and often overlooked.

She didn't offer her full story. Not yet. But Stephen could see it in her eyes: she was someone who had already carried much and who had more to prove than most.

Stephen leaned back slightly, studying her with growing respect. Her answer wasn't rehearsed. It wasn't the polished ambition of someone seeking status. It was steady, thoughtful, grounded in something real. He liked that.

"I appreciate your candor, Miss Fidler," he said, his voice warm, sincere. He paused, then added with a touch of curiosity, "You strike me as someone who's been underestimated before."

There was a slight smile tugging at the edge of his mouth.

"As for expectations," he continued, "I intend to make sure you're set up to succeed not just placed in a windowed corner and expected to smile politely. This department will be yours to shape, with guidance, of course, but also with room to grow into something meaningful."

He gestured loosely with his hand, as though drawing a larger picture in the air. "Women clients have needs, preferences, questions that many of our male bankers have never considered—frankly, have never been taught to consider. I believe that you, with the right support, could help build something new. Practical. Dignified. Necessary."

His gaze held hers.

"I hope you'll say yes."

Estella held his gaze for a moment, weighing not just the offer but the sense of trust behind it.

She gave a small, deliberate nod.

"Then yes, Mr. Masters. I accept." No dramatics just the calm assurance of a woman who knew the value of opportunity when it came.

Stephen's smile deepened, the first genuine one she had seen stretch across his face since entering the room.

"Excellent," he said simply. "I believe you'll make a fine addition."

Just then, a white-gloved waiter approached, wheeling a gleaming dessert cart with polished brass rails and glass domes that revealed a tempting array of confections; delicate tarts, sugar-dusted cakes, and individual trifles layered in crystal dishes.

Stephen gestured toward it with a gentleman's ease.

"Would you care for something sweet, Miss Fidler? I'm partial to the lemon tart myself though I'd argue the chocolate custard gives it a proper rival."

Estella allowed herself the faintest laugh, her shoulders easing just slightly. "For today," she said, "I think I'll try the tart. It seems like the right kind of bold."

Stephen arranged for his driver to take Estella home. She hesitated at first, reluctant to accept the kindness, but quickly remembered the earlier shopping trip and the abundance of parcels that had nearly overtaken the back seat of the automobile.

Together, they stepped into the grand, high-ceilinged foyer of "The Club", the marble floors gleaming beneath their shoes. Stephen motioned toward a crested bench near the entrance. "Please, sit. I'll summon the driver."

Estella nodded, smoothing her skirt as she took her seat, the day's events still settling around her like fine dust.

He returned a moment later, pausing before her with a warmth in his expression that hadn't been there when they first met.

"I'm very glad you came to see me today," he said.

Estella rose and offered a sincere smile. "Thank you, Mr. Masters. For the opportunity. I won't take it lightly. I'll work hard, for you and the bank."

He gave a slight nod, appreciative of her resolve.

Just then, the doorman gestured toward the front. The automobile had pulled up at the curb below. They descended the stone steps together, side by side. The city bustled around them, but for a brief moment, it all felt hushed.

Stephen's driver stood at attention, ready to open the door.

"Until next time," Stephen said, his voice low, steady.

Estella met his eyes. "Until next time."

And with that, she stepped into the automobile. As the vehicle eased into motion and pulled away from the city's heart, she glanced back only once to see Stephen already turning toward the tall doors, making his way back to the world he never quite left.

She sank gratefully into the padded seat of the automobile, though the comfort of it pressed awkwardly against the weight in her chest. As the car weaved past the tall buildings, she gave the driver only a brief description and pointed to a landmark—just enough for him to find his way. She would not have him stop in front of Nora's home. Not with neighbors watching. Not with questions waiting behind half-drawn curtains. She couldn't bear the pity. Or worse—the judgment.

The driver didn't argue. He helped with her parcels, setting them quietly along the curb. She nodded in thanks without lifting her eyes, already bracing herself for the walk to the front steps, the silence she would meet there.

She clutched the folds of her coat tighter, as if doing so could hold in everything that now threatened to spill over. Frances, John, Florence—each name a wound she carried just beneath the surface. They were gone now. In the care of the state. In the hands of strangers. No matter how many times she told herself it was temporary, that it was for their well-being, the ache never left her. It clawed at her in the quiet, in the click of a closing door, in the hush that had taken over every room.

She stepped off the curb and steadied herself. There was no time to fall apart. She still had errands to run, a story to hold together, and the slimmest hope that someday, somehow, she might bring them home again.

As she made her way down the street, she caught the eye of many, but none more than Nora who was sitting at the top step of her rowhouse.

"Well-well, look at ye, missy, all dolled up with more frillies. I can see with me own two eyes and I'm wantin' to hear all yer news."

Nora helped Estella into the front room with the packages she was carrying. She handed a plain white bag with handles to Nora that had a box of pastries Stephen had wrapped. She noticed him handing the bag to the driver after lunch and didn't realize it was for her until now. It was the least she could do for Nora and her husband, who had kindly taken her into their home.

She couldn't wait to share the entire day with Nora. Estella filled her in with every detail. They were both surprised by the turn of events. Estella described her training that was to begin in the morning at the downtown location. She would be working closely in all areas of the bank to learn the inner workings and departments so she could set up a Ladies' Department or women-only lounge within the new bank that was to open in Overbrook. The location would be very close to commute to, but she reassured Nora that she would look for a home for her and the children as soon as possible. She had not wanted to wear out her welcome of her gracious friend.

Neither Estella nor Nora knew much about banking, certainly not the significance of leading a Ladies' Department. Estella had seen articles in the newspaper now and then, discussing interest rates or economic markets, but she had never paid much attention to them. It simply never occurred to her that banking was something she would be part of, let alone a woman at the helm of it. But Stephen had assured her otherwise.

He had spoken with quiet conviction about the growing importance of financial services tailored to women, widows managing estates, young working women needing to save, and wives learning to navigate accounts independent of their husbands.

"This isn't just a desk and a title," he had told her. "It's a gateway."

Estella had always paid close attention to the headlines surrounding the women's suffrage movement, clipped articles, bold photographs, marches down Broad Street. The growing noise of change. The rights and freedoms women were fighting for; votes, voice, and visibility, weren't only political, they were practical. They would shape futures. Open doors. And now, unexpectedly, Estella was stepping through one of those doors.

She couldn't help but think that if she had possessed this kind of independence earlier, if she'd known how to manage money, to read the fine print, to ask the questions, her story, and her children's, might have unfolded differently. But that didn't matter now. Because change had come. And she was ready to meet it.

The two women continued chatting as Nora helped Estella hang up her new dresses and unpackage the rest of the accessories. It looked like a regal Christmas, with all the empty wrappers and boxes.

Nora also recognized that these outfits were not uniforms. Never one to hold back her thoughts, she blurted out, "This fella kinda gotta fancy for ya, doesn't he?"

Estella turned bright red as she recalled the day of the accident as the two locked eyes and for a moment, she felt something that had long escaped her consciousness but quickly dismissed it as the moment at hand.

She quickly replied with a defensive tone, "He is very passionate about his responsibility and duty to his position and values his customers and their needs. I'm fortunate, if you can call it that, to have stumbled into him that fateful day."

When they were all talked out Nora invited Estella to have supper with her and her husband, but she kindly declined, wanting to bathe and prepare herself for her big workday in the morning. She also did not want to be in the way of Mr. Murphy when he returned home from his hard-working job at the mill.

JOB TRAINING
Estella | Philadelphia | Summer 1910

The streets were bustling with automobiles and a stream of delivery wagons and people in nearly every direction that the eye could see. Up until this time Estella had been unaware of the city's vast activity and work ethic. Her eyes had been opened as if for the first time and she fit right into the buzz. Dressed in her fine new clothing, she had an air of confidence and walked upright and proud. Her thoughts of her children, though, grounded her in the focus of her mission. Today, she promised herself, was the beginning of a new and exciting journey. She felt a sense of energy that propelled her forward.

As she approached the prominent facade of the bank building, she felt a twinge of nerves. The imposing multi-story structure was embellished with ornate columns, pediments and large windows. The main entrance stood out because of an elaborate crescent made with a mix of marble and granite, signifying the status of a financial institution. It gave the feeling of strength, power and prestige on approach. The doorman tipped his hat and held the door open as she stepped inside, her footsteps echoing faintly in the quiet threshold. As she came across the massive doorway of this prestigious building, it opened into a spacious banking hall adorned with high ceilings, elaborate woodwork and large marble counters. She would spend the next month learning the positions and functions that would empower her to lead up a very important department in the newly created Overbrook branch.

As Estella walked to the marble counter, she caught sight of Ruth making her way toward her and felt a sense of relief. At least there was one person that she was familiar with and who knew why she was there.

"Good morning and welcome," Ruth warmly greeted Estella. "Let's find you a place to sit and call yours for the time you'll be with us in our main branch. We have a lot to see and accomplish today."

Estella followed along and the women stepped through a doorway that led to an area behind the countertops. Here there were rows of desks set back and out of sight from the main hall. Ruth led her to a desk that was adorned by an oversized window that looked out on the street-level business district. Here she placed her bag in a desk drawer and hung her shawl on a nearby hook.

Ruth knew her way around the bank from her many years of service. Estella learned that she grew up in a bankers' family and took a deep interest from a young age, often coming to work with her father, whom she adored. She knew everyone and frequently stopped, introducing various employees to Estella, indicating the need for them to share information pertinent to her position.

After the introductions and tour of the bank offices Ruth wound back to an area with a large steel lift. She pressed the button on the outside and the doors of the lift opened. She pulled across a fencing apparatus and the women stepped inside, closing the doors behind them. Pressing another button, it carried them quickly to another floor. As they walked off the lift, Estella recognized this as the waiting area outside Stephen's office. Now it made sense about the different entrances and the mazes of hallways and floors that were all interconnected.

Ruth escorted Estella into Stephen's office and told her, "He'll will be with you shortly," and turned to walk out the door.

Estella sat quietly by herself for the first time since she had arrived and took a deep breath in and sighed out with relief. Her mind was swirling with so much information. She was surprised at how fast the time had gone as it was nearly one o'clock.

Stephen stepped inside of the office and greeted her kindly, "So my dear, how was your first morning on the job? Did Ruth take care of you? Why don't we ride the lift to the underground restaurant below for a quick bite to eat and you can tell me all about it. I have another place I'd like to visit with you today afterwards."

The doors of the lift opened to reveal the famed "Rathskeller", one of the city's celebrated social establishments. At the time, it was considered the most elaborate and artistically adorned restaurant of its kind in the United States. True to its German origins, the name *Rathskeller* suggested a tavern or restaurant tucked beneath ground level, a place of warm lighting, hearty food, and spirited conversation.

Estella and Stephen stepped into the expansive room, her eyes sweeping across the vaulted ceiling, richly detailed columns, and the subtle hum that still lingered in the air despite the late hour. Time was short, so Stephen led them to the far side of the room, toward the wood-paneled bar, an opulent stretch of dark oak adorned with intricate carvings, beveled mirrors, and ornate brass fixtures. They took a seat at the grill counter, where the scent of roasted meats and spices still lingered. Though the peak lunch hour had passed, the remnants of a busy service were evident. Staff moved swiftly, clearing dishes, resetting tables, and restoring order to the lively space.

A large man in a white apron, clearly the cook, emerged from behind the counter with a warm nod.

"Mr. Masters," he said, recognizing Stephen immediately. "And Miss, welcome."

He presented them each with a printed menu, thick paper and elegant script, featuring the day's remaining specials. Estella scanned the offerings, still slightly awed by the setting. She had never eaten anywhere quite like this before. Yet here she was, with Stephen, being handed a menu.

Estella glanced around and noticed a pretty side room.

Stephen noticed her attention and told her, "That is the ladies' dining room and a few steps below that is for both gentlemen and ladies. We'll have to return sometime when they have live performances at the dinner hour."

The walls were all decorated with oil paintings. For being in a basement, it was well lit and bright. It had a very warm and cozy richness to it. She could see this being a retreat for many people from the chaos of the streets above.

Famished from the busy morning she was glad to see the food being placed before them so rapidly after they'd ordered. She picked up half of the grilled sandwich and took a large bite of the cheesy goodness. Stephen smiled to himself at her big appetite while he also devoured his sandwich. They ate quickly and didn't waste a moment getting back to work. They didn't return to the lift but rather walked up a short set of steps and were at street level where Stephen's driver was waiting for them. Both took a seat in the back and Estella noticed her bag and shawl were neatly set to the side.

The automobile pulled away from the curb, the rhythmic hum of the engine settling into a steady pace as they made their way out of the city.

Stephen turned slightly toward Estella. "I thought you might like a proper look at the bank where you'll be working—perhaps within the month, maybe sooner. A little tour, if you're willing."

Estella nodded, grateful for the gesture. The idea of seeing it made everything feel more tangible.

For a while, they sat quietly, watching the city unfold beyond the windows. They spoke easily, discussing the responsibilities of the role, the daily routine, the types of clients she might encounter. The city passed by in a familiar blur, people on corners, wagons and carriages weaving through traffic, the occasional burst of streetcar bells.

Then, without warning, the automobile turned down a street she knew too well. The mill row. Her block. Estella's heart gave a small flutter in her chest as her eyes caught the narrow stoops, the lines of laundry, the windows she had looked out of so many evenings.

Stephen, caught up in explaining a staffing detail, didn't seem to notice. Estella kept her gaze forward, sitting very still, her fingers lightly tightening in her lap. She was relieved when they turned again and left that stretch behind, the rows of soot-darkened homes giving way to quieter streets.

Soon, the city began to soften. There were fewer buildings, more trees. Open green parks flanked the roads now, with wide walking paths and benches nestled beneath budding branches. The air itself seemed to shift. Eventually, the automobile came to a smooth stop in front of a handsome stone building—stately but inviting. The sign out front bore the name of the bank in elegant lettering, carved deep into its facade.

Stephen stepped out first and turned to offer Estella his hand.

"This," he said with quiet pride, "is where your next chapter begins."

The bank was fully built, but just not open for business yet. It had been a welcome site for many of the nearby residents who would benefit the most from not having to travel into the city center to conduct their usual banking business. The two of them walked up the steps to the arched entryway. Once inside, Stephen led Estella across the large open banking area to a set of elevators. They went down to the lower level which opened into the Ladies' Department.

Stephen explained, "This area is very important for our new clientele, and we want to make it an environment where women can learn finance while feeling safe and being fully supported."

Estella stepped away from the front counter and walked slowly toward a bronze plaque mounted at the center of a quiet sitting area. Above it stood a bust of Susan B. Anthony, the suffragist's features cast in determined stillness, her gaze unyielding. Etched into the plaque below were words Estella had never seen in person, only read about in newspaper columns and books borrowed from neighbors:

> "Woman must have a purse of her own, and how can this be, so long as the wife is denied the right to her individual and joint earnings?"

Anthony had written those words in a time when a married woman's income legally belonged to her husband. Even now, Estella knew, the idea of a woman having her own account, her own say, was still met with skepticism in many corners of society. She reached out and let her fingertips brush against the bronze, the metal cool beneath her skin. The words settled into her chest with quiet weight.

Behind her, Stephen watched the moment unfold. Sensing her reaction, he stepped closer and said gently, "Perhaps you shall be our first customer."

Estella turned, a slow smile spreading across her face, one of quiet pride and growing resolve.

"That would be quite an honor for me," she said, her voice steady. "More than you can imagine."

There was a sentiment that Stephen sensed she was guarding closely to herself. He guided Estella into a corner office that had windows at ceiling height since they were in the lower level of the bank building. He told her, "This shall be your office. Let's take a seat and open your first account."

She started to sit at the visitor's seat and Stephen motioned her to the other side of the desk and said, "This is your office now."

There were so many questions, not to mention concerns about whether she would be able to perform the tasks required, but she would put every effort forth to make it work. There was no other choice. Stephen showed her some of the set-up procedures and took out a file for Estella to open her own account. She was eager to begin and learn to be financially independent while assisting other women in the journey. This would become her refuge and a place to earn a decent living while also securing a better future for her children.

Once Estella completed the file she glanced up at Stephen and slid the folder back to him.

"Congratulations on being the first customer of the new Ladies' Department. How would you like to join me for coffee nearby? I know a great little place, a tavern, around the corner that serves the best homemade apple pie. I rushed you through lunch. Let this be in celebration of your new journey."

She smiled at his kindness and said, "I'd be more than happy to join you, thanks."

The two departed the bank together and Stephen approached the driver. "We'll be walking to the tavern. Please come around and get yourself a meal, which I'll take care of while we finish our business."

The driver nodded eagerly as Estella and Stephen walked along the tree-lined street toward the tavern.

Upon entering there was a large bar area with patrons seated all around. Stephen appeared to know his way around and led them toward the back of the building to an area with tables and chairs. The dark wood walls gave a cave-like, cozy feeling with the flicker of candles glowing on each table. Glancing back, Estella could see daylight streaming in the front windows of the establishment. She must have been hungrier than she thought as the aroma of the daily offerings were tempting her taste buds. An older buxom waitress with graying tendrils peeking out of her covered head approached them.

"What'll it be, Mr. Masters, the usual?" she asked.

He nodded with a smile and replied, "Yes, Maggie, the warm apple pie with shaved cheddar and hot coffee, please. My colleague, Miss Fidler may want to know your other delicacies."

Estella glanced at Maggie with a smile and said, "The 'usual' sounds good for me too, thanks."

Then, turning to Stephen with a hint of playful curiosity, she added, "You must come here frequently."

Stephen chuckled, lifting his glass in a small toast. "Guilty as charged. It's hard to stay away when they know your order before you even sit down."

Estella relaxed into the moment, the formality between them softening just slightly. For all the newness of her world, this felt... familiar. Natural. And perhaps, the beginning of something she hadn't quite expected.

"The building process has been a huge undertaking. I like to keep a close eye on the work, so I found myself tempted many times as I passed by here. I have a home nearby, but mostly I stay downtown, close to my office. This has been a wonderful retreat to get quick refreshment. So, tell me, Ms. Fidler, what brought you out to look for work?"

She had been uncertain about sharing her story with Stephen but felt that his warmth and concern were from the heart. After a momentary pause and reflection, she shared her devastating story with him. Just as she was in the middle of telling him about the children being taken away after the fateful day they met, Maggie returned with the pie and coffee, quickly serving them, as it was apparent they were in deep conversation.

"Please, go on and finish your story," he pressed.

She said, "This is what got me thinking about our chance encounter, your contact card, and that fate would have me come to you for a job. I never felt so helpless and lost in my life. With the good grace of my neighbor and your generosity, I am seeing a future that will help me provide for my children. The criteria of the Children's Aid Society were that I have decent housing and income before my children would be able to return to me. I am genuinely touched by your decency in giving me the opportunity to achieve those conditions."

He spoke, his voice steady and sincere. "I knew I saw something different in you that day—a determination, a kind of driven desire that refused to be deterred. It intrigued me. And then, just as I was trying to place what it was, I saw the automobile coming straight toward you. You didn't even notice the danger. I didn't think—I just reacted and pulled you to safety.

"But afterward, I couldn't stop wondering what had you so focused, so intent. It's a rare quality, and one I deeply admire. Now, it all makes sense. There is no greater force than a mother fighting for her children.

"I want you to know, I'll do everything in my power to make sure you meet the criteria, quickly, so you can bring your children home from the orphan asylum."

For a moment Estella had tears well up in her eyes. With gratitude she said, "I will work very hard for your bank and make the Ladies' Department the best one that has ever been organized. More than ever, I want to help other women not fall into the same fate and lose hold of their home or children at no fault of their own. Now sir, you know my story and I'm very eager to learn yours, please share it."

He didn't speak much about himself and threw himself into work most of the time to avoid the sadness he fought against. However, Estella had shared a very raw part of her life, exposing herself to him, and for the first time he opened up.

"I lost my wife about a year ago. She was expecting our first child—just a month from her due date—when she fell ill with a fever. We lost them both.

Like you, I felt helpless. I spiraled into a darkness I wasn't sure I'd ever climb out of. The only way forward was to pour myself into the bank. This dream of a Ladies' Lounge—it was hers. She believed in a space where women could rest with dignity, feel welcomed in the world of commerce. It became her other unborn gift to society.

While designing the new building, I had the architects revise the plans to include the lounge—something never before seen in this city. That decision gave me direction again. And hope. A chance to shape something beautiful from sorrow."

"I'm very sorry to learn of your wife and child. I can't even begin to imagine how difficult that was to endure."

Stephen nodded in agreement and said, "Those that are left behind in the aftermath remain for a reason and we're lucky if we find out what that is and pursue it full heartedly. I, too, fully believe in fate and that day we both met was no accident. I'm sorry that you and your children were abandoned and left to sort things out. These scars will heal over time, and I promise you that better days are ahead for your family."

With that he suggested they get started back into town.

The two of them made their way to the front of the tavern where Stephen's driver was awaiting their return.

Stephen told the driver, "See to it that Miss Fidler is taken home. I want you to return for her in the morning at a time of her choosing and bring her back to the new bank. I'll walk home from here, thanks."

Stephen reached his hand out to Estella and when she responded, he took his other hand and embraced hers warmly to convey his promise. Their eyes met once again, sharing a warmth she had never felt before, a deep respect and affection for each other was developing.

A bit uncomfortable in the moment, Estella glanced down and returning her gaze upward, said, "Thank you for everything you're doing for me. I am eager to begin work and look forward to returning in the morning."

For the first time since Aaron vanished—leaving her to carry the weight of everything alone—Estella felt a flicker of control return to her life. The day had moved swiftly, full of errands, inquiries, and possibilities she hadn't dared consider just days before. Her mind buzzed with all that had transpired, and though the anger and hurt still lingered, something quieter had begun to settle in its place.

That night, as she knelt beside the borrowed bed and whispered her prayers, she gave thanks—not for her hardships, but for the strength to face them. She thought of the children sleeping in a strange place, their small bodies, unaware of the fragile plans she was building for their future. She whispered each of their names as if sealing a promise.

And yet, just beneath her gratitude, a shadow stirred—an unspoken fear that things might shift again before she could make them right. But she was too tired to wrestle with it. Instead, she lay down, wrapped in the illusion of progress, and drifted into sleep—unaware that by morning, everything would begin to change.

She awakened early to dress and be out of the way of her kind hosts. She had eagerly shared the news with them over the evening meal. They were so thrilled for her and that all was falling into place. She kindly asked both to keep it private and not share with anyone in the mill community. She had many reasons, but above all she knew deep down that if Aaron showed up on the doorstep, she would not take him back. His abandonment was one thing but leaving her with nothing and losing her children was more than she could forgive. His fate was forever sealed.

She made her way down the steps of Nora's home, glancing at what had once been her home next door. She turned in the other direction and walked to the busy street where Stephen's driver would be awaiting her. She never let him come directly to Nora's and didn't want the busy-body tongues wagging in the mill community. It was devastating enough that Aaron had walked out and never looked back and she had decided she was not going to add to that gossip.

She hurried along with better care now and crossed the already bustling street. Delivery wagons, automobiles, and people making their way to transportation, jobs and more were all about. She spotted the driver waiting for her on the corner. Walking over she got in the automobile. She sat back in silence gazing out the windows and felt comforted when they passed the last set of rowhouses and reached the edge of the city where the view now changed to wide-open expanses of trees mixed with open fields.

She thought to herself about the children and how much they would enjoy running and playing in that open space. The idea of it brought a smile to her face and for a moment it brought them close to her once again. She wondered about them nearly every waking minute of the day, what they were thinking and feeling and how in the blink of an eye they were snatched away. This memory was like a splash of ice water, and she came to her senses as the driver approached the bank.

She climbed the set of stairs leading to the new building. A doorman pulled open the door and she entered. Although the bank was not yet open for business, the final finishing touches were being carried out within the sturdy walls preparing for the grand day ahead. She started her path across the wide lobby and headed to the elevators. Just as she was ready to press the button Stephen came out of an office door at the end of the corridor.

Pleased to see her, he spoke up, "I'd like to go over a few agenda items with you in my office."

She headed down the hallway toward him and he gently took her hand into his and guided her to a soft seat in front of a large desk of burnished wood. He came around and sat at the desk. Behind him were tall windows that faced out onto a large grassy area with shade trees dotted throughout. It was a bucolic setting that she rarely saw while living in the rowhouse section of the city. It gave her a sense of peace and calmed her nerves.

He couldn't hold back and said, "You look quite lovely, Estella, and I do hope you had a good drive here. I've been thinking about your situation since we parted company yesterday. I am making it a priority for you to find immediate housing so that you begin the process of getting your children back as soon as possible."

Surprised and touched, she responded, "I will need more time and earnings to do that properly."

"You represent women in your roll at the bank and have already shown the capability to serve them well. Before you can assist others, it is imperative that your well-being and security are established. As you are aware, I keep a home out here and would like to offer it to you. It is well appointed and ready to move into. Of course, I will return to my other residence, making it a proper home for you and your children. I hope you can agree with this arrangement."

Estella sat silently for a moment deep in thought. She wanted to say yes, but instead, "This is a very generous offer but a part of me wants to wait and properly save to find an apartment until I can purchase a home for me and the children."

Although she was still young and perhaps a bit naive, she was determined not to fall into the same trap she had with Aaron. Stephen's offer of his home was generous—but it also gave her pause. After Aaron left, she'd made a quiet promise to herself: she would remain independent. Stephen had already honored that resolve by giving her meaningful work and fair wages.

She'd begun to imagine a future of her own making—scrimping and saving until she could afford a modest apartment near the bank. It would take months, maybe longer, but it would be hers. Not a gift. Not something that could be taken away. Earned, and therefore solid. Safe.

Not surprised by her response he said, "I thought you might be reluctant to accept my offer considering what you've experienced. Therefore, I'd like you to consider taking out a loan. We can begin the process now. I want to make it very clear that this will be a top priority. This is a financial institution capable of finding the means for you to purchase your own property. We can make this happen quickly. Shall we begin?"

Estella never expected such generosity or kindness toward her. She answered Stephen, "I'm honored and would definitely consider this option." Tears began to well up in her eyes in a wave of emotion at the thought of a home she and her children could live in and that belonged to them.

Stephen pushed back his chair, came around the desk and offered her his handkerchief to dry her eyes. He gently put his hand on her shoulder in a gesture of comfort.

He stirred a reaction in her that was difficult to suppress. She wondered if he felt the same toward her. She dried her eyes and apologized for her emotions spilling out in an effort to gain composure. For a moment she caught herself going to a place they both might regret.

Stephen spoke up, saying, "We best begin with the loan paperwork. I can get this processed quickly. We need to find a home that is available for sale. At a minimum it will need to have three bedrooms. I insist that you borrow furnishings from my house nearby. I'll arrange for it to be delivered until you're able to order your own. Of most importance is acquiring the house so that you can approach the Children's Aid Society and begin the process of having your children returned. They will no doubt need to have proof of your living arrangement and work to ascertain that you can properly care for the children."

A light tap at the door turned their focus to Stephen's assistant, Ruth, who had been standing in the doorway. Stephen had arranged for her to come out of the city to continue to work and train Estella in several areas of the new establishment.

Her entrance was timely as Stephen announced, "I have some business to attend outside of here. Ruth can assist you with the loan process, which shall also be a part of your training. We are ahead of schedule with the building and most likely we will be opening the doors within a month now. It's prudent to focus all our attention on this main location. Let's all plan to meet at the tavern for lunch at 1 p.m. Ladies, good day."

Ruth sat down beside Estella in the other soft chair and glanced over her application for a loan. There was not much information aside from her name and current residence and employment. She just needed to sign and date the bottom of the page while Ruth signed as a witness. Both ladies finished up in Stephen's office and Ruth led Estella over to the loan department office on the other side of the bank. She wanted to expose Estella to the many facets of the bank to have a good overview to serve her new clientele. Strangely though, Ruth left the loan paperwork on Stephen's desk.

Ruth said, "Mr. Masters will need to give it a final review and sign off on it. He'll take care of walking it through the proper channels for approval. Don't be surprised if things happen rapidly. He's a man of his word and doesn't stop until he accomplishes what he has set out to do."

After meeting several of the employees in the loan department, they headed back to the main floor of the bank. There were more employees here today and a lot of activity behind the counters. Ruth continued making brief introductions and was well acquainted with the staff. Estella met bank tellers, bookkeepers, accountants, loan officers, security guards and was given a brief overview of each position. This was all a part of her training. Ruth gave her a rundown on how the Ladies' Department of the bank was going to be operated and the people she would need to interact with daily on behalf of her clientele. This entire banking process was a well-oiled machine from behind the scenes. Although this department was a newly created vision of Stephen's, it was obvious how much thought went into it to bring it to life. Estella thought back to what Ruth told her in Stephen's office earlier. He made things happen, especially when he saw it as something good for all.

The morning passed in a blur of handshakes, introductions, and polite conversations. So many names, so many roles, each carrying weight in the carefully structured world of banking.

By late morning, Ruth left Estella in her new office with a warm smile and a few parting instructions. At last, there was a moment of quiet.

Estella exhaled slowly and looked around the room—hers. Modestly appointed but sunlit and well-positioned, it already carried the faint scent of ink, paper, and possibility.

There had been little time to reflect on the swirl of activity, so she sat at her desk and opened a fresh notebook. With practiced neatness, she began to jot down names, titles, and responsibilities, anything she could recall from the morning's meetings.

These were not just colleagues. Some would soon work under her. Others she would need to work with directly, representing not just her department, but the women who would soon walk through its doors. It was becoming clear: this wasn't just a job. It was a quiet revolution.

Every effort was being made to establish this bank as the first in the region to include a Ladies' Department, a place where women could ask questions without ridicule, learn without shame, and make decisions about their money with dignity. If it was to succeed, it needed more than polished counters and polite staff. It needed trust. Comfort. Respect.

Estella felt the weight of it, but not with fear. With purpose.

She was already becoming keenly aware of her duties and of the foundational workings of the bank itself. The more she learned, the more determined she became to not only master her role but to become an advocate for other women like herself. Women who had never before been given a seat at the table. Now she had one. And she intended to make it count.

A low growling rumble from hunger made Estella acutely aware of the time to set things aside and meet Ruth, as planned earlier. The ladies met up with one another at the front entry. They stepped outdoors to cooler than expected temperatures. The earlier bright blue skies were now covered in grey clouds.

They made small talk along the short stroll. As they turned the corner, the tavern was in sight, as was Stephen's automobile. They entered the dimly lit establishment and were led back to the seating area. Stephen immediately stood up and pulled out the chairs for both ladies then took his seat.

Before Stephen could begin, the waitress appeared and spoke up, "Our lunch specials today are roast beef with the usual potatoes and carrots or a hot turkey sandwich with gravy and potatoes. What'll it be?"

They ordered their food, and the waitress was off to task. The tavern was quieting down, and most of the diners were finishing up and making their way out. This was Stephen's motive for choosing one o'clock to have lunch. The less crowded dining area was more relaxed, making it easier to carry on discussions. He was curious about how the morning went and asked for an update.

Ruth said, "We visited most of the departments of the bank today and made introductions. Estella has a good demeanor with the others, while also commanding respect for herself. She quickly learns names and positions. I think she is going to make a fine department."

"I'm glad to have this update and am not surprised with her capabilities. Do you care to add anything, Estella?"

"The morning was well spent, and Ruth has been a wonderful mentor to me. I'm grateful for her experience and tutelage. I have greater appreciation and understanding of the bank and the department. And how was your morning?" Estella asked.

"I'm glad for this update and the two of you are working well together. As for my morning, it has paved the way for the direction we will take this afternoon. We will need to enjoy lunch together rapidly. I'll need Estella to accompany me to several houses I have arranged for my realtor broker to show to us this afternoon. They are nearby. However, to save time, we will have my driver take us to them. I trust the loan application is in good order and in process," Stephen stated matter-of-factly."

Both ladies smiled and Ruth glanced over at Estella and remarked, "See, that man doesn't let the grass grow beneath his feet. You've been advised and have witnessed him in action."

They all laughed aloud and shortly after the waitress came along, juggling three full plates of food on her arms and served the hot lunches. Without any more discussion they began to enjoy their meals.

The driver patiently waited outside of the tavern. Stephen pulled open and held the large wooden tavern door for both Ruth and Estella to walk through. Ruth wished them a good afternoon and turned and walked back toward the bank while the two of them got into the back of the automobile. They pulled away from the curb and were on their way to see three potential properties that Stephen had arranged with his realtor friend nearby. Along the way he gave Estella a brief history of the area in hopes of stirring her interest in finding a suitable home for her family.

As the automobile rumbled along the dirt thoroughfare of Sixty-Third Street where much of the commercial activity bustled, Stephen pointed out landmarks along the way. To their right, the tracks of the Pennsylvania Railroad, known widely as the PRR, ran parallel to the road, a steel artery connecting the suburbs to the heart of Philadelphia. Electric trolleys clattered past at regular intervals, shuttling people to and from the city with efficient frequency.

Not far ahead stood Overbrook Station near City Line Avenue, a modest yet well-traveled hub. The station even housed a post office, which had helped spur the surrounding development. Small businesses had sprung up around it like seeds in fertile ground, drawing trade and opportunity.

As they passed Lafferty's Market, a striking red brick building in the Pompeian Italianate style and one of the earliest commercial structures in the area, Estella took it all in with wide, thoughtful eyes.

The automobile slowed to a stop outside a smaller, neatly kept building just beyond the main cluster of shops.

A man stepped out of the doorway and approached the car. With an easy grin, he opened the front passenger door and climbed in beside the driver.

He turned toward Estella in the back seat, tipping his hat. "My name is George Samson," he said warmly. "And I'm pleased to be showing you around today. Mr. Masters mentioned you might be looking for a home nearby, and I've lined up several properties I think you'll find interesting."

Estella returned the introduction. "It's a pleasure to meet you and I'm appreciative of your time to show me around."

Estella offered a gracious smile, her heart quickening with a mix of excitement and disbelief.

A home. A real one. Her own. The car pulled away from the curb, and for the first time in a long while, the road ahead felt wide open.

George gave a more detailed history of the Overbrook Farms area as they drove ahead. He pointed directly across from the Overbrook PRR Station to a brand new, ornate building, The Drexel Apartments of Overbrook, built in the Tudor Revival style. There was such a demand for housing because people wanted to leave the industrialized city. The area was in its prime and it was obvious to Estella that this was the reason the bank had decided to move outside of the city center.

There was a laundromat, medical and dental offices, and other services all along the street. Of particular importance was the Overbrook Steam Heat Company. This company provided centralized heating systems which eliminated the high maintenance coal fired furnaces. This not only reduced pollution, but also the number of servants needed in wealthier homes. Their plant produced and distributed steam through a protected-pipe system into the cellars of the Overbrook Farms.

In 1892 the investment bank of Drexel & Company purchased about one hundred and seventy acres from the estate of John M. George. The farmland spanned from Fifty-eighth to Sixty-sixth Streets, nestled between City Line and Woodbine Avenues, with the Pennsylvania Railroad, Lancaster Pike, and Marion Road threading through its heart. The Drexel group commissioned developers to build Overbrook Farms. They advertised a venue that rose to two hundred and fifty feet above the level of the city, ensuring good drainage, coolness in the summer, pure air, all of which contributed to good health for the residents.

The elegantly appointed single and twin houses attracted upper-middle-class and wealthy owners with modern amenities including electric lighting, pure spring water, modern landscaping and grand curvilinear streets with sidewalks lined with streetlights. They even had their own locally operated telephone exchange with most private homes having a telephone. In the planning it was recognized that more affordable housing was also needed and modernized rowhouses and large apartment complexes such as they passed by earlier were becoming a part of the area.

The driver slowed and pulled next to the curb in front of twin homes that lined the street. They were much nicer than the typical rowhouses with easier access to a large backyard from the front area. The three of them got out and walked up the set of stairs leading to the twin house to the right. Mr. Samson held a key in his hand and when they reached the top of the steps to the home he unlocked the door, which opened into a fully furnished living room. The light spilling in from the two large front windows reflected off the mirror that hung above the fireplace, giving the effect of overhead lighting.

Estella asked, "Does someone live here currently?"

George responded, "The owner bought and furnished this home for his wife's aging mother, but sadly she passed away recently. This home is available immediately with all the furnishings. The owner is eager to sell."

George encouraged Estella to walk around to see the entire home. She passed by a staircase that led upstairs, then through the dining room and back to the kitchen at the rear of the home. There was a door that led outside and another that led down to a basement. She took notice of the modern switches on the walls that were the latest for electric lighting. She walked back to the set of stairs and headed up to the bedrooms. It was now obvious that no one lived here. There were no wall hangings or personal items. It made it very easy to visualize her and the children living here together. She was in awe of the bathroom with the modern upgrades and clean steam heating. There was another door at the end of the hallway that led up to an unfinished attic.

Estella asked George if the other two homes they were going to visit were furnished and available immediately. He replied, "I showed you this one first for those reasons and it made the most sense to come here initially."

"What is the price of this with and without the furnishings?" she asked.

George hesitated before speaking, his tone measured. "The owner was hopeful to get about $2,500 for the home," he began.

"It's fully furnished, top to bottom. I do believe, though, that he could be enticed to take a payment of $2,000 for everything, provided the sale is immediate and without delay."

He glanced at Estella, gauging her reaction.

Mortgage lending was still relatively new, slow-moving, often entangled in red tape, and rarely extended to women without a male guarantor. The idea of an immediate purchase was both a rare opportunity and a heavy pressure.

Estella stood quietly in the front room, her eyes sweeping over the modest yet well-kept furnishings, the clean lines of the woodwork, the warmth of the space. She could hardly imagine affording a home like this. Two thousand dollars. It might as well have been twenty.

The silence hung between them until Stephen, who had been quietly watching her face, finally spoke.

"Estella," he said gently, "if this home interests you... I can assure you the funds will be made ready. Your loan would be processed immediately."

Estella turned to him, her lips parting slightly, caught between disbelief and the rush of possibility. This wasn't just a house. It was stability. Respect. A place to bring her children home. And it was hers to claim if she dared.

She felt a pang in her stomach, a bundle of nerves, at the very thought of having her own home for her and the children. "Yes, I would like this home very much and do not need to see the others," she added.

Without hesitation George said, "I'll have the papers drawn up and we'll plan to begin the purchase immediately. I suspect I'll have the keys in your hands in a few days".

They walked out the front door and stood on the small, covered porch looking down the steps to the street below. George proceeded to lock the door of the house. He then pointed out that nearby was the Overbrook School within walking distance for her children. The three of them walked down to the awaiting automobile. They drove back to George's office, near the train station, and they all got out to complete the necessary signatures to proceed with the purchase. George felt confident he would secure the seller's signature by the next day and all would be a smooth process ahead.

FOSTER CARE HOME
Florence, 3 months later | Amish Farm | Fall 1910

Sister Theresa came out from a weekly meeting with a group of local supporters who she now led to the front entrance of the orphanage. They had been working on a plan for months to reduce costs by placing children in foster homes, giving them a more family-like environment to thrive. When she returned to her office, she summoned Sister Henrietta to bring Florence to her.

The children had spent the morning practicing penmanship along with reading activities. The boys had been separated from the girls into different classrooms.

Sister Henrietta greeted Florence and asked her to come along with her to the office. She looked scared, as if she had gotten into trouble for something.

Sister Henrietta could sense her concern and told her, "You haven't done anything wrong. Sister Theresa wanted to visit with you."

They walked down the long dark hallway toward the office. Florence hung her head down as she longed for the warmth and love of her mother that was lacking in this environment. This place was the opposite of that feeling and she could not easily hide her feelings like John and Frances.

Sister Theresa sat at her tall desk as the two of them crossed over the doorway into the office. In her stern, cool demeanor she asked Florence to take a seat. "Please have Florence's personal items brought here at once and that will be all now," abruptly dismissing Sister Henrietta.

Sister Theresa went on to tell Florence, "We've arranged for a farm family to take you in. We believe it will be a better home for you."

With big eyes Florence looked back at Sister Theresa and softly asked, "What about John and Frances? They are coming with me, aren't they?"

Sister Theresa replied abruptly, "No, they will not be joining you. It is in everyone's best interest that you go with this family, while your brother and sister remain here."

Florence began to cry and begged to say goodbye to her brother and sister. An automobile was in front of the orphanage as she was led down the long, dark corridor. Sister Henrietta met her and carried Florence's doll and bag of clothing. She kindly and gently handed Florence her doll, which she immediately clung to while sobbing uncontrollably. Once before, Sister Henrietta was assigned the cruel task of escorting a child from the asylum and now would have to accompany Florence on a ride that would seem to be an eternity for both.

Sister Henrietta and Florence climbed into the back of the waiting automobile. They pulled away from the orphanage and the driver took them to the main train station. Aside from hyperventilating gasps of air from all her crying, Florence was silent as she stepped away from the automobile with Sister Henrietta. It felt like she could hardly breathe. Her world was once again coming unraveled from all she ever knew. Sister Henrietta tried to put a comforting hand on her shoulder, but she pulled away and clutched tighter to her doll.

Several trains passed by as they stood patiently along the station's sheltered overhang. Finally, the right train arrived and the two of them climbed up the tall steps and took a seat. It was an express train that would take them to Parkesburg, Pennsylvania. A fear swept over Florence as the train began to move, and she trembled. Her entire body ached from the thought of losing her mother and now her brother and sister were being snatched away. She wondered why all of this was happening without any way to make it stop.

The train slowed as it approached stations along the route, but did not stop. It made one at a station to pick up and let off a few passengers and quickly continued to the destination. It crossed through many wooded areas until it reached open fields with large farmlands. It was like nothing she had ever seen before. The train began to slow up as it approached Parkesburg. There appeared to be a large town over the hill in the distance. Tall smokestacks reached high into the sky billowing out dark smoke. The train neared the town and passed over a bridge looking over the town.

There were some frame houses and small businesses, but the imposing Parkesburg Iron Company was the main attraction. It became clear that it was the main industry for this town far from the big city. There was a big demand for their high-quality charcoal iron tubes that were used in steam engines.

The train came through a main street in town and on either side were buildings. One that stood out had unusual towers adorning each side. It was the newly built hotel and saloon. There were many people walking on either side of the street coming in and out of the shops. A restaurant came into sight along with The Oyster and Boarding House, drug store and a movie house.

The train came to a full stop with a jolt, and Sister Henrietta gently motioned for Florence to step down.

Florence hesitated, then carefully descended the last step, her shoes clicking softly against the pavement. She stood still for a moment, staring down at the steel rails that had carried her to this unfamiliar place. She felt small. Lost. Afraid. Questions flooded her mind. Where was she? Who was coming for her? Would she be staying long? Would she ever see her siblings again?

Sister Henrietta took her hand and guided her to a nearby staircase that led beneath the tracks, allowing them to cross safely to the other side of the busy street. Florence followed wordlessly, her heart pounding in her chest. They emerged into a large open space flanked by rows of parked automobiles. The air smelled faintly of oil and dust, mixed with the distant scent of something sweet—perhaps a bakery or street vendor nearby.

Sister Henrietta suddenly picked up her pace, her gaze fixed across the lot. Florence looked up and followed her eyes. On the far side, standing quietly beside a dark grey covered buggy drawn by a single horse, were a man and woman dressed in plain clothing. Their posture was still, their faces unreadable beneath the wide brims of their straw hat and bonnet.

Florence clutched Sister Henrietta's hand more tightly as they approached. The woman stepped forward slightly. The man nodded once. No words were exchanged at first, just the weight of the moment settling over them all like a hush before the turning of a page.

She asked, "Are you Amos and Sara Blank?"

They quickly replied with a head nod and flatly stated, "Yes, we are."

Sister Henrietta introduced Florence to her new family while also handing the small bag of clothing to Mrs. Blank. Sara took hold of the bag and coaxed Florence to come stand by her side. Florence hesitated for a moment. Sister Henrietta told Florence that Mr. and Mrs. Blank were going to be her new caretakers and to behave and try to fit in with her new family. She walked with the couple, who helped her step up into the buggy. She sat on a flat wooden bench with Mrs. Blank and once she was settled, Mr. Blank slapped the reins, and the horse took off along the street shared with the train. She saw Sister Henrietta cross the same roadway heading back to the train station.

This ride in the buggy took nearly the same path as the train and passed by the same buildings. She took notice of a park with many people, and children playing and shouting with joy. It was the newly opened Crystal Spring Park. It reminded her of the park she and her mother and siblings would visit in Philadelphia, but this one was much bigger and more active. She wondered if perhaps she would come here to play.

They then came upon an intersection that had a strange looking object in the center. It was a horse water fountain and for a moment the buggy stopped, and the horse drank the water from the large bowl. From there they turned down the road and passed beneath the train bridge that had carried her into town earlier. The street was lined with trees and the bustling of the town activity began to fade.

The horse pulled the buggy with its passengers into the countryside. It opened into fields as far as the eye could see, with an occasional house alongside the roadway. Tall grass in the adjacent fields swayed in the breeze and some fields were filled with tall stalks of corn. Florence looked out to her left and saw the sun beginning to set lower in the sky. She immediately thought of what her sister Frances had told her about if she could see the sun or moon and stars that they were all looking at the same ones, bringing the three siblings near to one another. The breeze from being in the buggy and the fresh air seemed to give her a little boost of energy. The sound of the horse's hooves on the hardened earth was rhythmic and the horse picked up the pace when it came to the rolling hills, bringing them faster away from the town.

They began to descend one of the hills and a large building came into sight. It appeared to be a church. It was here that the horse turned away and to the right onto another road. Florence glanced over and saw a small stone building that had numbers "*1836*" at the top. She was taking in all the scenery. The horse powered up another hill and on the other side she saw a cemetery dotted with headstones amidst the farmlands. The horse finally turned up a long lane leading to a tall white house with a porch. There was a smell in the air that got stronger as they approached the farm and it was not pleasant. It seemed to be coming from the barn area further away from the house and it permeated the air. Amos spoke a verbal command, pulled back on the reins and the buggy came to rest. Sara stepped down from the buggy and helped Florence down to the ground. She spoke to Amos in a language Florence didn't understand and he replied in the same. With one hand grasping Florence's and the other clutching the sack of clothing, Sara guided her toward the back steps of the house. Behind them, Amos turned the buggy and drove away.

Florence was frightened as she stepped into the unfamiliar home. The scents, the silence, the absence of electricity—all of it felt strange. Foreign.

Sara bent down and gently removed her own shoes, then looked up at Florence and said softly, "We leave our shoes here."

Florence obeyed, slipping off her scuffed shoes and placing them beside Sara's by the door. Together, they stepped across the threshold into a large, warm kitchen.

The room smelled of baked bread and something stewing, food that had clearly started earlier. The wooden floors creaked softly underfoot.

"Would you take the plates and set the table?" Sara asked kindly, already turning her attention to the food.

Her voice was calm, matter-of-fact, as if Florence had always belonged there. Florence nodded but stood staring at the stack of plates, unsure of what setting the table meant. Back home, meals were often a hurried affair, eaten from mismatched dishes or shared from the pot.

She carefully lifted the stack of plates and carried them to the long rectangular table in the center of the room. Unsure of what to do next, she simply placed the plates in the middle and stood frozen, her eyes scanning the unfamiliar space.

Sara glanced over but said nothing. She continued preparing the food—slicing bread, ladling stew—then called gently, "Florence, would you bring these to the table, please?"

Florence moved quickly and quietly, following instructions, placing the bowls and platters of food down where she thought they might belong. Just then, the back door opened and shut with a soft thud. It was Amos.

He removed his boots at the door, just as Sara had, then entered the kitchen. He was tall, with a quiet, gentle presence, and said nothing as he took his seat at the head of the table. He looked at the disorderly arrangement of dishes and said nothing, though it was clear he understood.

Florence stood near the side of the table, unsure whether to sit, to wait, or to speak. She felt the weight of her ignorance and the ache of missing home.

Sara stuffed a basket with warmed bread and finally came to the table, and she coaxed Florence to sit on the bench opposite her.

Amos led them in prayer, giving thanks for the day and asking the Lord to bless the bounty before them.

Florence watched carefully as Sara passed the large platter of meat to Amos, who filled his plate with several slices. Sara passed more of the prepared food, while also putting portions of each on Florence's plate. The ham, potatoes and string beans smelled good, and the warmed buttered bread was a nice side.

The meal was eaten in silence. Florence did not have much of an appetite, but she remembered Sister Henrietta's parting words to behave herself. She had learned at the orphanage that it would have been disrespectful not to eat all that was given to her. It wasn't difficult to do with this delicious assortment of foods.

After the meal, Amos remained seated, and Sara got up from the table and asked Florence to help her. They both cleared all the plates from the table while Sara began to wash the dishes and put up the food.

She set out three small dishes and cut slices of a juicy-looking peach and strawberry pie and slid one onto each plate. She asked Florence to carry them to the table. This time she understood the placement of the plates better. She returned to get the third piece of pie while Sara poured three cups of chicory coffee.

The pie was delicious and both Amos and Sara drank the hot, dark liquid in the cup. Florence was hesitant to try the coffee but lifted the cup to sip on it. She was surprised by the bitterness and set it back down. She knew she was not going to be able to drink it.

Once they finished the pie Sara got up and took the full cup of coffee and asked Florence to help with the dishes again. Amos stood and walked over to an oil lamp, lighting it with a wooden match and took out a book to read while the ladies cleaned up in the kitchen.

Once all the supper dishes were cleaned and put away, Sara led Florence up the stairs that were just off to the side of the large room. The hallway was dark and the glow of the lamp that Sara held lit the way. She walked to the end of the hall and into the doorway of a small room with a single bed on the opposite wall. There was a small, round, knotted rug alongside the bed. The window had a plain blue cloth that came down and across it for privacy and to block the light.

Sara walked over to a tall wooden wardrobe with drawers and set the oil lamp atop. She opened one of the middle drawers, revealing neatly folded clothing and removed a white cloth night dress for Florence. To the side of this wardrobe on the wall hung two plain dresses, one blue and the other a pale green. Nothing else adorned the walls. The room was stark; it did not even have a mirror.

Sara asked Florence, "Do you need help getting into your night clothes?"

Florence quietly whispered, "No, thank you."

Sara stepped over by the doorway and turned her back, giving Florence a moment to undress. She recognized the child might be frightened and gave her a little space. Florence removed her clothes and pulled the soft white night dress over her head. It was a bit long and went down past her ankles, just touching the floor. When she was finished dressing, Sara returned to her side, pulled the quilt down and motioned for Florence to climb beneath the covers. When Florence was tucked under the quilt, Sara sat down beside her.

Sara broke the silence and said, "I know this is all strange to you. I will help and care for you. Please call me Mamm, which you will hear other children do with their parents. And you may call my husband, Daed. You've had a long day and sleep should come quickly."

Following a quiet bedtime prayer, Mamm Sara rose, collected Florence's clothes, and offered a gentle goodnight. As she crossed the room with the oil lamp, its golden glow dwindled, fading into shadows at the threshold.

Florence quietly said, "Good night, Mamm."

Florence lay quietly in her bed and tears welled up in her eyes. She got up and pulled the curtain away from the window next to her bed and tucked it behind the small hook it had laid on previously. She knelt on the floor and gazed out the window toward the barn. There was a bright full moon rising and she thought of Frances and John at the orphanage. She wondered about her mother and thought about how they used to read stories to one another at bedtime. Her heart ached and longed for them. There were no words to describe the big hole in her heart. Nothing made sense. She felt chilled and decided to get back beneath the covers for warmth. Aside from the moonlit sky casting a light glow across her ceiling, the room was dark. The shadows that danced on the walls frightened her. She missed her sister Frances and her protective brother John, who would always calm her worries at nighttime. These thoughts gave way to a torrent of tears. Florence cried herself to sleep.

***

Mamm Sara stood in the doorway of Florence's room. Daylight was streaming through the window, yet Florence did not stir. She did not remember leaving the curtain pulled back. She walked across the wood floor and gently tapped Florence, who lay there still. Sara felt the heat coming off her small body and when she pulled back the sheet found her soaked in sweat. She immediately ran back down the steps, fetching a large pitcher of water and a cloth. There was no time to waste as Florence was burning up with fever.

She returned to Florence's side and pulled back the quilt. Florence's little body jerked from what seemed to be a sob. Her nose was so stuffed full, she could barely breathe. Her mouth was agape, trying to get air. Mamm Sara dipped the cloth into the cool water and wiped Florence's forehead to help lower her temperature. Worry came over Sara and she prayed quietly beside Florence.

Unsure if she could hear her, she said, "I'll make some tea and be back up with some biscuits too."

Sara hurried down the stairs to make tea for Florence and was met by Amos' worried expression. He had been out in the barn since before sunrise milking the cows and was accustomed to returning to a prepared hot breakfast.

He asked with concern, "What is it? Is the girl unwell?"

Sara seemed frantic. "She is, and I need to tend to her immediately. I've not seen anything like this from being well to this ill overnight. Please go to the Weaver's and ask for Rebecca to come and help me."

Amos dashed to put on his boots and headed to Weaver's farm just across the hayfield. Meanwhile, Sara poured hot water from the kettle on the wood stove into a cup with honey and lemon. She gathered a few biscuits on a plate and was back up the stairs to tend to Florence.

Thankfully, removing the quilt and cooling her head with the cool wet cloth had helped to bring her temperature down. She dipped the cloth back into the water and placed it atop Florence's head, letting it rest there. She opened her eyes briefly, looked up at Mamm Sara and closed them again.

She tried to rouse her, "I've got tea and biscuits, shall we try some?"

Her eyes opened momentarily, and she tried to sit up, but her head wouldn't lift off the pillow. Mamm went to the wood dresser across the room and opened the top drawer, removing a large quilt. She folded the quilt several times, making it like a big pillow. She used this to bolster Florence's head. She knew it was going to be critical to have Florence sip liquids. She was burning up, red hot with fever, and was becoming dehydrated.

Florence opened her eyes once she was sitting upright. Mamm Sara raised the teacup in front of her and quietly spoke, "You need to sip on this tea. It will make you feel better."

Florence just stared out far away as if in a daze and sipped the hot tea that Mamm raised to her lips. She had no energy or will to do anything and felt lost in a flood of sadness. Everything she had known and loved was gone, stripped away and she could not process or make sense of her world. It was as though she had awakened from a bad dream and was still inside of it, unable to escape. She was utterly helpless and at the mercy of these people she knew nothing about.

Mamm Sara was sitting beside Florence on the bed, refreshing the cool rag on her forehead every few minutes. This helped bring down her temperature. She turned slightly away from Florence and in a hushed voice prayed. Afterwards she pushed up from the bed and went to the window and pulled on the bottom panel to lift it up, allowing a whoosh of fresh cool morning air to enter the room. It caused Florence to shiver and reach for the quilt, pulling it up closer to her neck for warmth. She came back and sat down next to her and lifted the cup to her lips for her to sip slowly.

It wasn't long before Sara heard Rebecca quickly coming up the stairs and into the room with her and Florence. She had a look of concern on her face and said, "I came as quickly as possible when Amos arrived with the news."

She wasted no time.

Rebecca crossed the room swiftly, her plain skirts whispering against the floorboards, and knelt at the side of the small bed where Florence lay. The girl's skin, flushed and clammy, was hot beneath her trembling fingers. But the cool compresses resting on her brow had already begun to ease the worst of it. The fever was still there, but not climbing. Rebecca reassured Sara that she was doing all the right things to help the child get better.

Sara folded the cloth again and dipped it into the basin of water on the washstand. "There now," she whispered. "You rest, my child. We'll see this through."

She reached for the wooden chair and pulled it closer to the bedside. From that moment on, she rarely left it. Rebecca visited with her daily and came with prepared meals so Sara didn't have to leave Florence's side.

The first day passed slowly, with no rhythm but the rise and fall of Florence's breath.

She was quiet, too quiet—save for the soft whimpers that came now and then in her sleep. Her body shivered, then stiffened, then relaxed again. She drank in tiny sips when coaxed, but mostly she drifted. In and out. A world of shadow and murmuring voices.

Sara sat beside her, hands busy with cloth and spoon and prayer. At times she sang under her breath—old hymns in German that Florence didn't understand but seemed comforted all the same.

To Florence, it felt as though she were floating, far away from her body, from the farm, from everything she knew. The world was distant and blurry. The room smelled of vinegar, lye soap, and honey. Voices hummed low and soft, blending with dreams. Sometimes she felt herself crying but couldn't feel the tears. Once, there was a sharp pain in her chest, then the peace of slipping under again.

On the second day the fever climbed again with the sun.

Sara changed the linens, washed Florence's face, and murmured to her in both English and Dutch, hoping the child would stir, would speak. When Florence tensed and moaned in her sleep, Sara rested a firm hand on her chest and prayed aloud.

"Heavenly Father, I trust You. This child is not mine but Yours."

The day was hot, and Sara opened the window to let in the breeze. The scent of cut hay and warm earth filled the small upstairs room. Downstairs, the house was quiet. The Weaver boys had been sent to help Amos with threshing. It was just Sara and the child now. A sacred watch.

When evening came and the light faded, Sara lit the lamp. She sat by the bed and dozed upright, waking at every shift in Florence's breath.

The third day brought stillness.

Florence no longer tossed or cried out. Her breathing was slow and even. The flush had faded from her cheeks, leaving her pale and hollow-eyed, but cooler now—no longer burning.

Sara slipped in and out of the room all day, keeping vigil with quiet hands. She changed the bedding, smoothed the quilts, hummed under her breath. Every now and then she reached for Florence's hand and whispered prayers over her fingers.

When Florence stirred that afternoon, her eyes fluttered halfway open. The world was blurred and golden, as though she were waking inside a dream. She heard a chair creak, a spoon in a cup, and then—Sara's voice, low and steady beside her:

"Heavenly Father, may my child not fear, for Thou art with her."

Florence drifted again, not fully awake, but not as far from the surface as before.

By mid-morning on the fourth day, the change was clear.

Florence opened her eyes fully, blinking against the light pouring in through the freshly washed windowpanes. The room smelled of morning and something baking downstairs—bread, perhaps, or apples. Her throat was dry, her head heavy, but the fever had loosened its grip.

Sara returned just as she stirred and moved quickly to her side.

"There now," she whispered, brushing the hair from Florence's damp forehead. "Welcome back, my child. You've been very brave."

Florence managed the faintest nod, her lips parting as though to speak, though no words came yet.

Sara didn't press her. She dipped the spoon in the teacup and held it to the child's mouth, steady and patient.

Florence swallowed, then closed her eyes, safe now under the soft quilt and the steady presence of the kind woman she knew as Mamm.

Mamm asked, "Are you hungry?

She nodded her head vigorously, indicating she was famished.

Mamm Sara was relieved for this good sign and went downstairs to prepare some food for Florence.

She hurried about to the kitchen, grabbed a glass jar of homemade chicken soup and began to heat it. She managed to take a wooden tray and fill it with fresh warm bread, hot tea, soup and a small side bowl of oatmeal drizzled with honey. It seemed like a lot of food, but Florence hadn't eaten for days and needed to regain her strength. Mamm took the stairs back up to Florence's room. She walked across the room and set the tray of food on the chair next to the bed.

Florence was already sitting up with the quilt pulled back. The food smelled delicious and Mamm handed her the cup of chicken soup. She could sip or spoon it – the reason Sara put it in a cup instead of a bowl. It would get her started eating again. The warm savory liquid seemed to be the magic potion she needed. She set the cup down and picked up the bread and took a big bite, chewing it well. The oatmeal was the next food she tried. She ate until she was full and lay back on the folded quilt that propped her up.

In a raspy voice she quietly said, "Mamm, thank you for caring for me. I'm sorry to be so much trouble."

Mamm had to look away before she answered, blinking back the tears that welled suddenly in her eyes. Her voice trembled as she spoke, but she kept it gentle.

"Dear child, we are grateful for you and thank the Lord He shined on you and made you well," she said, reaching out to smooth Florence's hair. "You've been asleep on and off for four days. We feared the worst, but we kept watch over you."

She paused, then added quietly, "We saw you clutching your chest in your sleep—so restless, so fitful. We could only guess it was a heart ailment."

Florence lay still, trying to make sense of it all. Her limbs felt heavy, but her mind stirred with the ache of memory. She wondered if it was quite possible her heart had broken—splintered from the sorrow of missing her family, from the weight of everything that had happened. The sadness she carried was deep and unspoken, and though she was only a child, she had known more loss in recent weeks than many did in a lifetime.

She turned her head slowly toward Sara. "Mamm," she asked softly, "may I go outside?"

Sara smiled through her sadness, brushing her hand gently across Florence's cheek. "Of course, girl," she said. "Let's get you dressed and out into the fresh air."

She moved with care, helping Florence with her clothes, wrapping a shawl around her thin shoulders.

Outside, the world waited—quiet, green, alive. And for the first time in days, Florence was ready to step into it again.

HOMECOMING
Frances & John, 4 months later | Philadelphia | Fall 1910

The crisp bite of autumn had arrived, not only in the air but in the landscape itself. The trees, once lush with summer green, were now adorned in shades of gold, crimson, and amber.

Summer slipped away quickly, almost without warning. Like a thief in the night, it vanished, taking with it the warmth, upheaval, and the first steps into a life Estella never expected. And yet, in the wake of all that had unfolded, there was a silver lining.

Estella had thrown herself into her work at the bank, and her efforts had not gone unnoticed. She had earned a reputation as a woman who "took no nonsense"—sharp, efficient, and deeply committed to the clients she served, especially the women who were learning to navigate their financial independence for the first time. It was this very strength, this quiet resolve, that Stephen had first seen in her. And now, months later, his instinct had proven right.

Estella wasn't just surviving in the Ladies' Department—she was shaping it. Growing into a role that once seemed like a distant dream. And though the world outside was changing with the season, inside the bank, Estella Fidler was just beginning to bloom.

Estella arose early on this mid-week morning. In fact, she hardly was able to sleep thinking about the day to come. She was finally going to have her children return home where they belonged. The process with the Children's Aid Society was laborious and felt to her like an effort to keep the children distanced from her. She persisted and kept after the organization, but she had to endure numerous interviews. Recently though, the final inspection of her new home is what she felt sealed the deal on the final approval and release of her children back into her custody. Today, she thought to herself, was the beginning of a new life for all of them.

She thought about the predicament and the devastating consequences that had befallen her family at the whim of her husband, Aaron, who had not been heard from since the morning he left for work and never returned.

It was only later, through a kind Children's Aid assistant handling her case, that she discovered the full extent of the betrayal. In their effort to trace kin and keep families intact, the Children's Aid Society had located Aaron's parents. Estella learned, to her horror, that it was his family, wealthy, well-connected, and until then unaware of their three grandchildren, who had intervened.

She recalled their hatred toward her, how they had opposed the match from the beginning. They had judged her harshly, and now, emboldened by their means and social standing, they seized the opportunity to act.

Estella would never forget the moment she saw the open file left on the assistant's desk—left, perhaps, with intention. While the woman excused herself from the room, Estella leaned forward, compelled by a force stronger than fear, and read the neatly typed notes that pierced like knives: character attacks, unfounded accusations, and cold assessments of her fitness as a mother. *Neglectful. Unstable. Unfit for visitation.* The words blurred as her vision swam. So this was why the letters had gone unanswered. Why every request to see her children had been met with vague delays and hollow apologies. They hadn't forgotten her—they had written her off.

She sat frozen in the chair, her hands trembling in her lap, numbed by the terrible clarity that she had been tried in absentia and found lacking. And for what? Poverty? Abandonment by a husband she could not find?

Only later—much later—would the fuller truth begin to surface. It was Nora's nephew, a city police sergeant, who tracked Aaron down during an off-duty inquiry. He had been living in a boarding house across town, under another name, with a woman who worked and cleaned there. He hadn't disappeared at all—only abandoned them quietly and moved on. And yet, it was Estella who bore the sentence, the silence, the separation.

What she had lost had not come all at once—it had been taken in pieces, behind closed doors, and signed off with the thump of a stamp.

Instead of her usual short walk to the office, she turned in the opposite direction and made her way to the trolley station. After purchasing a ticket, she hurried across the street to wait for the city-bound transportation. Stephen had kindly offered the use of his automobile and driver, but she had graciously declined. It felt like too much—too difficult to explain to her children, and especially to The Children's Aid Society. She couldn't risk giving anyone a reason to question her ability to care for the children.

Estella had hoped for the express trolley, but the next one to arrive made numerous stops along the route. She passed by the old mill community and immediately thought of Nora and the kindness she had often extended to her and the children. She knew that if Nora hadn't helped that they would've been homeless and then who knows what may have happened. Both ladies exchanged newsy letters, monthly or whenever time allowed, to keep in touch. The Murphys' were happy for Estella and congratulated her on getting back on her feet in such successful fashion and finding a way to get her children back.

The trolley clattered along its route, pausing for passengers at each corner, until it finally reached Estella's stop near the Children's Aid office.

She hopped off the trolley and paused at the curb, steadying herself. The city hummed around her, automobiles clattered by, voices echoed off brick buildings, but all of it faded into the background.

Estella took a deep breath, then stepped forward toward the tall stone building rising ahead of her. The sign above read: *Children's Aid Society.*

Her heart pounded with nervous excitement at the thought of being reunited with her children. She crossed the long, open waiting area, her steps deliberate, her hands trembling slightly as she joined the reception line. After what felt like a lifetime, she was led down a quiet corridor to an office at the far end of the building. She was asked to wait. The minutes dragged.

Finally, a caseworker entered and sat across from her, opening a file and glancing through its contents.

"The children arrived later than expected," he said kindly. "But they'll be brought in shortly."

Estella nodded, holding herself together. You've waited this long, she reminded herself. A few more minutes is nothing.

Then—soft sounds. Shuffling. Footsteps just outside the door.

The doorknob turned.

Frances and John stood in the doorway, wide-eyed, frozen for a breathless moment.

And then, all at once, they moved.

They rushed into Estella's arms, and she wrapped them up with a cry that came from the deepest part of her soul. They clung to each other as if nothing else existed, as if letting go again was unthinkable. Tears and laughter poured out of them all—raw, unstoppable, cleansing.

Estella finally pulled back slightly, brushing the hair from her daughter's tear-streaked face, then looked past the caseworker. Her expression shifted.

"Where is Florence?" she asked, voice low, urgent.

The joy in the room paused—tilted by the weight of one name not yet spoken.

"It was in her best interest to be taken to a foster home where she has adjusted well." he answered flatly.

Estella was stunned for a moment, then spoke up. "I want my daughter returned to me. I've fulfilled all the requirements, have suitable employment, a home and a loving environment for all three of my children."

"We've only approved of your older two children being returned on a trial basis to ascertain the possibility of the third child," he reminded Estella.

She felt a wave of ice come over her as he didn't even bother to mention the children's names. She felt as if his words were threats and that, at his whim, it was possible all her children could again be taken away without warning. He was obviously hand-picked for this job and was clearly a cold, insensitive person. She did not want to destroy the happiness she felt because Frances and John were witnessing this encounter with the caseworker. She decided that this man was a stone wall, and she would have to return at another time to get Florence. She could see no amount of reasoning was going to make a difference.

They were quietly led out of the office—not through the grand front doors of the Children's Aid building where hopeful families still sat waiting, but instead through a narrow hallway that led to a side entrance opening into a back alley.

Estella couldn't help but take notice.

It felt deliberate—an attempt to avoid attention, to slip them out unseen. She had once believed this place stood for hope, for support, for holding families together. But now, after everything, it felt more like they had been processed, wrung dry, and quietly released—like unwanted laundry from a back door chute.

And yet, as they stepped into the sunlight together, John holding her hand and Frances clinging to her arm, Estella lifted her chin.

They may have been pushed to the margins—but they were together again. And this time, they would not just survive. They would thrive.

She vowed silently, fiercely, as they walked into the street: I will not rest until I find Florence.

Nothing would stand in her way.

They all hugged briefly again until Estella pushed away and leaned down and whispered to them, "Are you ready for an adventure to your new home?"

Frances and John both nodded their heads eagerly and smiled while each took hold of their mother's hand and walked out to the sidewalk together. She looked for the trolley labeled "Overbrook" as they passed them by. Finally, it appeared and, with the children following along, they all hopped onto the trolley. The journey out of the city was mostly in silence while the three of them sat together. Clinging tightly to one another, the warmth and love they felt needed no words. As they passed by the mill area the children recognized their old home and looked concerned when they did not signal to get off at this stop. Estella told them she had found a better place to call home.

The trolley finally came to a stop at Overbrook Station. Estella got up and the children followed along. She pointed out the shops during the walk home. Lafferty's market was one where she told the children that they would really enjoy visiting to pick out some favorite treats. When they got down to the next street, they turned the corner, and Estella caught a glimpse of the bank. She didn't want to mention that to the children yet. This was their first journey to the new house, and she wanted to build excitement in them when seeing home for the first time. A home that was never going away from any of them again.

Suddenly she stopped on the sidewalk, looked up at the tall twin house and said, "Welcome home!"

The children screamed with excitement as they dashed up the steps to the front porch, their feet thudding with anticipation. They stood patiently at the door, eyes shining, waiting for their mother, who followed close behind. Estella pulled the key from her bag, slid it into the lock, and then stepped back.

"Go on," she said with a smile, inviting them to turn the knob themselves.

They pushed open the door and stepped inside, falling into a hush of awe as they caught sight of the fireplace in the front room, the warm heart of their new home.

"Would you like to see your bedrooms?" Estella asked, already knowing the answer.

The children bolted up the stairs. At the landing, Estella gestured toward the first room. "That one's mine," she said, encouraging them to take a peek.

Large windows filled the room with soft light and looked out over a peaceful backyard oasis dotted with tall trees. One stood out—a blazing red maple in full glory, its bold color framed by neighboring evergreens. It gave the illusion of stepping into a quiet park. As they passed the doorway, a faint scent of rose water drifted from the dressing table with its elegant tri-fold mirror.

"Go ahead," Estella urged gently, "Pick a room."

There were three more down the hall. John darted straight to the end room, the one with a view of the street and sidewalk below. Just as Estella had expected.

Frances, thoughtful as ever, chose the room beside John's, leaving the one closest to Estella for Florence.

For a moment, Estella paused at the doorway of that last, quiet room. The sight of the empty space pulled at her heart, a stark reminder that Florence was not yet home. The joy of this long-awaited day dimmed slightly under the shadow of her absence. It wasn't how Estella had imagined it.

But she didn't let herself linger there. She smiled, pushing the ache aside.

"Is anyone hungry?" she called out, her voice bright, lifting the mood once more.

The children could already smell the delicious aromas coming from the kitchen below. Estella had started a ham, potatoes and green bean meal before she went downtown to greet the children. She figured on all of them being tired, hungry and wanting to visit with one another. It was one of their favorite meals.

They took to the stairs and didn't waste time finding the kitchen. It was bright with windows on all sides. In the corner was a round table, already set with a lace tablecloth, utensils and dishes. It faced out over the same beautiful red leafed maple they saw from the second-floor bedroom window. Everything looked brand new in the kitchen and very modern compared to what they had known before.

Estella instructed the children to take their seats while she brought the bowls of warm food to the table. Their laughter softened as they watched her move about the kitchen with quiet purpose, each gesture filled with care.

She opened the large wooden icebox with its heavy double doors. Inside, a thick block of ice sat at the top, keeping the shelves below cool. She reached past a glass bottle of milk and pulled out a crock of butter, still firm and pale. Returning to the table with a basket of warm bread wrapped in a clean towel, she set it down and encouraged the children to spread the butter while it was still soft enough to melt.

From the cast iron, porcelain enamel stove, she ladled steaming helpings into the bowls—ham, tender and savory, nestled alongside buttery potatoes and slow-simmered green beans. The scent alone wrapped around the children like a memory. On the back burner plate, a pie sat cooling—its flaky crust golden and slightly cracked.

They ate with eager delight, savoring each bite. This was the food they associated with home—not just nourishment, but love. There was no fear, no threat of punishment for leaving something on their plate. Only laughter, soft conversation, and the simple joy of being together. For a moment, the room held nothing but warmth, and it truly felt like home.

The place setting where Florence would have been seated would remain set, patiently awaiting her return. Once they finished enjoying time together over the meal, Estella asked Frances to help her with the dishes. Once all but Florence's setting was removed, they brought them over to the sink and set them down into soapy water to soak.

Estella returned to the stovetop and sliced into the warm apple pie. The crust flaked away perfectly, and she put one slice on each plate. John and Frances both returned to the table with the pie and enjoyed the sweet indulgence together.

Estella asked the children if they'd like to see their new school and perhaps find the park nearby to run off some energy before the sun dipped below the rooftops. It had already been a full day for all of them, but she wanted them to know exactly where the school was. Part of her agreement with the Children's Aid Society required immediate enrollment, and Estella was determined to follow every instruction to the letter. Nothing could be allowed to jeopardize Florence's return.

Eager and curious, the children dashed out the front door and down the steps to the sidewalk, calling back to her as they went. Estella followed behind, her heart lightened by the sight of them, safe, joyful, and bounding forward into a new chapter.

They walked for about ten minutes until they reached a large, grey stone building of the Overbrook School. Rounding the side, they caught sight of a spacious playground and recreation area tucked behind the school. Without waiting, the children took off running toward the seesaws, their laughter echoing in the late afternoon air.

Estella found a nearby bench and sat down, taking a moment to revel in the simple beauty of her children playing freely together. The day had unfolded better than she could have imagined.

Still, she remained keenly aware of the reality she faced. It was important that the children knew how to get to and from school on their own. As a single mother, a rarity in her time, she had to be precise and vigilant about her schedule. Every decision mattered. The scrutiny from the Children's Aid Society lingered in her mind, a constant reminder of how fragile this reunion could still be.

She felt the invisible eyes of the system watching her, judging her choices, her worth. But for now, she watched her children instead. And for a few moments, their laughter drowned out everything else.

John and Frances decided to dash over to the swings and try them out. They swung higher and higher laughing, giggling and talking aloud about going up and over the top bar and back down again. Leaping off the swings midway, they came down to try out the ladder steps alongside the swings. They looked like monkeys swinging from vines.

They liked their new school, especially the grassy recreation area where they could run freely and just be children again. Estella stood from the bench and called them over. The light was fading, and it was time to head home. As they walked, she took the same route she always did, hoping to help them learn the way on their own. Soon enough, they'd have to walk it without her, especially with the growing demands of her new job.

Just before turning onto their street, Estella paused and pointed down the road toward the grand stone building where she worked.

"That bank over there," she said, her voice steady but full of feeling, "is the reason we have a home now."

The children turned to look.

"I'm going to take you there this weekend, when it's closed. I want you to meet my friend and co-worker, Mr. Masters. If it weren't for him, we wouldn't be here. He helped me get a loan so I could buy our house. And I have a respectable job, one that lets me care for you properly."

She knelt slightly so they could see the seriousness in her eyes.

"I want you to get a good education. Work hard. Learn all you can. So that one day, you'll be able to do the same, not just for yourselves, but for others."

Frances nodded solemnly, and John took her hand. Estella stood tall again and led them the rest of the way home, the glow of a streetlamp catching the pride in her eyes.

They continued their walk until they came to the rows of twin homes. She told the children to dash between the twins and head straight back to the yard. She knew they would want to race ahead of her. When she caught up and met them in the backyard she climbed the steps to the rear kitchen door. There was a small hook underneath the railing where she had hidden a key. She showed the children how to let themselves in the house.

She went on to tell them they would practice this again before she let them do it on their own. The door led into a small mudroom off the kitchen. There was a door at the end of it that had a small toilet room with a sink. She instructed John to go and wash up while Frances went upstairs to bathe and dress for bed. He could go second after her for a bath. It was such a luxury to have a second toilet room in the home. One that took very little time to become accustomed to.

Estella turned on the gas stove top and heated water for tea. She poured the boiling water into the teacup to let it steep. She sat for a moment while the children readied themselves for bed and stared at the table setting that belonged to her daughter, Florence. She would get the children enrolled in school and head into the office and use the telephone to begin the search for Florence. She wondered where she was and how she was being cared for and by whom. She was a quiet and reserved girl that never shied away from anything, yet she was never far from her brother and sister. Florence's day would come to return home where she belonged.

Estella climbed the stairs and while the children finished preparing for bedtime stories she dressed and readied herself for the end-of-day ritual together. She sat at her dressing table and gently pressed the rosewater-soaked cloth across her brow and along her cheeks and down to her neck. It removed the grime of the day and cleansed her skin leaving, a gentle fragrance behind that lingered long after. She looked at her reflection in the tri-fold mirror and felt as though she had aged numerous years over the last several months. But it mattered not, and she pushed herself away, getting up and crossing the room to stand by the warm radiator beneath the window. She pulled the long drape aside and gazed up at the sky. The night was lit up by a bright overhead moon surrounded by stars. In the background she could hear Frances and John chatting away. She could only surmise they had found the collection of stories she'd left in their rooms. She wondered which one they would decide to read together for story time.

She joined the children in John's room at the end of the long hallway. They patted the bed and moved aside to make room for their mother to join them. She nestled between them and asked the children which book they had chosen to read. With great excitement, John held up the hard-bound copy of The Wizard of Oz written by Frank Baum.

Pleasantly surprised, Estella took hold of it and began to read to them. They took turns reading aloud to one another, something they had always done before drifting off to sleep. No matter what happened during the day, good or bad, it was a ritual they had grown to love, transporting them to another place all together. They would continue to read this book for several more weeks. Poignant to all of them in unique ways was at the end of the story when Dorothy repeated, "There's no place like home," and it left them all wondering if it was all just a bad dream or whether it was real.

Awakening early to dress for the day ahead, Estella quietly descended the stairs, allowing the children to sleep a bit longer. Today would be lengthy for all of them and she wanted them to start with a hearty breakfast. She sipped on her hot coffee as she busied herself in the kitchen, making lunches from the supper leftovers to send along with the children. She had the stovetop ready to cook the eggs when the children came down into the kitchen.

She showed John how to toast the bread over the gas flame of the stovetop using a long-handled fork while she started cooking the eggs. They all preferred them over easy or, as Frances liked to call them, dippy eggs.' They all sat together at the kitchen table and enjoyed their meal.

Estella with the children headed out the back door to make their way to school. She was glad that at least John and Frances would be together during the day while she worked at the bank. She encouraged the children to lead the way. They climbed the steps to the landing and entered the front doors of the school building. They had a choice to go up or down a set of wide stairs. They chose to go downstairs, and it was a good choice as it came out to an office area on the ground level in the rear of the building.

Once the children were enrolled, she gave them a reassuring hug and kissed them on the cheek and told them to work hard and have fun. It was difficult for Estella to turn and walk away and equally hard for the children. The emotional turmoil from the last time she left them in the care of trusted adults was not a good memory for any of them. They would have to overcome those fears and grow together in the coming days, putting that misery behind them.

Estella welcomed the cool morning breeze as she stepped back out of the school and crossed the street toward the office. She spotted Stephen's driver idling at the curb. Perhaps he was heading into town. The security guard stationed at the door recognized her and promptly unlocked it, letting her slip inside before official hours.

She made her way quickly through the quiet lobby and down to her office, settling into her familiar morning rhythm. Estella valued this early solitude. The stillness gave her space to move through her start-up tasks without interruption, ensuring her staff could begin their day on steady footing. There would be enough distractions once the office came fully to life, this quiet window was her way of staying one step ahead.

But today, her mind was elsewhere. As she organized papers and turned on her lamp, she reminded herself: Today is the day. She would begin the formal process of reclaiming Florence.

With resolve tightening in her chest, she sat down, took a steadying breath, and prepared to make the call that could bring her daughter home.

Stephen stood in the doorway of her office. She hadn't noticed initially, and he spoke up. "You must be fully absorbed in your work today. I trust all went well with the children yesterday."

Estella looked up from across her desk with concern in her eyes. Stephen was somewhat taken aback and wondered if the children were not well. She went on and told Stephen how wonderful it was to have her children at home. Then after a brief pause, she explained the situation about Florence.

He came into her office and took a seat to listen closer and inquire how he could assist her in locating Florence to bring her home with the others. They brainstormed with one another like when they often conversed for hours after the close of business. This was different and more personal now. He insisted that she take all the time she needed for her inquiries. The women in her department were trained to handle most situations. He would make sure she was not disturbed today. He would advise the lead officer before he departed for his downtown meeting.

Before leaving her office, he got up, came around to her side of the desk and reached out for her hands. Holding them strongly in his he looked into her eyes and promised her that he would do everything he could to help her. She knew the conviction of his words and thanked him once again for his compassion for her and the children.

As he walked out, he turned and told her, "You know where to find me. I'll return in the afternoon, and I'll be eager to learn more about your queries."

He pulled her office door closed. The staff were arriving and were surprised to see Estella's door closed. It was something she never did, and they treated it with great respect, as she had always shown the same to them.

She began making calls to the downtown Children's Aid office. Fortunately, she had the use of the bank phone system, and they had records of previous calls to get her through to the proper contact that would be familiar with her case. She had to make several calls before she finally got hold of the helpful individual who had left the open file for her to read. She immediately recognized the woman's voice at the other end of the line.

The assistant interrupted the conversation. "Madam, I know your case well. But I've been instructed by my supervisor not to discuss this with anyone, especially you. I can tell you that the foster program is something the agency and orphanages have been pushing for a very long time to alleviate the overwhelming burden on the system. They are very secretive and closed-lipped about where the children have been taken. Not even do I have access to those records.

I wish I could be of more help to you, but quite honestly, there isn't anyone in this office that knows about that end of things. I will keep a close watch over your file and if I learn anything new, I know how to contact you."

Estella's heart sank as the news settled over her, resonating deep in her soul. She couldn't comprehend how an agency tasked with protecting children and supporting families could so easily become the force that tore them apart. It seemed a cruel contradiction, one that shattered the very bonds they claimed to uphold.

She pushed away from her desk and rose slowly, smoothing the front of her long dress with trembling hands. Crossing the room, she moved to the tall windows, where the light filtered in through the glass. She needed a moment to breathe, to gather herself.

Her thoughts turned immediately to Florence. Where is she? Is she warm? Safe? With kind people? The questions multiplied, pressing in from all sides, unanswered and relentless. The ache of uncertainty was almost too much to bear.

Just then, the telephone rang, slicing through the silence. Estella walked back to her desk, lifted the earpiece, and spoke into the receiver.

Stephen's familiar voice came through, calm and steady. He didn't need to ask, he could tell by her tone that the morning had brought no good news.

She filled him in, her voice subdued but controlled. When she finished, he said gently, "I've wrapped up my meetings. Let's meet for lunch at the tavern in thirty minutes. My driver will bring me from the city."

The offer, simple as it was, felt like a lifeline.

Estella opened her office door and took a few moments to tidy up tasks that required her attention. It was the last day of a short week due to the holiday, which often meant a flurry of end-of-week activity—accounts to reconcile, final approvals to sign off on. Much of it was routine, but it still needed her signature before the close of business.

After checking in briefly with a few members of her staff, Estella chose to take the stairs to avoid lingering conversations. She needed air, space, and time to reset before lunch with Stephen. The security guard saw her coming and held the door open. She stepped out into the crisp fall air. Low, dark grey clouds hung overhead, matching the mood that had settled over her since morning. The cool breeze brushed across her face, reviving her spirit slightly as she made her way down the sidewalk toward the tavern.

Not seeing Stephen's car yet, Estella continued walking, letting her feet guide her as her thoughts untangled. She had become a familiar figure in Overbrook, especially among the women who came to the bank for guidance and to open accounts. A few of them passed her on the street, nodding and offering warm smiles, gestures of mutual respect and quiet solidarity.

She turned down a side street and looped through the small park behind the trolley station. The clouds had begun to break, and shafts of sunlight streamed through, catching on the last of the golden leaves. Estella stopped, closed her eyes, and offered a silent prayer—for Florence's safety, and for a path to bring her daughter home.

A sudden burst of laughter pulled her from her reverie—children racing ahead of their mothers, their joy spilling across the walkway as they ran toward the merry-go-round. For a moment, she simply watched, the weight in her chest lifting slightly.

Turning back toward the main road, Estella walked with more ease, her spirits buoyed by the small reminder of joy and the progress she had already made. She had brought two of her children home. That was no small feat.

As she neared the tavern, Stephen's car pulled up to the curb. He stepped out and greeted her warmly. Together, they entered the

familiar tavern and made their way to their usual table at the rear. It
was busier than usual, filled with the low hum of conversation and
clinking glasses, but Estella welcomed the distraction. For the first
time all day, she let herself exhale.

Stephen started the conversation while at the same time placed
his hand atop of hers. The warmth of his touch was comforting. "I'm
very sorry about your daughter and how she has been treated. I know
it's the last thing you expected.

The waitress arrived, interrupting their conversation with a soft
smile as she placed their beverages on the table and recited a few of
the day's specials. After placing their orders, the conversation picked
up where it had paused.

"I'm truly grateful for everything you've done for me and my
family," Estella said, her tone measured but warm. "Right now,
though, I feel like there's little more that can be done, at least
according to the assistant I spoke with earlier. She's been candid
with me from the beginning, and she seems to understand the inner
workings of the organization enough to know that pressing further
might be fruitless."

She paused, swirling the liquid in her glass thoughtfully.

"I'll keep thinking, keep trying. I'm staying in close contact with
her. She's promised to let me know if there's any new information.
Apparently, everything is kept extremely secret, meant to protect the
child and the foster family. I can understand the need for that kind
of secrecy if a child is in danger. But in Florence's case, it's clear there
was no harm. They approved the return of John and Frances without
hesitation."

Stephen listened quietly, his expression softening. He could see
she had turned over every possibility in her mind, trying to accept an
unthinkable situation. He also sensed she'd said all she wanted to for
now.

Wanting to ease the moment and lift the heaviness, he leaned forward with a gentle smile.

"Would you and the children like to join me tomorrow at the zoo?"

She smiled at the thought of it and replied immediately without thinking. "Of course we would. I've read about the spectacle of it and have always wanted to take the children. That would be a sweet adventure. Thank you!"

The waitress returned with bowls of piping hot stew and warm bread. "Ya be needin' anything else?"

Both Stephen and Estella gestured to her all was well, and she hurriedly raced off to take care of the full tavern.

The two of them continued their conversation, allowing the hot food to cool off before they took the first bite. They planned on meeting at the trolley station in the morning to get an early start to the zoo. She looked forward to introducing the children to Stephen and sharing the day together. They continued with lunch but knew the time was too short to linger over dessert. They needed to return to the office and finish out the day which would take them in different directions. Estella would need to close out the accounts and hurry off to the school to greet the children after their first day of attendance.

Heading back to the bank, they could feel rain droplets beginning to hit their face. Thankfully the tavern was not far from the bank and the two of them took the steps up to the entrance, racing inside to escape the cold, wet thrashing assault of rain. After they crossed over the main floor, Stephen headed to his office and Estella to the elevator to return to her department below.

Her return led to a flurry of activity and before she knew it, she needed to be on her way to the school to pick up the children. She had not even had a moment to allow the morning endeavors to creep into her thoughts or wonder about the children at school. Although the extra-long weekend would be welcomed, there was a lot more to achieve before it could be savored. She tidied up her desk and locked up on the way out.

Most everyone had departed for the day, and Estella wasn't far behind. As the elevator doors opened with a soft chime, she stepped into the hushed hallway. On a whim, instead of heading straight for the exit, she turned and made her way toward Stephen's office. Something compelled her, just a quick good night, if he was still there.

Peering around the doorway, she saw him look up from his desk almost immediately. Their eyes met.

"Please, madam, come in," he said, rising and walking around his desk to greet her.

"I can't stay," she replied quickly, offering a warm smile. "I need to pick up the children from school. I just wanted to say good night—and that I'm looking forward to introducing you to them tomorrow."

A quiet beat passed between them.

Something unspoken hung in the air, suspended as if held in profound stillness.

Neither of them moved, but both felt it, that quiet pull, the unmistakable current that had grown stronger with every shared glance, every conversation steeped in mutual respect and neither dared name.

Stephen, ever composed, held his posture steady. But inside, he was grateful she didn't stay. The temptation to reach for her, even briefly, had become harder to resist. It had been years since he'd felt this way, since before his wife passed, and he hadn't expected to feel it again.

What Estella didn't know was how deeply she had stirred the still waters of his grief. And if she were honest with herself, her own thoughts had started to wander too.

The moment broke as she gave him a gentle nod and turned to go. Her cheeks flushed warm as she descended the slick stone steps outside, the cool evening air brushing her skin like a balm.

She hurried down the street, her heart beating faster than she cared to admit, just in time to meet her children.

As she got closer to the school, she could see the doors opening wide and children happily dashing down the steps and making their way home. Some lingered around the large trees in a grassy area of a courtyard on the side of the school building. Others dashed behind the school and headed to the playground.

She waited patiently at the familiar corner, and at last, both John and Frances appeared. The moment they spotted her, they broke into a run, calling out joyfully. Estella opened her arms, welcoming them into her embrace. Their faces were filled with happiness, brimming with stories from the day.

She listened closely as they walked home together, their voices tumbling over each other with excitement. They skipped along the sidewalk, chatting all the way, and in no time, they reached the house. With a burst of energy, the children raced ahead, darting along the side yard and up the steps.

Estella followed at a slower pace, her heart full. She was so grateful to be home with her children again, especially with the long holiday weekend ahead. The timing felt like a small grace. Only one thing weighed on her heart, the absence of her youngest. If only Florence was here to enjoy this too.

The children bounded upstairs to change into their play clothes and were out the door again moments later. Estella called after them, "Don't go far and be back in about an hour for supper!"

She turned her attention to the kitchen, where the cooler air inspired thoughts of warm, hearty food. Filling a large pot with water, she set it on the stove to boil. In another pan, she seared a cut of meat, then added it to the bubbling water along with chopped carrots, onions, and potatoes. A simple stew, humble, comforting, and perfect for the weather.

As the savory aroma began to fill the house, Estella felt a deep sense of contentment. There would be enough food for tomorrow, and even more after that. She was already making plans to take the children to the market over the weekend. It felt good, empowering, to have her own money again, enough to buy what they needed… and now and then, something she simply wanted.

Estella made herself a cup of tea and retreated to the living room. She hadn't yet had the time to sit and enjoy this lovely room. The large windows always seemed to allow the light to fill the room with warmth. She wondered if she would use the fireplace or even hang stockings for the children at Christmas like the ones she saw in pictures. She sat in a Victorian wing-backed chair next to the fireplace and set her tea on the side table. She picked up a book that Stephen had recently loaned to her: "The Private Life of Marie Antoinette," written by a Madame Campan. She began to read and completely lost herself in the pages of the book. It was a peaceful moment that settled her entire being. A journey elsewhere that took her across the ocean to a different place in time.

Her empty teacup and the happy chatter of the children coming through the door brought her back to here and now. She closed the book, saving her place with the silk bookmark sewn into the spine, then joined the children in the kitchen.

She could see with their rosy colored cheeks that they had enjoyed themselves immensely and had expended a lot of energy. They sat down for a savory meal together and shared the adventures of the day. The best part, of course, was the small park tucked away at the end of the street. Estella had not even noticed it before. She was pleased that they were fitting into their new home and area very well. Perhaps the children were more resilient than she imagined.

She realized there was a lesson for herself in their ability to overcome the hardships they had endured.

Once they were through with supper and the dishes washed up, she asked the children to join her in the living room; she wanted to establish new routines that would bond them together, creating lasting memories in the years to come. Estella turned on a brass table lamp. John ran to the other lamp on the opposite side of the room and turned it on, making a nice cast of light. The days were growing shorter and the convenience of these new electric lamps and bulbs were welcomed.

They sat on the long couch together and Estella began to tell the children about the zoo trip they were going to take the next day. They listened to her with great interest as she told them about the animals that were there. More importantly she told them about Stephen, the man who she worked for at the bank. He would be meeting all of them at the trolley station for their ride to the zoo together.

Estella glanced over at John and said, "Can you get the book from the table at the end of the couch, sweetheart?"

John sprang up eagerly. "The Tale of Mrs. Tittlemouse!" he said with delight, already familiar with the title. The well-loved copy had been loaned to them by one of Estella's dear friends.

As he returned with the book, Estella smiled and said, "Please let Frances start the book for us tonight."

Without hesitation, John handed it to his sister, who settled in and opened to the first page. As Frances began to read, the room grew quiet with anticipation. More than the story itself, the children were captivated by the charming illustrations, each scene bursting with color and the delightful antics of Beatrix Potter's woodland characters. After every page, Frances held up the book to show the two-page spread for all to see the world come to life.

When she reached the end of a section, she passed the book to their mother, and they continued taking turns reading aloud. It became their gentle rhythm, voices changing, laughter bubbling up now and then.

Midway through the tale, Estella gently marked their place and closed the book.

"Oh, please, just one more page!" the children begged in unison.

But Estella shook her head, her tone soft but firm. "It's been a full day and tomorrow promises to be just as exciting. You need to wash up and get into your night clothes. I won't be long behind you, so hurry, please."

Reluctantly, they stood and walked off down the hall, still smiling, the story lingering in their minds like a lullaby.

Estella sat for a moment, taking in all the good feelings. She had so much to be grateful for. She stood up and turned off both lamps. She could see through the tall windows the glow from the gas street lights below. She felt safe and secure as she gazed out the window. She took the stairs and made her way up to her bedroom. She drew the drapes closed, feeling the warmth of the radiator. Sleep would come fast for all of them.

She went to check on both John and Frances, who were already tucked under the covers. John's room at the front of the house had a nice cast of light from the street lights. She pulled his drapes closed, creating a dark cave of rest. She wished both a good night. When she got beneath the covers she thought about Florence. She drifted into deep sleep while whispering one of her favorite poems, "Cradle Song" by Thomas Dekker:

> Golden slumbers kiss your eyes,
> Smiles awake you when you rise;
> Sleep, pretty wantons, do not cry,
> And I will sing a lullaby,
> Rock them, rock them, lullaby.
> Care is heavy, therefore sleep you,
> You are care, and care must keep you;

Sleep, pretty wantons, do not cry,
And I will sing a lullaby,
Rock them, rock them, lullaby.

THE GREAT WAR
Politics | Amish Farm | Spring 1915

Once again, the fields had been planted, and the spring crops were beginning to paint the landscape in vibrant green. Talk of promising yields, corn, wheat, and more, filled the air as Amos, Jacob, Isaac, and the other men gathered near the market outside the auction barn.

They had returned to inspect the strong workhorses soon to be brought through the sale. With the recent expansion and purchase of a neighboring farm adjoining the Weavers' property, it had become necessary to find suitable animals to manage the growing land.

Jacob Weaver's eldest son, Isaac, his and Rebecca's first married child, was beginning a new chapter with his young wife, Mary. Their local community, bound by faith and tradition, had come together to help the young couple build their new farmstead from the ground up.

Nearby the men heard a commotion and loud expressions of surprise and horror as a delivery truck unloaded a stack of the Philadelphia Public Ledger alongside the New Holland Clarion Newspapers.

Splashed across the front pages read: "LUSITANIA TORPEDOED! Mammoth Cunarder Sunk on Irish Coast."

It wasn't long before all the newspapers were snapped up and sold, mostly by the English, but Isaac had been curious enough and was able to pick one up, returning to the men who had accompanied him to the sale on his behalf. Silently they read the headline and article together, standing closely to one another to take it all in.

The story read:

"LONDON, May 8– The Cunard liner Lusitania, which sailed out of New York last Saturday with more than two thousand souls aboard, lies at the bottom of the ocean off the Irish coast. She was sunk by a German submarine, which sent two torpedoes crashing into her side while the passengers, seemingly confident that the great swift vessel could elude the German underwater craft, were having lunch.... The British admiralty is discouraging the publication of surmises and guesses regarding the dead and injured. Even before the crude details are known, the British press is asking editorially what the United States will say to this event and how she will hold Germany to the "strict accountability" mentioned in previous diplomatic correspondence."

There was a growing buzz in the crowd, whispers swelling into anxious conversation: the United States might finally be pulled into the Great War in Europe. Until recently, such a possibility had seemed unlikely. President Woodrow Wilson had maintained a firm stance of neutrality, and most Americans had agreed, this was not our war.

The diverse makeup of the American population, with millions of citizens having emigrated from Europe, made it difficult to even choose a side. Many supported Britain and France, while large populations of German and Irish Americans leaned toward the Central Powers.

The war, which had begun on June 28, 1914, with the assassination of Austrian Archduke Franz Ferdinand by a Serbian nationalist, had set off a chain reaction. With Germany's encouragement, Austria-Hungary declared war on Serbia a month later. Russia stepped in to support Serbia, and then France backed Russia. On August 1, Germany declared war on Russia—and within days, Britain joined the conflict after Germany invaded neutral Belgium.

Given the complicated ties to the warring nations, it made sense that America had remained on the sidelines. It was a nation of immigrants, many of whom still felt strong allegiances to their homelands.

Still, the U.S. had played a powerful role behind the scenes. American factories produced weapons, munitions, and goods that helped keep the Allied war effort alive. Banks thrived on loans made to Britain and France.

But now, a headline had shaken the American public. The sinking of a passenger vessel, reported with growing outrage, was seen by many as an outright act of hostility. Citizens questioned whether the time for neutrality had come to an end. And some wondered aloud if Britain might use the tragedy to push America into action.

Amos and Jacob spoke in low voices; their words edged with concern. The others sat nearby, quietly listening as the two men speculated about what the news might mean for their community. If the United States were to enter the Great War alongside her allies, the Amish would face difficult moral decisions. How could they remain true to their belief in nonviolence without being drawn into the broader conflict? And how could they stay outside of mainstream American society while still securing legal recognition as conscientious objectors?

One of the main reasons their ancestors had come to America was to avoid the compulsory military service that plagued Europe. The threat of war now made those old fears feel fresh again.

The Amish were descendants of the early Anabaptist movement in Europe, a group that had broken from both Catholic and Protestant traditions. They believed baptism should be reserved for adults who had consciously chosen their faith, and they held fast to the principle of separation from the world. For those beliefs, many early Anabaptists were executed as heretics. Others fled to the remote mountains of Switzerland and southern Germany, where they survived by farming and worshipping in homes rather than formal churches, a tradition that carried through the generations.

In the 1720s, the Amish had begun settling in Pennsylvania as part of William Penn's "holy experiment," a promise of religious freedom and tolerance. Now, nearly two centuries later, the very ideals that brought them here were being tested once again.

Amos espoused his concern by stating to the men, "This will test the core of our faith in all that we hold true and believe in Jesus' teachings, which prohibit fighting, even in self-defense. There is also our belief in the separation of church and state. We must remain outside the conflict without entering the mainstream and, if necessary, secure legal conscientious objector status."

Jacob and the others agreed with Amos. Jacob added, "I recall my Daed talking of the Civil War when the United States began a conscription service. Some Amish boys got exemptions for farm deferments with conscientious objector status. Others were required to report to Army camps. The drafted Amish who refused to enter armed service were sent to these camps and often subjected to abuse. Of more concern for our families is that some of the boys who were pulled away never returned to their communities after they served. We must keep watch on the news and prepare ourselves for what appears to be the inevitable."

A sudden clamor from within the sale barn, just across from where the men had been deep in conversation, snapped their attention back to the present. Though talk of war and headlines had stirred the morning, they had come with a clear purpose, and if they didn't move quickly, they might miss their chance to bid on a good horse or two.

They made their way into the auction area, skipping the usual inspections of the animals beforehand. No matter, between them, they had enough knowledge to make sound judgments as the horses came through.

The auction was in full swing. Horses were paraded through the ring, one after another, sold off to the highest bidder with the sharp crack of the wooden gavel and the auctioneer's chant ringing through the rafters: "SOLD!"

Then came a pair of light tan Belgian draft horses. Isaac's eyes locked on them instantly. He had attended many auctions with his father and the other men of the community, but he had never bid himself. This would be his first.

As the bidding began, he felt his heart race. Steadying himself, he raised the sale number he'd registered earlier. The numbers climbed fast, but Isaac remained firm. With each bid, his confidence grew, until at last, the final call echoed:

"SOLD!"

The hammer dropped. The horses were his.

The older men clapped him on the back in quiet approval, their pride visible in their smiles. A flush of satisfaction warmed Isaac's face. He had stepped into a new role, provider, husband, farmer, and passed his first real test.

They lingered for a few more sales, letting the buzz of excitement settle before heading home.

Isaac headed out of the sale barn and over to the cashier to make the payment for his new team of workers. He couldn't wait to get home and share the news with Mary. Newly married, they had so many dreams of having a family together and this was a step in the right direction. He had been saving up his hard-earned dollars from his carpentry work alongside his Daed.

Once he made payment and received his ticket to retrieve the horses, he walked back to the group of men sitting at picnic tables beneath the shade of a large oak tree behind the sale barn. He sat down at the end of the table where they had left an open seat for him.

The men had waited for him to join them in fellowship and share in a meal together. After the appropriate prayers and thanks were given, they got into the picnic baskets that Rebecca, Sara and Mary had packed for the trip to town. The women knew it would be a long day ahead for them and their appetites would be big. The men enjoyed the fellowship.

After the meal and some light conversation, the men made their way back to the buggy. Amos, Jacob, and Isaac had traveled together to the sale barn, anticipating a purchase and wisely bringing the necessary tack to transport the horses home.

Once the pair of Belgians were released to Isaac, the men wasted no time in readying the animals for the journey.

The clouds above were beginning to gather, dark and heavy with the promise of rain. It would be a blessing for the crops, but less so for the long, damp ride ahead. Still, the day had been a success. Spirits were high, and the buggy rolled steadily forward, full of good news to carry home.

The original plan had been to return directly to Isaac's farm with his new pair of work horses, but as the weather turned foul and rain lashed down in heavy sheets, Isaac made the decision to drop Amos, his Daed, and Jacob, at their farm first. The road to his own place could wait a little longer.

Amos wasted no time once they arrived. He jumped down from the buggy and made a dash for the barn, eager to catch up on the evening chores.

To his surprise, the sound of steady movement and soft murmuring reached him before he reached the stalls. Inside, he found Florence and their neighbor, David, quietly finishing the last of the milking. Rebecca Weaver must have sent her son over, knowing Amos was away at the sale. The Weaver family could always be counted on when someone needed a hand.

Amos walked over and gave David a grateful nod. "Thank you for coming by to help. And tell yer Mamm we surely enjoyed the treats she sent along for all of us today."

David smiled and looked up at Amos. "Glad to help you out. Is there anything else you need me to do?"

"Appreciate the offer, but for now we're all caught up, thanks to your help."

The sound of the rain on the barn roof was beginning to let up. Streams of light began to shine in the side windows now. These afternoon showers were a blessing for the crops. Amos came out of the barn and looked out across his fields. A fog seemed to rise from the ground, creating a surreal scene above the landscape. He knew that soon enough the heat of summer combined with the moisture would make for a rich harvest season. David and Florence had finished up and came out to stand behind Amos and appreciate the same beauty of the land.

After a minute, David spoke up, "I'll see you soon," and was off running across the back field on the path to home.

Amos and Florence walked from the barn and toward the back of the house. In a quiet, soft-spoken tone he said, "Girl, you be fitting in well here and me and Mamm appreciate your hard work around the farm."

Florence shyly responded, "You're welcome, Daed."

Florence had been with the Blank family for five years. She knew she was loved and well cared for, but there was still a piece of her missing, a space in her heart that remained quietly empty. She often wondered about her real mother, her sister, and her brother. Would she even recognize them if she saw them again? Were they out there somewhere, trying to find her too?

Her last happy memory of them flickered like a worn photograph in her mind: a day at the park, laughter echoing around the swings and merry-go-round. Then, as if torn from a dream, came the next day, when they were all taken away in an automobile to the orphanage. She never spoke of it with her new family.

Still, she remembered the day she arrived, stepping off the train, meeting the Blanks, and the strange, hollow feeling that sank deep into her belly. Something had shifted inside her then. She had only faint memories of the illness that came soon after, of slipping in and out of sleep, of the soft voices of Mamm Sara and her friend Rebecca praying by her bedside each time she stirred.

Mamm Sara later told her just how sick she'd been, and that God had answered their prayers, sparing her. That moment marked a turning point. It was then that Florence began to trust Sara and Amos, to believe that she was safe, and that this might, somehow, be home.

Florence dashed to run up the stairs with Amos close behind. They removed their shoes in the small room off the porch. The meal that Sara had been preparing all afternoon reminded them both how hungry they were. After washing up at the small sink, Florence dashed into the kitchen to help her Mamm. She got busy setting the long table for the three of them. Sara had earlier taken the roast out of the oven and was beginning to carve thin slices.

Florence knew the routine well. She came over next to her Mamm and began to spoon carrots and potatoes that had been cooking alongside the roast into a bowl. Next, she sliced the warm bread that had been set on the back of the oven top to keep warm. Once the food was put on the table, they all came to sit on the long wooden bench together.

Amos shared the big news of the day from the sale barn. First, he was happy to say that Isaac had found a wonderful pair of tan, Belgian work horses that would be a nice beginning for his newly acquired farm. After sharing the gripping headlines splashed across the newspapers, the tone of the discussion seemed to change. Florence even picked up on the concern that seemed to come across her Mamm's forehead. This had been the first time she ever recalled her family discussing this sort of news.

She listened quietly as her parents spoke of a possible conflict that could affect the entire church community. She felt a sense of fear and wondered if she would once again be abandoned. Sara sensed the child's concern and immediately turned the conversation from one of war to the upcoming quilting affair that she and Florence planned to attend in the coming days.

In their spare time they had been working together on a new patterned quilt which was nearly finished. Florence was becoming very skilled at this task, which delighted Sara. She could see the child had a knack for it and took the time to master the stitches neatly. The group of ladies and girls that met weekly were working on a large project to produce several quilts for an auction that would happen at an upcoming fair. It was a nice time for the ladies to get together, and the young girls got to spend time chatting and sharing stories with one another.

Amos said, "I'm glad to hear about this project and happy that Florence is making friends. I'll look at your work after we finish up supper."

Florence smiled. "I'd really like to show you what we've been working on."

After they finished the meal Sara and Florence pushed themselves away from the table and without much thought about the routine, went about cleaning the supper dishes. Sara made the chicory coffee and cut three slices from a berry pie she had made earlier. She whipped some fresh cream and spooned it onto each slice of pie. A nice, sweet ending to the meal.

Amos asked Florence about school and when she would be finished. The children in the nearby community all attended the same small school building that was perfectly placed between the Weaver, Blank and now Isaac Weaver's farmlands. The whitewashed stone building had children from ages five through fourteen in attendance. There was an unmarried teacher, Miss Emma Yoder, who schooled the children. They learned the basics of reading, writing and mathematics.

Florence replied, "We will be finished with school in two weeks. If we need to do farm chores, we can let Miss Yoder know and she'll release us earlier."

Amos nodded his head in approval and said, "Thanks for letting me know." He appreciated her awareness of the needs required on the farm. She had only been with them for five years and picked up quickly on what needed to be done in any given situation.

It brought him to a subject he was discussing with the men today about hiring local male laborers. During the hay cutting and wheat shocking seasons, Amos had come to rely on these men for the heavy harvests. It was a busy time for the entire community and not having a large family, especially male children, put him behind. The crops and harvest time waited for no one and needed to be worked at the right time. It created extra work for Sara and Florence because part of the laborer's wage was two meals: one in the middle of the day and a second at the day's end. It was a busy time for everyone.

He spoke his mind on the topic. "We will again hire laborers to help in the fields this season."

Sara and Florence listened quietly as Amos described the details of the work ahead. Both women knew their roles well. Florence, though young, understood what was expected of her.

Florence wondered if her Mamm disliked serving these men as much as she did. They were often demanding—some barely courteous, banging their cups on the table when they wanted more. Though she said nothing, Florence had been taught to keep her thoughts to herself. Still, the discomfort stirred quietly within her, refusing to be stilled.

A part of her felt guilty for thinking this way. She had been raised to serve with a willing heart, and to pray for grace when her own fell short. She quietly resolved to bring her feelings before God later, asking for a change of heart, just as she'd learned in her Bible lessons.

As was usual, Amos got up from the table and lit an oil lamp, setting it on the small desktop in the corner of the room. Mamm Sara and Florence went about cleaning up the supper dishes and putting away the food that was left over. There was always extra.

Once all was cleaned in the kitchen, Florence asked her Daed, "Would you like to see the quilt that Mamm and I have been working on?"

He set down his pencil to mark the page in his record keeping book and got up and walked across the room. She unfolded the quilt and spread it out on the dining table. He could see that she had spent a lot of time meticulously stitching and creating a lovely quilt with her Mamm.

He smiled and told her, "You've discovered something of value, a gift, and it pleases me to see your craft developing so well. Nothing satisfies a parent more than knowing their child is a person of value, having a strong work ethic and a sense of responsibility, along with their faith."

Florence smiled and humbly looked down and thanked her Daed, who rarely made those remarks. It made the moment even more special. She and her Mamm looked at each other with warm smiles and began to fold up the quilt, putting it away for another time. Amos returned to his bookwork across the room and finished his journal. It had been a good, productive day for the family.

Mamm Sara and Florence took a seat close to one another, both sitting near the lit oil lamp. They each had a devotional book they kept notes in and read daily. Often on church meeting days, the ladies would take out and discuss some of their writings with one another afterwards. Florence enjoyed this activity as it was something she could understand since it was in English. The services were mostly in Old German, which she found very difficult to follow. This always made her feel a bit detached and different from the others.

Now, they quietly read together by the light until it was obvious to Sara that bedtime had come when she noticed that Florence had nodded off and let her book fall into her lap. She gently nudged Florence, who sleepily wished her Mamm and Daed a good night and went upstairs to prepare for bed.

***

Overnight, it seemed as though summer had turned the heat up a notch. The sun bore down earlier and stronger this year, making everything grow at record speed, especially the weeds. In the cooler hours of morning, Florence found herself in her favorite place: the garden. She knelt among the flower borders, pulling up the stray weeds that had crept in, then worked her way through the vegetable rows with a hoe, keeping them clean and tidy.

She could spend hours there in the quiet company of blossoms and earth, but today she needed to finish up sooner than usual. She and Mamm were planning a visit to Mary Weaver, joining the other ladies from their quilting circle. Sara was already busy in the kitchen preparing food to bring along and had started a pot of stew that would be ready by the time they returned. Amos was off working with Jacob Weaver for the day, and Florence knew Rebecca would offer him a proper mid-day meal, freeing Sara from that task.

Just as she was wrapping up in the garden, a joyful cackle rang out from the henhouse, one of the hens celebrating a fresh egg. Florence gasped, realizing she'd nearly forgotten her morning chore. With her basket still in hand, she dashed across the yard to gather the eggs for her mother.

After washing away the evidence of morning garden chores, both Sara and Florence readied themselves to head to the Weaver's. There was a very small mirror in the back room off the kitchen above the wash basin. Sara stood in front of it to straighten her white kapp and place her black bonnet over it, as was the norm when going outside. Soon Florence would be doing the same when she was a little older. Wearing the kapp came about from biblical teachings, an evident sign of a woman's commitment to living according to scriptural principles and a symbol of humility.

Sara picked up her basket of baked goods, ready to share them with the ladies at quilting group. Today wouldn't be their usual gathering spent bent over fabric and thread—they were putting the final touches on the quilts they had worked on so diligently through the long winter. Florence was especially eager to visit, curious to see Mary Weaver's garden, which was said to be filled with beautiful blooms. As a newly married woman, this was Mary's first time hosting the group—a special milestone she welcomed with quiet humility.

Sara and Florence walked across the field that bordered the Weaver farm. The day was gloriously beautiful—blue skies stretched in every direction, and the sun had begun to warm the air just enough to lift the dew from the rows of corn they carefully stepped between. Grateful to live nearby, they had arrived ahead of the others and spotted Mary in her garden beside the house. Florence dashed over, eager to see what was growing. She adored flowers most of all and was curious to discover what Mary had planted.

Mary happily greeted them. "Gude mornin'! Come Florence, let me show you some of my flowers."

It was no secret that the girl loved flowers. She saved seeds every year to be replanted the following season. Mary did that too and would soon be sharing her favorite ones with Florence.

"Look here," Mary said. "That's a blue jacket and grows like a weed sometimes, but not to worry, once it gets too hot it will go away altogether until next Spring. It looks pretty when it grows amongst the narrow leaf coneflower that's about to blossom with pink flowers. Would you like me to save you some seeds from both?"

Florence nodded her head with delight and spoke up quietly, "Yes, please, I'd like that very much."

"Okay, well come on, let's get washed up. You can give me a hand in the house."

It wasn't long before everyone started to arrive, and the ladies took their seats around the table where the first quilt had been spread out. Its geometric patterns were all throughout the quilt. The dark blues, purples, greens, browns and reds symbolized a devotion to God. It looked like a beautiful flower garden. The ladies used intricate stitching to make their designs unique.

For Sara, quilting was more than a skill—it was part of her upbringing, woven into the rhythm of daily life. Like many Amish women, she hadn't inherited the tradition from her ancestors in Europe; rather, it was something passed down by neighbors and shaped by necessity. The early Amish didn't come to America with quilting patterns in hand—they learned the craft after settling in this new land, where winters were long and bitter. By the time Sara was a girl, quilting had already become a cherished custom.

She remembered stories from her own Mamm about the days when fabric was so expensive it was used only for clothing. Quilting, in those early days, was done with scraps—carefully saved, nothing wasted. After the Civil War, when cotton and wool became more affordable, quilting shifted from purely practical to quietly expressive. For Sara, each stitch still carried purpose: warmth, yes—but also comfort, tradition, and a kind of quiet love passed from one generation to the next.

Florence sat at a small table off to the side, one that had been specially set up for the day's quilting. She had taken to the craft quickly and now found herself helping a few of the younger girls, guiding their hands through simple stitches on their own budding quilt projects. It was always a work in progress, but she enjoyed the company of the little ones—their chatter, their curiosity, their eagerness to learn.

Not all stitches were neat, and more than once they had to pull out crooked seams and try again. But that didn't matter. It was all part of the learning. The girls giggled and whispered as they worked, and Florence couldn't help but laugh along. There was something deeply satisfying, almost soothing, in the steady rhythm of needle and thread. Quilting brought her a sense of peace—and in moments like this, even joy.

The ladies worked on the quilt for several hours and the time flew by quickly. It was important to finish up today as the growing season was in full swing and quilting sessions would be put aside until after fall harvests. For this reason, it seemed to go on longer than usual. Florence was feeling a bit hungry, and her stomach began to protest with loud rumbling noises that caused the smaller children to chuckle.

The ladies began to put away their needles and thread and together folded up the lovely, finished quilts. Each one was uniquely patterned. One had a center quilted area with the rest of it remaining one solid color. It stood out from the rest. The quilts would fetch a fair sum at the upcoming auction and would become a part of the community collections.

Once all the quilts were put away the women all collectively set up the food that they had prepared and brought along to share with one another. It was a nice gathering and social visit that no one had to go to too much trouble to produce. There was so much good food and discussions. Above all else, the time together, laughing and swapping stories, was the highlight.

Florence, along with the other younger girls at the small quilting table, cleared away the dishes from their table and asked if they could go outside and play. The other ladies happily motioned for them to go and continued to chatter away. It almost made this day feel more like a Sunday.

The children dashed outside. It didn't take long for them to organize a game of tag. Using the back corner of the house as a safe zone and starting point, the children tugged at pieces of straw that Florence held in her hand. The girl to pull the shortest straw would be "it". Leah ended up pulling the shortest straw and while she counted to ten, the others took off in all directions. They laughed and played hard together, making lasting friendships.

Mary stepped outside of her house and called out for Florence. "Would you like to continue that tour of the garden with me?"

Florence did not hesitate. "Yes, ma'am, please."

They walked together toward the large vegetable garden, where rows of young plants stretched in tidy lines. Beside it was a smaller patch reserved for flowers and herbs—just for beauty, Mary had said with a smile. Though early in the season, many of her plants were already in bloom. One cheerful cluster caught Florence's eye: bright yellow petals with dark brown centers. "Black-eyed Susans," Mary called them. Nearby, tall stalks—some nearly reaching Mary's height—stood ready to burst open with bell-shaped blossoms. Florence leaned closer, enchanted by the soft pinkish-purple hue gathering at the tips, just moments from blooming into full glory.

Mary could see her take a keen interest and said before she could ask, "That's a Foxglove and as pretty as can be when it opens. You can keep it blooming for a long while if you can bring yourself to pinch off the flowers once they open."

Florence took it all in and was eager to learn more about the lovely flowers. "What are these tall green grassy stems coming up behind the Foxglove?"

"Those are gladiolus and will put out a tall flower from the center in many different colors. You can cut them and bring them inside to enjoy. I'll make sure I bring you some once they blossom."

She led Florence to the opposite end of the garden where she had a smaller section with many mounds of different green plants coming up. "These are the herbal plants that are my favorite thing to grow and dry," she said

Florence, curious now about the herb plants, asked, "What do you do with the dried cuttings?"

Mary was glad to share. "They are used mostly in cooking. Some of them, once the leaves get bigger, like this Lamb's ear, can be used as bandages to stop bleeding and clean a wound. I also found that it helps with insect bites that are hard to stop scratching."

Florence was thrilled to see all the different plants Mary was growing and asked her, "Do you suppose I could grow some of these plants too?"

Mary said, 'I'd be happy to share seeds and plantings if it's okay with your Mamm. We'll ask her before you leave today."

The time in the garden for Florence went by quickly, and probably for Mary too. Although Mary was a few years older than Florence, they both shared something in common with gardening and could easily get lost in conversation, talking about the plants endlessly. Mary looked away from Florence and noticed the women coming out of her home, preparing to depart for the day. It had gone by too fast and ended so well.

Mary nodded to Florence and told her, "You need to come back, and I can show you more in the garden. Let's check with your Mamm now, okay?"

Mary thanked a few of the ladies for coming and saw them off. Some had come in buggies from greater distances while others rode bicycles. Florence was so glad to live a field away and would find any reason to come see Mary and her huge gardens filled with so many surprises she wished to learn more about.

Florence and Mary together approached Sara.

"Mamm, Mary has been showing me her flowers and herbs and wanted to know if I could return some time and help her in the garden and if I could plant some of the seeds in our garden. Could I?"

Mamm Sara was hesitant in her reply. "The busy harvesting is coming up and we have a lot to prepare for in the coming months. There won't be much time to spare, but I'm sure we can find a bit for you to come visit and plant a few new things in the garden. So long as it doesn't mean more work that we can't keep up."

Florence would continue to hold out hope that spare moments might come during the long, hot stretch of summer, a time when Mary might again invite her to learn more about her gardens, which she so admired. Mary had offered to teach her whenever the chance came, and Florence tucked that kindness away like a precious seedling saved for another day.

The day had passed sweetly, the hum of conversation and the soft rhythm of needles stitching warmth into cloth still lingering in Florence's memory. She and Sara thanked Mary for her hospitality, and with their baskets in hand, began the walk toward home.

As they passed the garden path, Florence glanced over her shoulder to see Isaac stepping out from the barn, brushing hay from his shirt sleeves, making his way back to the house. He gave a polite nod in their direction, then quickened his pace. Florence smiled softly, imagining he was eager for a quiet meal after the bustle of so many visitors.

A wistful thought stirred in her chest, would she ever meet someone who loved her the way Isaac clearly adored Mary? Would she have a garden of her own one day, and a home filled with the scent of bread baking and the laughter of children?

If ever that day came, she thought, she'd want it to be just like Mary's world: peaceful, full of care, and rooted in love.

In silence, Florence and her Mamm walked home together. Not long after they arrived home, they got busy with their afternoon chores. Afterwards, Florence headed back out to the barn to help her Daed with the final milking. She was glad for the longer days of early summer. She hadn't felt the same pressure to hurry back before running out of daylight hours to finish up in the barn.

She had much to daydream about while milking. While she made quick work of the task, the flowers and plants that popped into her head took her to another place. It was in those moments that she wondered about her real mother, sister and brother. It was getting harder to remember them, but she could feel the love they always had for one another and that's what made her the saddest at times like this. She had to wonder if she would ever see them again. She kept these thoughts to herself. After all, Mamm and Daed Blank had become caring keepers. It wasn't the same love and warmth, but she convinced herself it was enough.

***

Florence found herself up and out of the house early to tackle her chores so that she could have a few moments to herself, tending to the garden that beckoned her each day. She used the excuse of needing to weed her well-tended garden and pluck a few things for the upcoming lunch meal. There was scarce extra time for anyone, now that the wheat harvest season started and would soon be followed by the hay cutting. The summer season was a very active time on all the farms.

Florence hurried back up the steps with a basket full of tomatoes and zucchinis to wash up. She knew full well that her Mamm would use them in part of today's lunch for the group of hungry field workers. She and her Mamm barely finished cleaning up from breakfast and tending to the morning chores before they had to start again, preparing the mid-day meal. In between, Florence squeezed in other duties, chief among them, gathering eggs, which had grown even more urgent with so many mouths to feed.

A long wooden table stood beneath the wide branches of the oak tree that shaded the entire side of the house from the blistering sun. Florence darted in and out of the kitchen, delivering plates heaped with food her Mamm had prepared to the waiting farmhands. She returned moments later with pitchers of coffee and cool water.

Each time one of the men banged his cup on the table for a refill, Florence winced inwardly. Though she kept a calm face, the crude clatter grated on her nerves. Since coming to live with the Blanks, this was her first real encounter with the outside world, and it wasn't what she remembered at all. These men were rough, loud, and unlike anyone she had come to know in her quiet, orderly life among the Plain people.

By evening, the final meal found the farmhands subdued and less demanding, worn down by a long day under the sun. Florence served the last round of food and drinks, making her final pass around the table with the coffee and water pitchers before slipping away to the barn for evening milking. She welcomed the quiet rhythm of it, the warmth of the animals, the steady sound of milk hitting the pail, and the chance to drift into her own thoughts.

Soon she would come inside to the comfort of a warm supper, and before long collapse into bed with heavy limbs and a grateful heart. The day had been long and trying, but full—and that, too, was something to be thankful for.

When Florence finished up in the barn and came outside, she noticed Mary coming across the field. She couldn't help but see the bright bouquet of tall flowers she was carrying across her arms. They must have been the gladiolus she showed her the day of the quilting gathering. Every color of the rainbow was in her arms. What a cheerful bunch of flowers. It made her smile and forget how tired she was feeling.

Running over to Mary, she smiled and said, "Those gladiolas are so beautiful! Are those for us?"

"Yes, I couldn't stop thinking about you when they almost all blossomed on the same day. I'll have more in a few days too. I wanted your family to enjoy them. Once the weather begins to turn cold, I'll dig up the bulbs to shelter them from the winter. I'll also have a lot of extra bulbs because they multiply and produce more in the growing season. That's why they're one of my favorite flowers."

Florence was thrilled with the beautiful gift and thanked Mary. "Would you like to sit down and have a cold drink?"

Mary declined. "No thanks, I've got to get back to my kitchen. I had a few moments to dash out but now I need to get back to putting up food."

She knew Florence had a lot of extra work as Isaac had been giving Amos a hand with some of it recently. She didn't want to add to the child's burden.

Florence, with flowers in hand, ran up the back steps of the house, setting them down for a moment to remove her shoes. She came through the screened door alerting her Mamm when it slammed shut. She called out, "Look, look at these beautiful flowers, Mamm."

"Oh girl, they are beautiful. Come here. Let's get them in some water to keep them happy."

Her Mamm pulled out a large pottery crock, filled it with water from a nearby pitcher, and gently placed the flowers inside. Sara carried the arrangement to the sink and set it beside the kitchen window, where sunlight streamed in. The natural light caught the petals, making the colors glow even more vividly. For a quiet moment, they both stood admiring the bouquet, letting its simple beauty speak for itself.

Florence told her Mamm, "Mary said these flowers have bulbs that multiply, and she would bring us some when she digs them up for winter. Won't that be pretty, to grow our own flowers like this next year?"

Mamm Sara was pleased that Florence was thinking ahead and was a natural gardener. "That will make a very beautiful garden for you to share with others," she said.

Mamm had been busy baking bread and preparing supper when Florence had come in with the flowers. She looked hot and tired from feeding the field workers for days on end. Florence stepped in to help her set the table and looked for anything she could to help her weary Mamm.

It was a relentless time of year, and, at times, it was difficult to keep up. But she knew it wouldn't go on forever and the cooler temperatures would be a relief in another month or two. Meanwhile there was a lot of work coming up in the hot kitchen that would be made even hotter with the big kettle of boiling water that would seal up the glass jars of food. The water boiled for days as the canning progressed, but the vegetables and preserves put away would serve them well over the winter months.

The door slammed and they heard Amos washing up his hands and removing his boots in the back room. He would be hungry and more than ready to sit down and have his supper. The long days of the harvesting season took a toll on him and yet he would have more work to catch up after the meal. He often discussed the daily harvests and which fields they would tend to in the upcoming days. The traveling workers had been a great help with all the extra crops but still left Amos with work long after they had gone for the day. He tallied up the numbers of workers and would pay them cash wages at the end of each day.

During supper Amos mentioned to Sara, "The traveling field workers were pushed off the land closer to town. They came by and asked if they could set up camp at the edge of our harvested wheat field, down by the road. I told them they could stay on until we finished up the last part of the work. Just a few more weeks. It seemed the right thing to do."

This was not too unusual, as this group of people were often called, "The Travelers." Amos and Sara were kindly to them but also wary. The townspeople had warned of their thieving and misconduct, although the Blank family had not encountered anything but their hard work. Amos had initially set boundaries that were abided by without challenge or question. There was a mutual respect they had for one another in their work ethic, yet with a separateness in lifestyle that enabled them to work well together.

Amos announced that the workers would be moving on to the potato harvest over the next week. This had been cringe-worthy news for Florence, yet she never complained. She would have to sit for days on end in the dark, cold basement, peeling potatoes while her Mamm would be up in the kitchen canning them to store over winter. Half of them were stored in the cool spring house where they would keep longer and be used as needed. Her Mamm would certainly be adding to the hearty meals she served with the fresh harvest. By this time, much of the potatoes from last winter's storage had been used up.

Once they finished supper, Amos retreated to his corner in the room to open his ledger. He recorded what the farmhand wages were paid under each crop, and the harvest amounts. He had to keep meticulous records so he could plan for the next season and decide on the rotating crops. Once he was caught up, he pulled out his book to read, taking a quiet moment to relax and reflect.

Once Mamm Sara and Florence were finished in the kitchen, they decided to go on the porch and read a shared book aloud. This evening, they read the inspirational stories of a young gardener who collected seeds through the years. Florence enjoyed reading these stories with her Mamm. She wondered if this is where her love of gardening grew.

As the day faded away to dusky skies a fog was visible across the lower field, no doubt where the creek meandered through the land. She could barely keep her eyes open until she caught a glimpse of flickering lights in the distance. It was the fireflies lighting up the night sky. They twinkled like stars, and it brought a spark of joy to her soul. She and her Mamm walked down the steps of the front porch to look at the blinking lights. She asked, "Do you suppose if we collected them in a jar, we could have enough bright light to read by?"

Mamm chuckled. "That's a good thought, but do you think it would be bright enough?"

With that they both laughed and climbed the steps together, coming across the front porch and into the house. Amos was in his chair, eyes closed, and his book laid across his lap. He startled awake and grabbed hold of his book when he heard the ladies come into the room. Both he and Mamm wished Florence a good night's rest and to remember her prayers. The new day would be upon them soon enough and the work was unending.

Florence had earlier opened her bedroom window to allow a fresh breeze to cool off her room. She climbed beneath her bed sheet, quietly saying her prayers. She always included her first family, keeping them close to her heart. As she lay still and was nearly asleep, she could hear lively music playing and singing voices coming from afar. She wondered if it could be the group of travelers that her father had kindly allowed to stay at the end of their property. It wasn't like anything she had heard before. The rhythmic hum of the music began to fade away as she drifted off to sleep.

***

The days were getting shorter and colder. Although it was welcomed after such a robust season of harvesting, storing and putting away winter food for themselves and the animals, it also made it more difficult to finish all the day's chores. Florence had returned to the small schoolhouse after the bulk of the harvests ended, but with the field corn needing to be tended, the children were given the coming week off to work alongside their families. It would be the last harvest of the season.

After the breakfast meal Amos was happy to see David, one of the older Weaver boys, along with his younger brother, James, coming across the field to help lend a hand with the corn harvest. Florence especially liked James as he was always kind to her and seemed to pay her special attention. He had not returned to school in the fall because he had completed all levels of classroom education. His learning continued in the work around the farm and apprenticing with his father in carpentry.

Amos went out to greet the young men who had come to help shock the corn. Mamm Sara and Florence would also be joining them after they finished up the breakfast plates. Preparations were needed to have a hearty mid-day meal ready to serve the hungry helpers and Mamm Sara would see to those later. The men greeted one another while they walked toward the barn. The large draft horses needed to be set up to pull the corn binder and wagon. The extra help would make light of the work and for that alone Amos was grateful.

The men set out into the field once everything was in good order with the horses and machinery. Mamm Sara and Florence soon joined them. Together, they turned their attention to the field corn. At first glance, one might think the corn was no good, its stalks dried out and brittle, appearing lifeless and spent.

But the work had just begun.

The draft horses moved steadily up and down the rows, pulling the binder that sliced through the stalks and fed them onto the wagon bed. Florence and Mamm Sara worked atop the wagon, adjusting and stacking the corn evenly into a growing pile. Their hands moved quickly, rhythmically, in tune with the horses' pace.

Walking alongside were David and James, who waited until a dozen or more stalks had accumulated before pulling them off the wagon to build teepee-like towers in the field. These were the corn shocks, neatly bundled stalks that would continue to dry under the open sky, soaking up the autumn sun and breeze.

Before long, the once-empty fields were dotted with rows of corn shocks, standing like silent sentinels across the countryside.

The repetitive work was hard, but necessary to sustain the farm for the long, cold winter to come. Later in the week, when the corn shocks had dried out, they would be moved undercover. The corn would be stripped off and the stalks cut up to be used as bedding or additional feed for the animals. Nothing went to waste.

This work went on for the next week or more, if necessary, until all was done. Everyone came out to help one another and, in return, Amos would assist both Weaver families on either side of his farm in the coming days. Florence always looked forward to the visits to Mary Weaver's as she always managed to come away with seeds or some sort of garden gem.

Mamm Sara hopped down from the wagon, leaving Florence to continue by herself. She had the hang of it but slowed the process down to allow David and James to catch up with the wagon and binder. Sara made her way back to the house to begin preparations for the meal.

Everyone would be hungry, and she had a great many dishes prepared in advance. She used her long counter, where she had been canning and putting away food from the garden earlier in the season, as a long tabletop for the hungry workers to serve themselves. This left space around the long rectangular table for all to enjoy the food and conversation before getting back to work.

She removed the hot savory beef and vegetable pies from the oven and placed them on round wooden discs. She opened glass jars of pickled eggs and placed a serving spoon inside. The potatoes were mashed, and a good portion of freshly made butter was added, making them even creamier. Sara took another glass jar with a brown liquid and poured some into the pan on the stovetop. She mixed some flour into water making sure it was dissolved and added the mixture while stirring the hot liquid. It became a delicious brown gravy for the potatoes and beef pie. The warm bread would be wonderful to sop up any gravy left behind on the plate. And then of course, there was everyone's favorite, Mamm Sara's shoofly pies. They were set out on the counter with freshly whipped cream to scoop onto the slices.

Mamm Sara's handwritten recipe book lay open on the counter to the page for Shoofly Pie, the same recipe her grandmother had once used to feed a house full of hungry children. The page was stained with drips and smudges; each one a trace of the sweet memories baked into it over the years. Though Sara could probably make the pie without glancing once at the page, seeing Mammi's familiar handwriting transported her back to those long-ago days spent in the kitchen with her sisters and grandmother, baking for what felt like days on end.

She was pulled back to the present by the sound of the back door swinging open and slamming shut behind the returning field workers. Their footsteps echoed on the floorboards, signaling the day's hard work would soon be rewarded and supper was well-earned.

Florence washed at the water basin, scrubbing her hands and face, then joined her Mamm in the kitchen to help with the final preparations. The men took their turns washing, then made their way to the table.

Mamm Sara waited until everyone had filled their plates and found a seat before she served herself. She took her usual place beside Amos, who sat at the head of the long wooden table. Once the silent blessing was said and Amos lifted his fork, the room came alive with the sounds of eating, laughter, and satisfied sighs.

It was as if they hadn't eaten in days.

Mamm Sara watched with quiet joy as they devoured the meal, hearty fare made from familiar ingredients, prepared with love. She took pride not only in the food but in the traditions passed down through generations, now being shared with Florence. Someday, she thought, that well-worn recipe book would belong to her. And Florence, too, would carry forward the stories and flavors of those who came before.

When the meal was finished, the men got up from the table and thanked Sara for the meal. They then walked outdoors and sat beneath the nearly bare tree which not long ago had offered shade from the hot summer sun. James laid his head back in the grass and looked up at the bright blue sky. He took in the white fluffy clouds that slowly moved and made shapes that reminded him of some of his siblings or funny characters. He laughed inwardly at the silly thoughts but then began to listen to Amos and his older brother David's conversation. There had been talk recently amongst the men about the likelihood of the United States entering the war that was far overseas.

Amos told David, "We will oppose any military action as we have done in the past. It does carry heavy consequences for us."

David nodded his head and asked, "Do you suppose James and I and my other brothers would be asked to participate?"

Amos thought for a moment. "It is entirely likely, and it must be respectfully declined by explaining our beliefs. It goes back to the late seventeenth century when our church started and Jacob Ammann, our founder, refused to serve forcefully in violence by the principles they stood for in peace. This position got them, and others burned at the stake. We came here to America to live quiet, plain lives. We are not alone since there are Mennonites and Quakers who are also believers in peace."

Now James was sitting up and intently listening to Amos. He asked, "What will happen to us when we refuse to fight in the war?"

Amos responded, "We do not know. There are now some groups of Amish working with the English to find a way to peacefully decline entering the conflict. There is a concern of retaliation to our community. We have been through this sort of thing before and in prayer we have been guided righteously, and we will continue to take that path, bring whatever it may to our people."

Talking to the young men, Amos recalled and shared with them about an elderly Amish minister who gave him, and many of his young friends, some wise advice. "This violence, if they're not careful, will unite people against us and the nations, in a way that is destructive for many generations to come. One need only look at the stories we read in the bible. It is not unlike that parable about the bad seed. The wheat and weeds illustrate to us the good and evil that co-exists in the world, which ultimately leads to the final judgment where the wicked will be separated from the righteous."

The loud slam of the back door jolted the men from their deep conversation, snapping them back to the task at hand, finishing the day's field work. The weighty topic they had been discussing was quickly set aside. It wasn't something they deemed appropriate to speak of in front of the women, it would only stir up worry and concern, neither of which could change what was coming. Still, it was a matter the men had to quietly prepare for.

Mamm Sara stood nearby with Florence, waiting patiently as the men returned to the freshly watered horses and readied them for the final push. The urgency was clear to everyone: they had to finish the corn shocking before nightfall.

As the sun dipped lower on the horizon, the air would cool, and moisture would begin to rise from the ground. If left unfinished, the shocks could grow damp, creating mold, a hidden danger that could prove lethal to their animals.

No words were needed. Each person understood their role, and the work resumed with a quiet determination born of necessity and experience.

Once this week was finished and the final shocks of corn were ready to be stored for winter, the day of rest ahead would be welcomed for the weary workers. This growing and harvest season had been good to them, and they had much to be grateful for. They were humbled by the rich bounty. None of this was ever taken for granted as each season had good and bad to contend with. The seasons ahead would prove difficult for this tight knit community as the United States came closer to entering the war.

CIVIL UNREST
Estella | Philadelphia | Winter 1917

It had been seven long years since Estella last laid eyes on Florence. Not a day had passed without thoughts of her—where she was, how she had grown, whether she still remembered her mother's face. It was as though a piece of Estella had been cut from her and left to ache quietly, unhealed. The wound no longer bled, but it throbbed in silence, especially in the still hours before dawn.

She dressed slowly that morning, bracing for the bitter February chill. The bleak, short days were wearing on everyone, their moods as gray as the sky. Still, she was grateful to live beyond the cramped, sooty streets of the city's heart, where tempers ran high and eyes held suspicion.

The newspapers spoke of unrest, of food shortages and rising prices, of mothers lining up for bread and fathers out of work. Though America had not yet entered the war, President Wilson had begun sending aid across the Atlantic to the Allies—England, France, and Russia. It was only a matter of time.

Philadelphia, one of the nation's great engines, pulsed with war preparation. Its mills roared, its factories churned out uniforms, munitions, and machines. Tanneries filled the air with their heavy scent, producing nearly three-quarters of the military's boots. Much of this labor was carried out by weary hands—immigrants who had crossed oceans in search of hope and now found themselves fueling a conflict that felt distant yet ever encroaching.

And through it all, Estella carried her own silent war. One that had no front lines or treaties. Just a mother's longing for the child taken from her—and the prayer that somehow, despite the distance and the years, Florence might still feel that love reaching across time.

She had never stopped trying. For years, Estella had reached out to the Children's Aid Society—writing letters, submitting inquiries, and pleading her case in person when she could. But the barriers always remained. Policies. Silence. Changing staff. Files that had been moved, misplaced, or "unable to be located." It was as if the doors had been shut and locked, and every knock she made echoed back unanswered. Still, she tried. Because hope, even dimmed, was the one thing they could never take from her completely.

The children, John and Frances, sleepily stepped into the kitchen and glanced up, saying, "Good morning, mom, what's for breakfast?"

Estella was happy to see her hungry children. "Hot oatmeal with apples and cinnamon."

John smiled and said, "Oh my favorite, thank you!"

They sat down at the small kitchen table to share their meal together. It was a good time to talk about the day to come.

Frances spoke up while waiting for her oatmeal to cool down. "Today we're visiting a government office downtown where my class will get a chance to meet with possible employers. We want to make a good impression because there's a good possibility for summer jobs to work on our skills."

Estella was happy to know her daughter would be able to work in a respectable position and earn a decent wage, preparing her for a good life ahead.

"Congratulations, dear," she said. "You are doing so well and we're all proud of you."

Frances had finished her schooling and was now attending the Drexel Institute nearby in a special program. Stephen had shared a promotional brochure from Drexel and encouraged Frances to investigate applying for the program. It boasted a secretarial school for women. It was the first official preparatory course that guaranteed employment as a statistical secretary by the Federal Civil

Service Commission. Students who finished the program would be eligible to apply for civil service jobs paying upward of $1,800 per year.

John listened all the while to his mom and sister as he devoured his oatmeal. He was eager to share about finishing up his schooling while also attending an apprenticeship program in electrical construction offered by The Pennsylvania Railroad, also known as just the "Pennsy."

Without going into the same detail, he shared, "We have an exam today, working to apply what we have been learning in the classroom to working with actual electrical engines."

Estella, without hesitation, said, "I'm very proud of you too John and all that you're learning. You and your sister will always be able to find employment no matter what happens. There are many people hurting and nearly starving from these skyrocketing food prices. The shortages of food and high costs have caused riots in other big cities, and it wouldn't surprise me if it got ugly here soon. The sugar mill workers have been on strike for weeks now and that isn't helping."

They thanked their mother for the hot breakfast and cleared the plates, washing them and setting them aside to dry. They then went about their daily routine, packing leftovers from last night's dinner for their lunches. There wasn't time to return home since they had begun these programs, and it was too long of a day to wait until dinner time to eat again. This made them think about the starving workers who couldn't afford to buy food.

Estella wished them a wonderful day ahead and headed into the office early. The cold, damp air and freezing sleet hit her face and felt like daggers. She tucked her scarf in tighter to keep the chilly air from penetrating her skin. She usually enjoyed a good brisk walk to the office, but she was not especially keen today with this wet mess. She was careful not to take too big a step and find herself down on the ground as she had experienced before. She made a mental note, reminding herself that this nasty, dank cold weather would eventually lead to a glorious spring bursting with bright flowers and longer days. In fact, she spied on the first signs of it in the slight greening of the lawn at the bank. In other places, small green sprouts were poking out of the earth that would soon have colorful little purple and yellow flowers. The crocuses were a sure sign that spring was near. Soon, daffodils and tulips would follow, brightening garden beds and window boxes alike. With that hopeful thought, she climbed the stairs from the street to the bank, the promise of the new season carrying her forward.

Henry, the older, more experienced security guard, was indoors today in the vestibule keeping warm. When he saw Estella coming up the steps he unlocked the door, opened it for her and greeted her in his jovial way, "Good morning to ya, Mrs. Estella."

She smiled and warmly said, "A good morning to you, sir. Thank you".

Henry appreciated that Estella always looked him in the eyes and spoke to him kindly. He could see that she was a decent, well-mannered person. There were others who were not so kind and barely gave him a glance. That made him very much feel like he didn't matter. Henry was up in years and returned to work after his dear wife had passed away. They had been married for forty years. Stephen had known his wife well since she had worked for him as a housecleaner over the years. He attended the funeral service and after visiting with one of Henry's daughters he offered the older man this security job.

Estella made her way into her dark office area. She could do it with her eyes closed, she thought to herself. She unlocked the door and began preparations for the day. She had to prepare the ledgers and cash drawers for the tellers who would arrive in two more hours, ahead of their first customers. She had earned a reputation as a tough yet fair supervisor. She had learned all the positions, training the tellers and other clerical staff and was not opposed to stepping in to assist when there was a need. She recently trained an assistant to step in for her so she could take a few more breaks and use some of her well-earned holidays. Stephen was a huge influence in making this happen.

A young bank messenger, Frankie, tapped lightly at Estella's open door and said, "Ma'am, Mr. Henry wanted me to bring this to you. He said you'd be very interested."

She motioned for him to come in and he walked over to her desk, handing her a copy of The Philadelphia Inquirer. "Thank you, Frankie. Where are you off to today?"

He was shy around her and softly said, "They have me running bills to some shopkeepers downtown."

"Well, you stay warm and dry and thank you for my paper."

He stepped out of her office, leaving Estella alone with the morning paper still open on her desk. Her eyes locked on the headline. Though stunned, she couldn't say she was surprised. Everything had been building toward this moment.

> The Philadelphia Inquirer, February 21, 1917
> "1 Killed, 14 Hurt, When Hungry Mob Fights Policemen
> –
> Wives of Sugar Refinery Strikers Lead Attack; 4 More May Die"

The month before, over two thousand workers from the Franklin Refining Company and the William J. McCahan Sugar Refinery had walked off the job. They were demanding modest but vital changes—ten cents more per hour, double pay for overtime, and Sundays off. For such long hours and grueling labor, it seemed a small ask.

But the strike dragged on. As days turned to weeks, families were stretched to their limits. With food supplies already strained by wartime hoarding and overseas shipments for the Great War, prices soared. Households teetered on the brink. Some were already starving.

Beef and chicken had all but disappeared from the markets. Even the humble staples like potatoes, cabbage, spinach, and parsnips were vanishing. Just weeks ago, a pound of produce cost two and a half cents. Now it was fourteen.

The desperation was no longer political—it was personal.

Earlier in the month, headlines from New York had reported housewives rising up. In protest, they'd vandalized carts and grocery stores and marched straight to City Hall, chanting in English and Yiddish:

"Give us bread. We are starving. Feed our children!"

When women in Philadelphia heard the call, they responded in kind, launching their own food strike. Many of them were wives of striking sugar workers. With babies on their hips or bundled in carriages, they marched to Front and Reed Streets. Armed with pepper shakers, they flung red pepper at the mounted police and their horses. It started as a defiant act—but it quickly became something far more explosive.

The sugar strikers joined in. The crowd swelled to more than two thousand.

Then bricks and rocks began to fly.

Then gunfire.

The first shots rang out from a revolver. No one could say exactly where. Policemen ducked for cover inside their patrol wagons, returning fire blindly into the crowd. Rooftop snipers opened fire, while protestors charged with whatever they could grab.

Children were trampled. Women were struck with clubs. The chaos raged for nearly two hours.

In the middle of the mayhem, one woman's cry rose above the rest—a raw plea of desperation:

"Our children and our husbands are not getting enough to eat! If we have potatoes and onions and a little barley, we can do without meat forever but with potatoes at seven cents a pound when they used to be two or three, and onions at sixteen cents when they were five or six, we cannot live!"

As Estella sat with the paper trembling in her hands, her eyes wide and unmoving, a soft knock came at the door. She didn't respond at first. The weight of the words she had just read anchored her in place.

Stephen stepped quietly into view, hesitating when he saw her. She was clearly engrossed in the headlines; her face etched with alarm. He didn't speak right away. He had read the same article earlier that morning—and now, seeing the fear in her eyes, he felt that same weight settle more heavily on his chest.

She managed to speak. "Please come, come in and sit down. Have you read –"

He cut her off, "Yes, it is not surprising, yet we'd hoped it wouldn't come to this. I fear that this, along with other large cities feeling the pressure of gross inflation and the inability to take care of the people, will lead us exactly where we didn't want to go."

"Do you mean getting the US into the war?" she asked.

"Exactly."

Estella remembered that her daughter Frances was headed into town today and would already be there soon. She filled Stephen in on that conversation and then asked, "Do you think it will be safe down there with all of that unrest?"

Stephen responded with a calm and confident tone. "Of course she'll be safe in that area of town. The security measures will be heightened after that news, and everyone will be on alert. I do understand your concern though."

Stephen looked at Estella lovingly. These quiet moments they stole before the others arrived were precious to him—more than he could admit aloud. Over the past two years, their connection had grown deeper, layered with unspoken emotions and the kind of understanding that only time and shared experiences could cultivate.

He often thought back to the moment when the line they had carefully skirted for so long quietly dissolved. That evening, like so many others, they had both lingered after hours. Estella had sent her employees home, struggling to balance her ledgers and increasingly frustrated by a small but persistent error. She decided to clear her head by walking upstairs, forgoing the elevator for the peace of the stairwell.

The building was nearly empty. She found herself drawn to the dim light at the end of the corridor. A warm glow spilled out from Stephen's office, the door slightly ajar. She stepped softly inside the threshold and saw him hunched over his desk, reading through papers. He looked up and smiled, and at that moment, something shifted.

"What a lovely surprise to see you at this late hour, dear," he said gently. "I thought you'd gone home."

"I needed a moment," she replied softly, stepping in and placing her tea on the coaster at the edge of his desk.

He stood and pulled a chair out for her. In the quiet of the room, time seemed to be still. Their eyes met, lingering, searching. A truth long buried rose to the surface. They drew close, their hands finding each other in a natural motion, as though they'd always known the way.

Stephen brushed a lock of hair from her face. His touch was reverent, as if he feared the spell might break. They kissed, tender at first, then deeper, as the years of longing gave way to undeniable emotion.

In the warmth of his office, they surrendered to the moment. They embraced each other completely—physically, emotionally, soulfully. It was not just passion. It was the profound discovery of something they had both been missing.

That night became the beginning of something neither had expected—something beautiful, complicated, and deeply human.

He held her close, their hearts beating in rhythm, wrapped in the quiet stillness that followed. In his arms, Estella felt the safety and warmth she had long gone without; something unspoken, something sacred.

They lingered in that moment, reluctant to let it pass. Slowly, they sat up, the weight of the world momentarily forgotten. Estella leaned into his chest, resting her head where she could hear the steadiness of his breath. Stephen wrapped his arms around her again, holding her as though the very act might make time stand still.

Then, softly, he whispered into her ear, "I love you, Estella. I want to make you my wife."

She stayed quiet, letting the words settle. Her hand rested over his, and she turned to look into his eyes. "I love you too, Stephen," she said gently, her voice threaded with both joy and restraint. "And nothing would make me happier. But we must wait—until the children are older, until they can stand on their own. I need to be their mother first."

Stephen nodded, understanding completely. There was no protest, only the quiet strength of a man who loved patiently. They held each other in silence; the room bathed in the hush of unspoken promises.

Stephen thought about the reasons she may have and came back gently, "I never thought I could love again, so the wait for you shall be my pleasure. I will do everything I can for you. Will you indulge me with your time and share in your children's lives until that time?"

With a devilish grin, she turned to look at him, "If you insist, I suppose I could do that. It won't be easy."

He rose and reached for her hand, his voice warm but practical. "Let's make ourselves more presentable before we head out and lock up. I know you need to get home to the children—it's late."

Still holding her hand, he stooped to gather their scattered clothing, then gently guided her toward a door at the far end of his office. Estella had always assumed it led to a storage closet or private file room.

But when he opened it, she paused in the doorway, her brows lifting in quiet surprise.

Inside was a spacious, elegantly appointed bathroom suite, far more than utilitarian. A marble sink stood beneath a polished mirror, and beyond it, a dressing area and tiled shower. It was quiet, clean, and thoughtfully arranged.

Stephen noticed her expression and offered a small, self-conscious smile.

"I often work late," he said. "Some nights I don't bother going home. The house is—" he hesitated, "too quiet. This space lets me wash up, reset, and sometimes escape... from the silence."

Estella turned to look at him, her eyes soft with understanding. She said nothing, but her hand gave his a gentle squeeze before stepping inside to freshen up. Their connection now went beyond longing. It was layered with compassion, shared sorrow, and the kind of intimacy that didn't always require words.

The two departed the bank together, locking up the solid doors. Stephen took hold of Estella's hand, and he walked her toward her house. He knew she wanted to get home for the children. Whatever she had walked away from in her office earlier she would have to wait until morning.

A crisp chill lingered in the evening air, sharpening their breath and painting a sheen of frost on the rooftops. The ground had dried since the morning's icy start, and the cold now felt invigorating rather than biting.

When they reached Estella's home, they paused beneath the dim glow of the streetlamp. Their eyes met, and without a word, they leaned into one another—sharing a kiss that was both tender and reluctant, followed by a long, lingering embrace.

Neither wanted the moment to end, but reality always waited.

Estella, ever mindful of her children, stepped back with a quiet smile. She was a mother first and Stephen, with no trace of resentment, honored that fully.

"There will be more evenings," he said softly, brushing a strand of hair from her cheek. "This is just the beginning."

She nodded. "Good night, Stephen."

"Good night, my love."

He turned, his coat collar pulled up against the wind and walked into the quiet night toward his own home. Estella stood at the doorway for a moment longer, her hand resting on the latch, a quiet warmth glowing in her chest despite the chill.

WORLD WAR
Promise | Philadelphia | April 6, 1917

The days were growing longer, a welcome reprieve from the dark, frigid months of winter and the grim headlines of riots fueled by food shortages and soaring prices. Overseas news remained bleak, casting a persistent shadow over the home front. Yet despite the unrest and uncertainty, something in the air had shifted, subtle but undeniable. There was a glimmer of hope, the suggestion of brighter days ahead.

Spring was making its entrance. Bright green leaves unfurled with confidence, and clusters of tulips, azaleas, and a chorus of other blooms pushed through the soil, bursting with color. Nature, unbothered by human hardship, was coming into its own again.

News of the Zimmermann Telegram would send shockwaves across the nation. Written in January 1917 and intercepted by British intelligence, the telegram was a secret diplomatic communication from the German Foreign Office proposing a military alliance with Mexico. Its contents were staggering: if the United States entered the war against Germany, Mexico was to join forces with the German Empire—and in return, Germany promised to help Mexico reclaim Texas, Arizona, and New Mexico.

British cryptographers cracked the code and, after carefully choosing the moment, delivered the decrypted message to President Wilson on February 24. Just days later, headlines across the country screamed in outrage:

Germany Plots Against the U.S.!

American frustration had already been mounting. The British naval blockade had crippled German supply lines, prompting Germany to resume unrestricted submarine warfare, breaking its prior pledge. The United States responded by severing diplomatic ties with Germany in early February. Now, with the Zimmermann Telegram made public and its authenticity confirmed by German Foreign Secretary Arthur Zimmermann himself, any remaining illusion of neutrality was shattered.

The memory of the Lusitania's sinking the year before in which one thousand one hundred ninety-eight passengers, including one hundred twenty-eight Americans, were lost to a German U-boat, was still fresh in the minds of the public. Coupled with rising food prices, labor unrest, and now the blatant provocation revealed in the telegram, the tide of public sentiment could no longer be held back.

On April 6, 1917, the front page delivered what many feared and others demanded:

U.S. Enters World War!

This Friday was a very busy day at the bank and at most service-oriented businesses. Estella dashed out the door for work and she knew what the day would bring as a matter of routine. Although she was looking forward to spending time with her family and Stephen on the weekend, the day's news would certainly have a way of changing the tone. Taking to the steps, she reached the landing to find a very seriously faced Mr. Henry who was ordinarily very chipper.

Holding the door for Estella, he spoke up first, "Mornin' Mrs. Estella. I sent the messenger to your office with the news first thing and it's not good. Seems we're at war with Germany."

"That is bad news, but I fear it's been a long time coming. Appreciate the warning. Have yourself a good day and weekend ahead, Mr. Henry."

She could always count on Henry to fill her in on all he knew and to share a kind exchange of words. She made a beeline downstairs to her office. She saw the paper in the box by her locked office door. She immediately grabbed it, unlocked her office and tore into the news. It would impact everyone, no one was exempt. She especially knew it would have ramifications within the banking industry as well. She looked forward to discussing it with Stephen over the lunch they had planned together, a favorite time they spent with each other, away from the demanding work, a private, intimate moment they came to enjoy each Friday.

She laid the newspaper down to collect her thoughts and whispered a poem she had memorized recently. It was titled "You Have No Enemies, You Say?" written by Charles Mackay in 1888. He was a Scottish poet, journalist, and author:

> You have no enemies, you say?
> Alas! my friend, the boast is poor;
> He who has mingled in the fray
> Of duty, that the brave endure,
> Must have made foes! If you have none,
> Small is the work that you have done.
> You've hit no traitor on the hip,
> You've dashed no cup from perjured lip,
> You've never turned the wrong to right,
> You've been a coward in the fight.

She couldn't help but think that the poem was written for a time such as this, a call to action, urging readers to join with the world, stand up for their beliefs, and not be afraid to make enemies in the process of doing what is right. The main theme was that a life of purpose and action, especially one that involves confronting injustice or standing up for what is right, will inevitably lead to opposition and, therefore, enemies. It hadn't made total sense until now.

Estella got up from her desk and made her way to the teller stations to prepare for the busy day ahead. It wouldn't be long until the other employees arrived, and she didn't want to get behind. Her assistant, Rose, had proven herself trustworthy and would soon arrive to take over some of the typical workload. The Ladies' Department was hosting a large seminar today for all their valued women customers. Much of the organization for this event had been taking place over the entire week in the large conference room across from the teller windows. A continental-style refreshments area would be set up by the caterer. These seminars were a huge monthly hit and taught women the principles of financial management.

Estella called Rose into her office as she usually did on seminar days. She wanted to discuss the current affairs and the impact it would have on the seminar. She stressed to Rose the importance of allowing open discussions, as the world situation would impact many of their customers. There would be a need for them to have time to share and, for some, learn for the first time that the U.S. had declared war on Germany.

Rose shared her thoughts. "We'll begin the seminar by addressing any concerns or questions about the current situation," she said.

"We've built in time for open discussion, it's essential. It will help build trust in the work ahead, even as we navigate unfamiliar territory."

Estella asked, "Will you let me know if there's anything I can do to assist before I head downtown for my meeting at the main branch? I plan to stop by for refreshments and mingle with the group, then quietly slip out and leave you the floor. I'm truly impressed by how professionally you've handled the seminars."

Though it hadn't been easy for Estella to hand over the reins of the monthly Friday sessions, she knew it was the right decision. She had poured long, hard hours into building the integrity of her department and creating a trusted program. But experience had taught her that learning to delegate was key. By entrusting capable leaders like Rose, Estella found the freedom to develop new areas of enrichment, giving her bank a critical edge and a growing reputation for innovation in the industry.

The morning went by like a blur and before she knew it, Estella found herself running behind. She had to wrap up a few loose ends, and upon poking her head into the seminar she was relieved to get an affirmative nod from Rose that all was going well. She knew that Stephen's driver would be out front waiting to take her to lunch downtown. It was always a mystery location. The elevators opened on the main level of the bank, and she strolled across the grand bank foyer smiling and wishing Mr. Henry a lovely weekend.

"Good day, Ma'am, wishing you all the same. See ya Monday," he said with cheer.

Dashing down the stairs, she saw the driver and said, "I'm sorry to keep you waiting."

He dismissed the apology. "Not a problem ma'am, happy to wait for you."

Estella leaned back into the comfort of the automobile seat, watching the city unfold through the window. The parks were bursting with spring color, tulips and flowering trees painting the landscape with hopeful hues. The driver navigated the crowded streets, weaving through the usual tangle of horses, wagons, automobiles, and delivery trucks.

As the city moved around her, Estella's thoughts turned to the recent headlines: The United States at War with Germany. A deep sadness settled over her. It wasn't the direction anyone had hoped for, but with the bold aggression aimed at the U.S., it now felt inevitable.

She knew the war would change everything. The days ahead would reshape households, industries, and futures. Businesses would pivot, and the roles women played would shift just as dramatically. The Ladies' Department at the bank, once seen as a modest courtesy, would soon become essential. With men called away to war, women would be the ones stepping forward to steady homes, take up jobs, and carry the weight of the workforce.

And Estella, she realized, would be ready to meet them—women like herself, trying to hold it all together.

The driver slowed his approach and pulled up to The Bellevue-Stratford, a French renaissance-style hotel also known as "The Grand Dame of Broad Street." It was considered the most luxurious hotel in the nation and possibly the world. Estella was quite surprised as she had only read about it in the papers. It boasted features such as the grand ballroom, Edison-designed lighting and hundreds of guest suites. The society page of the paper was always filled with pictures of charity balls, society weddings, and other lavish parties. U.S. Presidents from Theodore Roosevelt through Woodrow Wilson had visited. She felt a rising excitement and she wondered what Stephen had been planning.

Several men dressed in top hats and dark long tailed coats stood outside this impressive architectural gem and one approached the automobile, opening the door for Estella. He offered a hand and greeted her "Welcome to the Bellevue-Stratford, Madam."

She stood for a second, soaking in the moment. She turned and replied, "Thank you."

She climbed the final steps to the grand hotel entrance, where two identically dressed doormen opened and held the heavy doors for her. Estella nodded politely, maintaining her composure as she stepped into the opulence of the lobby.

The Gilded Age elegance surrounded her—marble columns flanked the corridor, and ornate chandeliers glittered overhead. Every surface gleamed with polished refinement, a perfect blend of old-world grandeur and the modern luxuries of the day.

She moved gracefully through the lobby toward the sitting area, her footsteps quiet against the gleaming floor.

Stephen, seated comfortably watching her approach, rose with a warm smile. She returned the smile, and as they reached one another, they greeted with a brief, familiar kiss, soft and sincere, a gesture that spoke of trust and quiet affection.

Holding her hands and looking at her he spoke softly, "You look radiant, Madam. Would you care to join me for lunch?"

Estella smiled back demurely, lowering her eyes flirtatiously, and replied, "I'd be delighted to share lunch in your company, kind sir."

Stephen seemed to know his way around this fine place and took Estella's hand and led her to the dining room.

The maître d greeted them with a polished smile. "Welcome, Mr. and Mrs. Masters. Right this way."

Estella felt a flicker of surprise, and something sweeter, at the sound of that greeting. Mr. and Mrs. Masters. It caught her off guard yet stirred something warm inside her. Clearly, Stephen was no stranger here; the staff recognized him easily.

They were led through the elegant restaurant, alive with soft clinking glassware and low conversation. The maître d guided them to a table near a tall arched window framed in intricate carvings. Fresh flowers and a single flickering candle graced the table, adding to the intimate ambiance. He pulled out Estella's chair, then handed them menus and listed the day's specials with care.

Once they were settled, Stephen leaned in slightly, his tone shifting with quiet excitement. "I have some news," he began. "I've arranged for Ruth to stay with the children this weekend... so we'll have time to celebrate—just the two of us. I've been planning this for months."

He smiled. "A romantic escape. I thought it was time."

Estella was pleasantly surprised. "Do the children know about this?"

He looked at her with amusement dancing in his eyes. "But of course they know. In fact, they've all been in on the scheming for quite some time."

Estella sat back, shook her head with a knowing smile. "What am I going to do with the lot of you? Generous, kind-hearted troublemakers, especially your meticulous sister and assistant, Ruth. I should have known something was happening. I've been so focused on running the department smoothly, I didn't realize just how much I've been missing out on the ones who matter most."

She had learned some time ago that Stephen's brilliant assistant was also his younger sister. They had grown up side-by-side in the banking world, mentored by their formidable and demanding father. Ruth was fiercely protective of her brother, sharp-minded and equally accomplished in her own right. Though she operated behind the scenes, she was unquestionably Stephen's right hand.

From the moment Ruth first met Estella, she liked her. That same day, she noticed a spark in Stephen, one she hadn't seen since before the loss of his wife. Quietly but purposefully, Ruth encouraged their bond. She often volunteered to stay with the children so the couple could spend time together—brief, meaningful getaways that offered a glimpse of a future they dared to imagine.

Though Estella and Stephen kept their relationship discreet, wary of workplace gossip and societal scrutiny, Ruth saw clearly what they shared: a love built on mutual respect, resilience, and deep affection. The children saw it too. They liked Stephen—more than that, they trusted him. They knew it was through his belief in their mother, and his connections, that they had access to educational opportunities once thought impossible.

Stephen was respectful of boundaries. He joined Estella and the children on weekends but never stayed the night, always returning to his home nearby. At times, it was difficult. But they managed—with patience, purpose, and the quiet hope of a shared future.

And soon, that future wouldn't feel so far away. Frances and John were on the verge of finishing school, beginning to chart their own paths in the world. Everything was shifting and, for once, in a direction that felt right.

Stephen leaned in slightly, his tone light but full of excitement. "I've arranged for us to stay right here at this hotel for the weekend—two nights, no interruptions. Ruth, ever the mastermind, delivered everything you might need. Clothes, toiletries, even your favorite hairbrush, I believe. Of course, the children conspired with her. Apparently, they had strong opinions about what you should bring."

Estella smiled, surprised and touched by the thoughtfulness behind it all.

"Madam," he continued, more formally now, with a glint of mischief in his eyes, "I'd like to invite you to join me this evening at the Academy of Music. The Philadelphia Orchestra will be performing under Leopold Stokowski's baton—Brahms' Hungarian Dances No. 5 and No. 6, among others."

He paused, savoring the moment. "And, what makes it especially exciting is tonight's performance will be recorded live by the Victor Talking Machine Company. A historic first."

Estella blinked, impressed and taken aback. "You're full of surprises, Stephen."

He smiled. "Only the best kind, I hope."

The waiter interrupted the conversation to take their order. "Madam, may I take your request?"

Estella answered, "I'd like to start with the Julienne soup. The Spring Chicken looks wonderful, thank you." Stephen also ordered the Julienne soup and chose for his entrée the Broiled Salmon.

They were in deep discussion about the current affairs and the United States entering the war against Germany. No doubt, most of the diners and everyone else were discussing the news.

Stephen had confirmed what Estella was thinking earlier. "We will have many changes coming in the banking arena and are well poised for it. I'm especially thinking that your department is going to grow rapidly. We will keep open discussions and stay ahead of the demands."

The waiter arrived with the soup, steaming bowls of vibrant vegetable medley in a delicate, clear broth. They savored each spoonful, the flavors as warm and inviting as the conversation between them. Soon after, the entrées were brought out, each dish plated with such care they looked almost too beautiful to eat.

When Estella finished, she set her fork down with the tines turned over—just as Stephen had once taught her, a subtle signal to the staff that she was done. Moments later, the attentive waiter returned to clear the table.

Everything about the experience was immaculate—refined, intentional, and impressively detailed. Estella took it in with quiet appreciation. She had come to enjoy places like this, to feel at ease in their elegance—though that hadn't always been the case when Stephen first began bringing her to his favorite establishments.

What once felt foreign now felt familiar, an unspoken symbol of how far she'd come.

The waiter returned with a tray of temptations and Stephen immediately knew what she wanted and took the liberty of ordering, "We'll share the Charlotte Russe and two coffees, thank you."

The waiter returned with a beautiful dish surrounded by delicate lady fingers, filled with Bavarian cream and topped off with luscious red and black berries. He laid down two dessert forks. It was a great end to this fabulous meal.

After sipping coffee and indulging in the rich dessert, Stephen asked, "Shall we see to our accommodations?"

Estella gave a quick nod of approval and smiled coquettishly as Stephen rose to pull back her chair. She stood, smoothing the pleats of her long skirt, and slipped her hand into his. Together, they walked toward the great hall, fingers entwined and stepped into the waiting elevator. The lift attendant took them silently up to the sixteenth floor. Outside room 888, Stephen retrieved the key and unlocked the door, revealing a spacious, luxurious suite beyond.

Estella drew in a quiet breath at the sight before her. The sitting room was awash in soft blue tones, its velvet furnishings positioned to face tall windows that offered sweeping views of the city below. It felt like a sanctuary perched above the clamor and chaos of the bustling streets. A lovely basket of fruit adorned the center of the coffee table, and above it, light shimmered from a magnificent Murano chandelier.

Her shoes sank into the plush carpet as she moved into the bedroom area of the suite. A lavish four-poster bed stood draped in bolts of velvet and silk. Original artwork graced the walls, each piece more striking than the last. For a moment, she felt like a princess in a grand palace.

She stepped to the threshold of the marble-lined bathroom, where a freestanding bathtub invited quiet reflection. The perfect place to relax, she thought.

Turning back, she caught Stephen watching her take it all in, a satisfied expression playing on his face.

He crossed the room and took her hand, guiding her gently to the velvet couch. As they sat facing each other, their lips met in a brief, tender kiss. He seemed thoughtful, almost solemn, as he reached into the inner pocket of his suit jacket and withdrew a small black velvet satchel, cinched with drawstrings.

Looking steadily into Estella's eyes, he said, "With all my heart, I love and adore you. When the time is right, I want to make you my wife. I hope you'll accept this ring as a symbol of my promise. My promise to love you, to care for you and the children, always. Will you, Estella, accept my promise of love?"

Estella was so moved; she could only sit in silence for a moment. A single tear slipped down her cheek, born of the deep, quiet joy welling up inside her. Stephen waited patiently, his eyes fixed on hers. At last, she spoke, her voice soft, but steady.

"I love you very much, Stephen Masters, for the love you've shown me and my children. Your gentle spirit and kindness to others never go unnoticed. I would be honored to accept your promise."

Stephen's shoulders relaxed in visible relief. He loosened the drawstrings and opened the velvet pouch, revealing a stunning yellow sapphire ring encircled by delicate diamonds. Carefully, he slipped it onto her finger. It fit perfectly.

Estella held out her hand to admire it, the gem catching the afternoon light streaming in through the tall windows. The stone sparkled brilliantly, alive with color. She pressed the ring gently to her heart, then reached for Stephen and kissed him—full of quiet gratitude and a hope she hadn't dared believe possible until now.

A gentle knock came at the door.

Stephen excused himself and stepped across the room. When he opened the door, a room service attendant entered with a silver tray bearing a chilled bottle of champagne, two elegant crystal flutes, and a porcelain dish filled with plump, crimson strawberries.

Once the tray was placed and the room quiet again, Stephen poured the champagne and handed a glass to Estella. Lifting his own, he said warmly, "To the love we share and the journey ahead," emphasizing the last word with a meaningful smile.

Estella raised her glass. "To our forever love. Cheers."

They clinked flutes gently and sipped, letting the moment settle around them like a soft blanket.

Stephen set his glass down and said, "Shall we explore the rest of the suite and maybe enjoy a bit of rest before our evening at the Academy?"

Estella nodded, and together they crossed the room to the grand four-poster bed. They turned toward one another, their movements slow and reverent. Stephen reached for the buttons of Estella's blouse, easing it from her shoulders, letting it fall in a whisper to the floor. She returned his gaze, unfastening his shirt to reveal the strong lines of his chest.

They moved with intention, shedding the last barriers between them, taking in each other fully. Their hands wandered gently, humbly, exploring the familiar and the new, until desire overwhelmed hesitation. What followed was tender and electric, as if something greater had pulled them into one another's arms. Wrapped in silk sheets and soft sighs, they surrendered to the depth of their love. A love hard-won and now freely given.

In the quiet aftermath, still tangled together, they drifted into sleep—safe, whole, and held.

This weekend was something Estella would cherish for the rest of her life. There was no question how much they loved one another. He always found ways to surprise her, and this weekend was the pinnacle. The lunch, fine hotel suite, promise ring, and the evening enjoying the orchestra together—as well as long strolls in the flowering spring gardens downtown—would be hard to top.

The idea that the children had been in on the entire scheme filled Estella with immense joy. But alongside the happiness came a familiar pang of guilt—her thoughts turning, as they often did, to her sweet Florence. She had tried again and again to find her, but each effort led only to dead ends. Even Stephen had used his connections, exhausting every avenue without success. Estella's heart ached with wondering. What did Florence look like now? What kind of life was she living? Was she safe—was she happy? And most of all, would her daughter even recognize her after all these years?

**

The United States sent over a million troops to Europe to fight alongside British and French forces. Daily newspapers brimmed with dispatches from the front, and a palpable shift took hold on the

home front. Americans rallied to meet the immense demands of
war. As men were deployed overseas, women entered the workforce
in unprecedented numbers, filling roles traditionally held by men.
Factories ramped up production of ammunition, vehicles, and
essential supplies for the Allied effort.

To galvanize public support, the government launched sweeping
propaganda campaigns. In 1917, Congress passed the Selective
Service Act, drafting men into military service. America's entry into
the war proved pivotal, helping to shift the momentum toward
Allied victory by November 1918. Yet the war's impact extended far
beyond the battlefield. It fueled momentum for women's suffrage,
planted early seeds for civil rights activism, and elevated the United
States as a rising global power.

Amid these months of upheaval and resolve, Estella's department
at the bank grew busier than ever. She rose to meet the challenge,
expanding her responsibilities, assisting a growing roster of clients,
and offering sound advice during uncertain times. Motivated by both
patriotism and personal purpose, she joined the Women's Liberty
Loan Committee, an initiative launched by the Treasury
Department in 1917 to involve women in selling Liberty Bonds.
These bonds were critical to financing the war, and the committee
recognized the persuasive power of women as civic leaders and moral
voices in their communities.

Advertising campaigns aimed directly at women appealed to
their sense of duty, framing the purchase of bonds as a way to protect
their families and help bring peace to the world. Estella worked
tirelessly in this cause, helping to nearly double the size of her
department while steadily growing her clientele.

The Great War reshaped nearly every facet of American society.
Life could never return to what it had been before April 6, 1917.
Prosperity touched many industries, and jobs were plentiful. Labor
shortages in northern cities drew thousands of Black Americans

from the South in what would come to be known as the Great Migration. Driven by a desire to escape economic hardship, racial violence, and Jim Crow laws, they arrived in cities like Philadelphia, Camden, and Chester in search of opportunity. Many found work in industries that others overlooked, becoming essential contributors to the wartime economy and to the shifting cultural landscape of the North.

There was a big price to pay by the big industrial cities for the success of the Allies in Europe.

The industrial boom came to an abrupt halt. The factories and mills were no longer supported by the high demands of war. Many closed while others laid off large numbers of workers. The other big challenge was the Spanish Flu epidemic that struck Philadelphia just as it did all over the world, but industrial cities were among the hardest hit by the pandemic. Although measures were taken to limit the spread of infectious disease in these densely populated areas, it did not matter. In October 1919, over a four-week period, the Spanish Flu claimed the lives of many more Philadelphians than had been killed in the entire war.

These challenges made Estella all the more grateful for her secure position at the bank. But not everyone on her staff was fortunate. Like many financial institutions across the country, her bank had been forced to lay off capable employees as the post-war economy slowed and workloads diminished.

Frances, however, had managed to secure a stable future. She had been working as a secretary for a judge in the United States District Court of Philadelphia. She'd begun as an intern at the court offices during the early days of the war, and upon graduation, was offered a permanent position. Unlike many sectors affected by the war's end, the court's operations remained steady. Frances was known for being quick to learn, well-liked, and highly respected, traits that ensured her continued success.

John, too, had found solid footing. He was in the midst of an apprenticeship with the Pennsylvania Railroad, one of the most well-funded and prestigious employers in the region. While many workers had been laid off following the war, John had graduated at the top of his class in electrical construction, and his skills were in high demand. His performance placed him on a promising path within the highly sought-after "Pennsy," offering him the potential for a lifelong career.

The post war days were tumultuous and demanded a steadfast ability to adapt and remain focused or risk being swept away by the steady commotion. Estella couldn't help but think about her earlier days, when she struggled to care for her children and then finding her way with the assistance of kind strangers. Perhaps, she thought to herself, this laid the framework for her ability to adapt now and be an example for her children. One thing she knew for certain was that life was going to happen, and it was up to the individual to make the best of it with whatever means were available. What remained was the capacity to remember not to get too far ahead without reaching behind to pull up the others who may have fallen in silent desperation. That's why she worked tirelessly in her position to boost other women in their quest for financial independence.

FRANCES AND JOHN
Respectable Positions | Philadelphia | 1920

Estella's children grew up before her eyes, entering the workforce and becoming productive young adults. They often shared breakfast before the start of a busy day and wouldn't see one another again for several days. Late nights or early starts changed the dynamics for them all. But this morning caught her off guard. John came downstairs with a packed suitcase. Returning to the kitchen table, he sat down.

At the same time both Estella and Frances blurted out, "Where are you off to?"

He smiled at their curiosity and replied, "The Pennsy has me working further out on the line and the hours are long each day. They've offered a few of us, mostly unmarried guys, to stay out there on assignment while putting us up in decent accommodation. We get higher wages and it's a good opportunity to grow into management positions."

They were happy to hear this good news and wished him well. "When do you think you'll be home?" asked Estella.

"I don't know, mom, but I'll keep you informed. I will call you at your office once they let us know more."

Frances spoke up, eager to share her latest news. "We've been especially busy with all the new Prohibition cases. There's something blowing up every single day. The rise in mob activity has led to a wave of arrests. It's almost comical. By day, we're knee-deep in bootlegging trials, and by night we're attending fundraisers, dinners, and galas where the so-called 'liquid gold' flows freely, as if the law doesn't exist."

Estella was not surprised by what she heard and just shook her head in disapproval. She was glad Frances could see the hypocrisy of the circumstances and remained on the peripheral. After all, it was Aaron's use of alcohol that she faulted for her predicament with the children and ultimate loss of her youngest daughter, Florence. She was not silent in reminding her children of that fact and that there was a time and place for one to enjoy an alcoholic beverage without it taking over a person's life and causing the ruination of others in the process.

Estella was not against alcohol consumption and worried what would happen after Congress passed the Eighteenth Amendment to the U.S. Constitution banning alcohol. She had an amazing gift for being able to look ahead at the consequences of specific changes in daily living.

Frances delighted in dressing in the most fashionable attire and adorned herself with costume jewelry. She felt it was important to put her best image forward on any given day. This day she was wearing her imitation pearls, necklace and earrings.

Estella knew this meant a big evening out and asked her daughter, "So where do you and your pearls have to visit this evening, young lady?"

"Another soiree to raise awareness and funds for upcoming elections," she quipped back. Please don't wait up." She was implying how long these evenings could go on and she was expected to stay late and make sure the attendees were able to make it upright to waiting cars that would whisk them safely home.

Estella had heard this before, but she never truly slept well until she knew her children were home. They would always be her concern. They all wished each other the best in the coming days ahead until they could join one another to share a moment like this again. Estella hugged John tight and said, "I'm very proud of the young man you've become. I know you will do good things always."

John told his mom, "I'll talk to you soon. I love you," and he was out the back door.

Frances also told her mom, "Thanks for always taking care of us. I love you too!"

Estella stood at the sink for a long moment before finishing up the rest of the breakfast dishes. She thought again about how quickly her children had grown up and were adjusting well to the responsibilities of adulthood. She had somehow worked herself out of her parenting position. She laughed aloud, as if that was ever possible.

***

Frances enjoyed her work over the last two years with Judge William Mulhorn at the United States District Court. He was a kind, upstanding family man nearing retirement, and he treated Frances with the warm regard of a surrogate father. Each day, she was called in to take shorthand notes of his meetings and conversations, later transcribing and typing them up to be ready on his desk the following morning. Over time, she learned that Judge Mulhorn had been raised by his uncle and aunt after the death of his parents, growing up in a bustling household with several other children. As a boy, he earned extra money after school by working in a law office, where the firm's owner recognized his potential and encouraged his education. That early mentorship led him to attend Dickinson School of Law and ultimately launched his distinguished legal career.

Judge Mulhorn called Frances to come in a little earlier than usual and asked her to take a few notes for him. He then finished and said to her, "I've shared a lot about my background and would be pleased to hear more about yours, if you don't mind sharing with me."

Although only a young woman, Frances exuded a graciousness from within that was complimented by an outer sophistication of poise and politeness. The judge recognized her as gentle and composed in all situations while standing strong in her values. She was refined and able to navigate professional and social situations with grace and class. She had an amazing ability to make everyone feel comfortable and appreciated. In her he saw a self-assured woman who approached life with purpose and grace. Yet he sensed a distance he could not quite read.

Frances obliged his question and responded, "I mostly grew up in the Overbrook area when my mother started working in banking for the Ladies' Department when I was a young girl. I have a younger brother, John, who currently works away from home for the Pennsy in electrical construction."

Judge Mulhorn interrupted her and asked, "And your father, does he work nearby?"

Frances, feeling somewhat awkward, simply said, "He abandoned us when we were young, and my baby sister is still missing."

Now feeling more awkward after receiving his answer, Judge Mulhorn apologized. "I'm sorry for digging into something I should have left alone. My curiosity got the better of me. A sense that there was something else unseen yet still unresolved, for lack of a better term."

Frances wasn't put off in the least. In fact, she spoke with quiet conviction. "Please don't apologize. It's something I haven't thought about in a long time. My mother says our lives have been much better since he's been gone. I didn't know him well, he was rarely home. But I do think of my sister every single day. We were all very close. Every effort my mother and Stephen have made to find her has led to a dead end. I fear we may never see her again."

Judge Mulhorn felt a slow sadness stir within him, one that quickly sharpened into a familiar, restrained anger. Earlier in his career, he had served in family court, a chapter he'd deliberately closed. The pain he'd witnessed, families splintered by systems meant to help, had left a lasting mark. He'd changed his judicial path for that very reason, knowing he couldn't endure such cases throughout his career.

He leaned in, asking more questions. Frances, surprised but willing, shared everything she knew. As she spoke, he began taking notes in the margin of his leather-bound notebook. His interest ran deeper than she expected. It felt almost personal.

The Judge said, "I know you'll be attending the fundraiser this evening and I want you to meet an associate and friend of mine, Attorney Jeffrey Alabaster. He's an up-and-coming lawyer with good connections in the family courts. He cares deeply for others. Too much at times. I will call him on your behalf. I'm sure he will assist you in locating your sister. Please be mindful as you well know the "parietals habent aures" at these functions.

Frances looked confused at his last words. He was known to make puzzling remarks to ascertain if his conversations were being listened to.

Smiling as he read Frances' confusion he spoke up, "It's Latin for the 'walls have ears.'"

THE ALABASTER'S
Connections | Philadelphia | Spring 1922

Jeffrey Alabaster stood out in the crowd, especially his towering six-foot, four-inch lean frame and jet-black curly hair. He saw Frances in the sea of attendees and wondered to himself how he had never laid eyes on her before tonight. William had described her perfectly. He made his way across the crowded floor and watched her for a moment as she stood and observed the participants. Perhaps her quiet, elegant stature amongst the grand standing politicians and their promoters made her less obvious.

He walked up to her and inquired, "You must be Frances?"

She smiled and immediately knew this was the one Judge Mulhorn had mentioned to her earlier in the day. "Yes, sir, you must be Mr. Alabaster. I'm pleased to meet you."

"Please, please, call me Jeff. Our mutual friend, William, described you well enough for me to spot you. He speaks highly of you and your excellent ability to keep him organized. I'd dare say you may have been the reason he hasn't retired yet."

It was odd for Frances to hear Judge Mulhorn being addressed as William.

"He's a kind person to work for and makes it easy for me to do my job. He has a depth of understanding and uncanny ability to see through the tactics of the younger staff. He's taught me a lot and I've got much more to learn from him."

It began with a conversation tucked into the corners of a crowded function hall—voices rising, laughter echoing off polished marble floors, the hum of professional gossip swirling like smoke above the heads of Philadelphia's legal community.

Jeff had approached her with purpose, though his voice was gentle. "William shared your story with me, and I believe I can find answers for your family, if you wish. It's best we meet, perhaps on our lunch break or away from listening ears to discuss the details. Would this be something you'd like to pursue—maybe tomorrow?"

Her eyes filled with quiet hope before she even answered, giving him the response he had hoped for. "Yes," she said. "Yes, I'd like that very much."

"Then let's plan to meet in Franklin Square at noon," he said, pausing. "Southeast corner. I'll ring you in the morning to gather more details about your sister. For now, I must do my usual mingling—but rest assured, I'd prefer to stay in your company. No doubt the gossip mongers are already at work." He smiled, gave a small bow of the head. "Until noon then."

Frances nodded, a smile pulling at her lips. "Yes. Noon it is."

She watched him stride away, effortlessly blending into the circle of colleagues and clients who moved through the room in practiced rhythms of conversation and charm. He was handsome, certainly—but it was his sincerity that lingered with her, the way his deep blue eyes had held hers just long enough to make her feel truly seen.

As the evening wore down and the last of the party-goers were ushered toward waiting automobiles—some helped along by tipsy laughter and too many sips of Prohibition-era spirits—Frances lingered. She made her goodbyes and stepped out into the cool March air, heart quietly stirred. She had made friends through her position with Judge Mulhorn, including other young women in clerical roles and secretaries who had graduated from the Drexel Institute alongside her. But none had looked at her the way Jeff had.

The next day, punctual as promised, Jeff arrived at Franklin Square. But March had its own plans, and the heavens opened with cold, persistent rain. They took shelter in a small café nearby. Jeff motioned to a table by the window, rain streaking the glass beside them.

"Let's get something to eat," he offered with a half-grin. "That is, if you've the time away from your work."

Frances smiled. "I'm famished, and Judge Mulhorn already told me to take whatever time I needed. He seems to think highly of you."

"Let's hope he's right," Jeff replied, his tone light but his gaze earnest.

Over coffee and warm bread, they shared more than the details of Florence's disappearance. Frances spoke of her childhood, her mother Estella's quiet strength, and the ache that never quite left her after Florence was taken. She reached into her skirt pocket and withdrew a folded document.

"It's all I have," she said. "Florence's birth record."

Jeff took it with the reverence of a man handed something sacred. "It's more than enough. I'll keep it safe."

From then on, they spent most of their lunch hours and many evenings poring through court records, hospital logs, and orphanage files, searching for even a whisper of Florence's whereabouts. The work was slow, often discouraging, but they pressed on. Their shared mission brought them closer, and between the lines of ink and dusty ledgers, something tender began to grow.

Judge Mulhorn, ever observant, took notice. With a glint of amusement behind his spectacles, he offered them just enough space to be seen together but not enough to invite scrutiny. "It's good to see two fine minds working side by side," he would say, though the twinkle in his eye betrayed that he saw something more.

By early summer, they had become nearly inseparable. What began as business lunches turned into late-night walks under gaslit lamps, visits to nearby public gardens, and evenings spent reading poetry or legal theory—often both. Frances admired Jeff's ambition and self-discipline, but even more, she appreciated the way he made her laugh, the way he listened.

For Jeff, Frances was like no one he had ever met—intelligent, composed, and full of quiet fire. He found himself looking for excuses to be near her, to hear her voice, to make her smile. He was falling in love with the very heart of her.

On a warm Sunday afternoon in July, after church and a long walk through the shaded streets of West Philadelphia, Jeff paused beneath a chestnut tree outside her mother's home. He turned to Frances and said simply, "I can't imagine life without you in it."

She looked at him, eyes wide but certain. "You don't have to."

A few weeks later, on August 12, 1922, they were married in a small ceremony at St. Luke's Chapel. Estella wept softly through the vows, her heart full of both pride and longing. Frances wore a cream-colored dress with lace at the sleeves and carried a nosegay of Queen Anne's lace and bluebells. Jeff stood straight and proud, his voice unwavering as he promised her forever.

What began in a moment of shared purpose had bloomed into love—quiet, strong, and enduring. The kind that would carry them through whatever came next.

In a celebration filled with joy, Estella and Stephen proudly introduced the newlyweds to the gathered guests.

"Please welcome," Stephen beamed, "Mr. and Mrs. Jeffrey Alabaster."

The wedding guests lingered long after the vows had been exchanged, eager to visit with the newlyweds and share in their joy. Laughter drifted through the garden as friends and family gathered in small clusters, sipping lemonade and sampling slices of the bakery's finest wedding cake—a gift from Frances' employer. Some danced to the strains of a fiddle and harmonica, others offered heartfelt toasts and quiet blessings. Jeff moved easily among the guests, his hand never far from Frances', while she beamed with the gentle calm of someone who had finally found her place. The celebration was simple, but full of warmth, and no one seemed eager for it to end.

***

Exactly one month to the day after their wedding, Jeff placed a call to Judge Mulhorn's chambers. He had hoped to speak with Frances but was met with William's familiar voice instead.

"What is it you need, my dear friend?" William asked warmly.

Jeff's voice held a spark of urgency and excitement. "I've come across something—something incredibly promising. I need to speak with Frances right away. Can you have her meet me downstairs in an hour?"

William chuckled softly, sensing the weight of the moment. "I'll send her down and I'll let you be the one to share the news. No need for her to return today. I suspect the two of you have things to do, people to see, and places to go. Godspeed!"

Frances, thinking she was running an errand to the communications division downstairs, was surprised to see Jeff waiting for her. She knew something was up with the look on his face and immediately went to him forgetting the immediacy of her errand.

He smiled and whispered, "I located your sister."

She looked at him, tears welling up in her eyes and asked, "Where? How? Did you see her?"

Jeff quietly took her hand in his, holding it tight and walking toward the front doors of the building. "Florence is in Parkesburg, where she has been since being placed in a foster family home."

He embraced Frances as tears streamed down her face. So many emotions welled up inside of her. She could barely compose herself. "We must go to my mother and share the news."

Jeff, already knowing she would want to share this news with her mother as quickly as possible, had arranged for Estella, Stephen and John to meet them at her mother's home in Overbrook. They made their way to the trolley station that would take them out of the city.

Along the way Frances asked, "Did you tell my mother the news?"

"No, I just told her we had important news to share, and it was imperative we all be together."

Though the trail had grown cold over the years, neither Jeff nor Frances was willing to give up the search for Florence. What had begun as a shared mission of the heart slowly evolved into something more deliberate, more strategic. While Frances combed newspaper archives and orphanage registries, Jeff quietly reached out to colleagues in the legal world—judges, clerks, even a retired city archivist who owed him a favor or two. Through back channels and carefully worded requests, they began to uncover what had been sealed, forgotten, or simply left to gather dust in locked drawers and closed ledgers. Slowly, pieces of a long-buried story emerged. And though they didn't yet know it, one of those buried records—filed under the wrong name and long since misplaced—held the key to everything.

The usual quick ride out to Overbrook turned into a question-and-answer session until finally the trolley arrived. She was so eager to share the news she lost her footing and luckily Jeff's quick, strong arm reached out to keep her from falling. He held her close, and she was comforted by his sheer warmth and reassuring strength, but most of all she was comforted by the love they shared with one another. They were both deeply committed to each other and let nothing stand in their way.

***

Estella and Stephen responded immediately to Jeff's request and wondered if there was possible news of Frances being pregnant. Estella spoke up, "If she were pregnant, couldn't this news wait until after working hours?"

Stephen replied, "Well, you know this generation and their exuberance. Perhaps an element of surprise is what they're hoping for. It does seem peculiar though."

Estella acquiesced. "Yes. Well then, I guess we can take off a little time to go and find out what it's all about".

On their walk back to Estella's home they passed by Lafferty's Market. Estella, in a last-minute thought said, "Let me just go in and pick up something from the bakery for all of us. I really don't have anything to offer them. It would be nice to have alongside a cup of coffee."

Stephen held open the door for Estella and they walked to the bakery. A delicious treat jumped out at both she and Stephen. Looking at each other knowingly, they smiled and glanced back at the shortbreads with a raspberry spread on top, one of their favorite indulgences for special occasions.

The bakery worker even seemed to know what they wanted, grabbing a small box and asking, "What'll it be today?"

Stephen politely asked, "May we have the last six shortbread jams, please?" He always got an extra one to keep things even—he was a numbers man, after all, and liked things to balance.

The shop attendant boxed the treats neatly, wrapped the package in crisp paper, and tied it with string. Stephen handed her the money and smiled. "Keep the change," he said warmly.

He and Estella arrived home first, since they worked nearby. They came through the back door, arms full. Stephen placed the box of pastries on the kitchen counter and made his way to the front sitting room, knowing Estella would want to tend to the lights, unlock the front door, and make everything feel warm and welcoming.

She started a large pot of coffee and carefully arranged the shortbread jams on her finest porcelain serving dish.

Soon, John appeared at the front door and stepped inside. He greeted his mother with a warm hug, then did the same with Stephen.

"I'm glad I was close by and could join in," he said. "Do we know what this is about yet?"

Just as he asked, a soft tapping came at the door. Jeff and Frances let themselves in, greeted with smiles and embraces all around. Estella poured coffee and offered the treats as small talk and laughter filled the room.

When the moment felt right, Stephen gently shifted the tone. "So," he said, looking at the pair, "to what do we owe the honor of this visit from you both today?"

Jeff exchanged a glance with Frances. She nodded to him to go ahead.

"When I first met Frances, it was through a mutual acquaintance, with the shared hope of helping her find Florence."

Estella gasped, her hand trembling as she set down her coffee cup. Stephen reached for her hand and held it firmly. John leaned forward, eyes fixed on Jeff, anticipation stirring in the room.

Jeff continued, his voice steady but full of emotion. "Through my connections in the family courts, I reached out to a trusted colleague in the Orphans' Court of Philadelphia County. After a long search, and some unexpected help, he was able to assist me in locating a crucial piece of information."

Estella's eyes welled up, her voice breaking as she blurted out, "Where is she? Can we see her? Is she all right? Is she nearby?" The questions tumbled out, her heart caught between hope and disbelief.

Jeff cut her off, "Please let me share the sequence of things and it will make more sense for all of us. I promise we will all get to see her, but we must carefully, together, come up with a plan. So hear me out first, okay?"

He looked at everyone, especially Estella and Frances, who understandably wanted to ask more questions. All nodded in agreement.

"This Orphans' Court acts as a protector of those unable to manage their affairs." He could see the anger flaring up in Estella as she had gone out of her way to prove she could care for the children.

"They hold considerable power to make decisions for families. Decisions that are often kept private and sealed, supposedly in the best interest of the child and the foster family. Originally, the goal was to offer housing and education to Philadelphia's poor white children. But in reality, many of these children ended up as indentured servants—a practice some now equate with slavery. The orphanages were overwhelmed, strained by waves of immigration, war, and deep poverty. Through no fault of your own, your family was swept into a system shaped by these harsh policies—policies many of us are now working hard to change."

He paused to take a slow sip of his coffee, then continued, "The Orphan Society was originally established to provide education and job training for children. Its primary mission was to steer 'fatherless' youth away from almshouses—grim institutions meant for the destitute, where conditions were often harsh and dehumanizing.

Many of my colleagues and I have been working quietly, behind the scenes and entirely pro bono, to challenge and reform what has become a deeply flawed and harmful system. I want you to understand that this is a highly clandestine organization, and what I'm about to share with you must remain strictly confidential.

Some of what we've asked of our peers could cost them their positions—or worse. I include myself in that risk. So, before I go on, I need to know: are we all in agreement?"

Everyone nodded, understanding fully what he had risked for the family.

Estella and Stephen both thought to themselves how they had often tried to find out information about Florence to no avail and felt stonewalled in exactly the way Jeff was describing the system. It was unimaginable what they had done to Florence and the family. They continued to listen intently.

Jeff said, "It appears that Florence was sent to an Amish family in Parkesburg, Pennsylvania. She has been with them for the last 12 years. I have a contact name and address. Amos and Sara Blank, a childless couple, who had reached out in good faith to raise a young child. It is a start to contacting her. We'll have to put together a plan of how we go about meeting with her. Any questions? Do you have any ideas?"

John spoke up. "I've worked in Parkesburg and beyond for the Pennsy, doing work on the electrical lines for the rails. I'm familiar with the area. I've spent many nights out there."

Stephen interjected thoughtfully, "I believe the wisest next step would be to open a line of communication by writing a letter to the Blank family. We could introduce ourselves respectfully and express a heartfelt desire to visit Florence. She deserves to know her family. There's no need to explain how we found her—not yet. A well-worded letter could open a door. Simply showing up unannounced might lead to us being shut out completely."

Jeff considered this and nodded slowly. It wasn't the approach he had initially imagined, but it made sense.

"I agree," he said. "Stephen's right. Direct communication is best. We've waited this long, and how we handle this now matters more than ever. If we go through the courts, they'll likely block us before we ever get the chance to see her. Reaching out to the Blanks directly and graciously gives us a real chance."

Estella got up and pulled out a drawer of the side table that was filled with writing paper and pens. She grabbed a book atop the table and sat back down. "Shall we begin drafting this letter?"

Dear Mr. and Mrs. Blank,

We have recently learned that our daughter, Florence, was placed in your foster care from 1910 to present. We appreciate that you have raised and cared for her as your own child. Florence's mother, sister and brother have missed her over the last 12 years and would very much like to see her, with your permission. Please write to confirm the day and time we can visit her.

Thank you for your thoughtful consideration.

Sincerely,

Stephen Masters

Friend to the Family

They all agreed it would be best if the letter was written and sent by Stephen, keeping Jeff's name far from prying eyes. He didn't want to be involved as an attorney with connections to the family courts. This felt like the easiest and safest way to communicate.

They were overwhelmed with gratitude for Jeff and the discovery he had made. The emotion in the room was unmistakable, thick with disbelief, hope, and quiet reverence. Estella and Stephen sat stunned, trying to absorb the weight of what had just been revealed. It wasn't the kind of news one might expect, like the arrival of a new baby but in many ways, it felt just as life changing.

Not a single day had passed without Florence in their hearts. She had lived in their prayers, in the silent spaces between conversations, in the wondering. There was so much they longed to share with her—birthdays, graduations, first jobs, trips to the zoo, holiday dinners, and wedding celebrations. So many moments that had come and gone without her.

And now, new questions filled the silence. What had her life been like, raised by an Amish family? What values shaped her? What joys and struggles had she known? It was a world so unfamiliar to them, and yet she had been part of it all this time.

A week had passed since they all met and devised a plan to meet Florence. They wondered if they would hear back from the Blank Family or if the request would be ignored. The waiting was difficult, and Estella walked home from the bank during her lunch break every single day to check the mail. She had hoped, as she did most days, that a letter might be waiting. But once again, there was nothing. Just the familiar ache of waiting, and the quiet resolve to keep going.

She climbed the steps inside to the second level and sat in the room she prepared for Florence years ago in high hopes she would return. The small bookshelf still stood by the window, its spines leaning slightly as if the books themselves were weary from waiting. She let her fingers trail over the familiar titles—The Tale of Mrs. Tiggly-Winkle by Beatrix Potter and the tattered fairy tale collection with gold-edged pages Florence had insisted on reading again and again. Each cover held a memory, each dog-eared corner a whisper of her daughter's voice.

The bed was made neatly, the soft pink comforter still in place, its silky trim slightly frayed from years of little fingers tracing its edge. Estella had straightened it countless times, smoothing the wrinkles with care, as if preserving its softness might somehow draw Florence back. A worn stuffed lamb rested on the pillow, its fur matted, one ear drooping—a silent sentinel in her absence.

She often sat in the small rocking chair by the foot of the bed, the same chair where she had once sung lullabies and combed tangles from Florence's hair. Now, it was her own thoughts she tried to smooth out—her own heart she tried to quiet. She would bow her head, whispering the same prayer night after night. That her daughter would be safe. That she would remember. That somehow, one day, she might return.

The room was still. But Estella could almost hear the echoes—of laughter, bedtime stories, the creak of small footsteps crossing the floor. It was the ache of memory and the fragile thread of hope that brought her back, again and again, to this room where love had never left.

Estella returned to the here and now, pulling herself from the tangle of memories. She quickly made her way down the stairs, smoothing her skirt as she went. There was still work to be done at the bank—ledgers to balance, documents to file.

Toward the end of a very busy week, Estella went home for lunch. In the mailbox she saw the letter she had been hoping for. She didn't wait to go inside the house and tore the letter open where she stood, reading the neat cursive letter written in pencil.

Dear Mr. Masters,

We were surprised to receive your letter requesting a visit to Florence. She is in good health and happy here. We have discussed your request with our church family and will agree to allow one of you to visit our farm on Tuesday in the first week of October.

Sincerely,

Amos Blank

Estella was stunned. She ran back to the office to share the good news with Stephen. She flew up the steps to the bank and Mr. Henry quickly leaped to open and hold the door for her. He'd never seen her so rushed to get inside. She quickly crossed the bank foyer and made her way toward Stephen's office. She poked her head in the door, and Stephen gazed up and knew immediately what she held in her hands.

"Come in, tell me the good news, Madam, he said."

She blurted out, "They've agreed for one of us to go and visit Florence on the farm next Tuesday."

Stephen paused before he spoke, thinking of his response thoughtfully. He said, "I believe you should be the one to go but, in a way, perhaps it's best if John goes first. He's familiar with the town of Parkesburg having worked there and would be more familiar with finding the place. And they were very close as young children."

Estella had thought the same thing about John. She asked Stephen, "Can you please ring up both John and Frances and tell them of this wonderful news?"

Stephen responded by picking up the receiver of his phone and placing the calls. He was happy to share this wonderful news and needed to confirm with John if he could take charge of this endeavor. It would require him to take off from his work which he could easily arrange. All was in good order for that fine Tuesday in October to come.

REUNITED
John & Florence | Amish Farm | Fall 1922

The first Tuesday in October arrived cool and foggy, with the bright reds, yellows, and deep auburn hues of the trees barely visible through the heavy morning mist. The crispness of autumn was a welcome relief after the long heat of summer.

John stepped onto the train bound for Paoli and took a seat by the window. As the train rattled forward, he gazed out over the rooftops, his thoughts drifting like the fog outside. It would be a long ride on the local route, with frequent stops along the Main Line. Paoli was the final stop for this leg of the journey. From there, he would transfer to the Thorndale/Parkesburg line, which would eventually carry him west to the state capital, Harrisburg—a route he knew well, especially of late.

By the time the train reached Paoli, the sun had begun to burn through the mist, revealing patches of blue sky—hints of a promising day ahead. John stepped onto the brick-paved platform, letting other passengers pass as he stood off to the side, choosing solitude over small talk. The night before had been spent in thoughtful discussion with his family, carefully going over ideas for his upcoming meeting with the Blank family and, hopefully, Florence.

He wanted to be sure nothing was left unsaid. His goal was clear: to convince the Blanks to allow Florence a visit from her family. And this first meeting—'his alone—was the first step in that direction.

As he waited, the fog that still clung to the tree line reminded him of the fog in his own memory. The days with Florence felt distant now. He had to reach back carefully, almost painfully, to find her there. He was certain he would recognize her, but so many memories of the orphanage—of their separation—were blurred, shrouded by time and sorrow. Maybe the mind let go of certain things because they were simply too heavy to carry.

He and Frances were devastated when Florence was taken. They, too, had been separated—he sent to the boys' side of the home. He had tried to be the protector, the guardian of his sisters. A role too heavy for a child to bear. In the end, he and Frances were the fortunate ones, reunited with their mother. But Florence had remained a missing piece.

He thought of what it must have cost Estella—what kind of pain she had endured all those years.

A voice interrupted his thoughts.

"Sir, is this where I catch the capital-bound train?"

He turned and saw a woman standing just behind him. He blinked, returning to the present.

"Yes, ma'am," he replied gently. "This is the place."

She replied, "You were so deep in thought, I'm sorry to have interrupted, but thank you."

"You're welcome". He wanted to return to his thoughts, but he recognized that this lady wanted to talk to someone.

Unsolicited, she started to share with John. "I'm headed out to see my family in Harrisburg. My aunt lives by herself and has invited me to come visit the State Capital and stay with her".

John had taken note of her travel bag and surmised she was on an extended trip. "That's nice, I'm sure you will have a nice visit."

He knew what was coming next. The lady asked, "So where are you headed to today?"

"The end of the line for me today is Parkesburg. I too am visiting family." It felt good to say that Florence was his family, even though they had not seen one another for twelve years.

She was just warming up and remarked, "Looks like you won't be staying long."

John was relieved to see the train coming, excused himself and wished the kind lady a good day of travel. He walked toward the end of where the train pulled into the station, trying to achieve a good distance from the chatty lady as he wished to return to his thoughts, uninterrupted. He waited for the other passengers to board and then stepped into the last train car. He took a seat again by the window and gazed out as he had done so many times before. He couldn't believe he had been this close to his sister for work and hadn't known her whereabouts.

The train continued its journey, and the rooftops faded and open fields abutting wooded forests came into view. John spotted four white-tailed deer dashing quickly across the open field, making their way to the safety of the trees. The colors of fall were brilliant, especially now that the fog had lifted and blue skies had been revealed as though a tall veil had been removed from this lush scenery. The countryside of Pennsylvania was breathtaking this time of year, John thought to himself, the perfect day to see his sister again. Also, this was her birth month, he recalled. His mother celebrated her birthday every year without fail. Estella felt it was important to remain connected in any way they could, and it was obvious now to John that she had done it to keep them together.

The train pulled away from the Coatesville station and John's stomach was in knots, knowing he could be passing by the farm where his sister had been living all these years. It was not long before the train slowed as it arrived at the Parkesburg station. Although John had been here many times before, it felt as though it was his first visit. He stepped down off of the train and heard the doors close behind him. He knew his way to the main street and would find transport to the Blank farm there.

John spotted the tall smokestacks from the busy iron company. He made his way on North Gay Street toward the post office and local bank. He knew there were often taxis for hire in this location.

Parkesburg was a destination for many people to come and shop and visit the nearby park. He approached one of the automobiles for hire and handed the driver a piece of paper with the Blanks' address.

The man looked up at John with a puzzled face and said, "Ya know yoos are goin' to an Amish place, doncha?"

"Yes, that's right. Can you take me there?"

"Get in."

The driver set the automobile into motion, passing by the hardware store and funeral home and down beyond the watering fountain. At the foot of Strasburg Avenue he stopped, staring out his window at the newly erected World War I monument that read:

This Monument Was Erected As A Memorial
To The One Hundred Parkesburg Area Soldiers
Who Gallantly Served Their Country
In World War I From 1914-1918

The driver then slowly headed out of town, away from the bustling streets and into the countryside. For a moment the driver's pause at the roadside memorial had John stop and think of the great losses the nation had experienced. He had been feeling sorry for himself at the loss of time with his sister, forgetting about those in his midst. His perspective shifted and he settled himself while taking in the scenic countryside now ablaze in fall color. It wasn't long before the automobile slowed up and turned right, passed a church on the corner and headed up a slight hill. John looked out the right side of the car at the rolling fields of freshly shocked teepees of corn. They appeared to be spread across the landscape as far as the eye could see. On the left of the automobile was an old stone building with "1836" etched into the top, just below the peak of the roof. John wondered if it was a spring house.

The driver took the final turn to the right. John inhaled deeply and let his breath out slowly as they drove down the long dirt drive toward the Blank family home. He saw a very neat and orderly barn off in the distance with black and white cows he later learned were dairy cattle. He spotted the huge draft horses in the pasture area. The driver stopped near the house. John settled his fare with him and stepped out of the automobile. He watched as he drove away. Turning, he looked over toward the whitewashed house and saw a man step onto the front porch and wave to him. John walked up to the front steps of the house.

Amos walked down the porch steps and greeted John with a firm handshake. His hands were unmistakably strong and callused from the laborious demands of farm life. Amos spoke first.

"Welcome to our home. I'm Amos Blank. Florence is inside waiting to see you."

"I'm Florence's older brother, John. Thank you for having me visit today."

John followed Mr. Blank up the porch stairs. He took a deep breath as Amos opened the door and stepped inside. John followed close behind. Sara was busily working in the kitchen while Florence sat at the long wooden table where meals were shared. Both ladies stopped and turned, immediately glancing toward John. When John and Florence first laid eyes on each other, both welled up with tears. Florence pushed back from the table and ran to John and grabbed hold of him. Together they held one another in an embrace that felt like home. Amos and Sara stood silently together taking it all in and keeping a distance.

John pushed back to look at Florence. He bent down, looked into his little sister's brown eyes and was the first to speak. "I've missed you terribly, sweet sister. Look at you, all grown up!"

Florence lowered her head shyly, looking back up at John with her big brown eyes and smiled. She said in a Dutch-English dialect, "Bruder, I've missed you very much."

Sara came over to the long table, placed several plates of food and interrupted, "I'm Sara Blank, welcome to our home. You've travelled far and must be thirsty and hungry. Here are a few goodies to eat. Would you like coffee or water?"

"Ma'am, I'm Florence's brother, John. It's so kind of you to have me come for a visit. No words can express how thankful I am for this time."

Sara nodded her head and asked again, "Anything to drink?"

John stammered, "Oh, yes, I forgot. Both would be nice, thank you."

John and Florence began to talk and visit with one another. It was as if no time had passed, and they were filling the gaps with stories and laughter and more. Amos and Sara just seemed to fade into the background while the two chatted away. John devoured the treats while sipping his chicory coffee. It was an unusual taste but was welcome after the long journey into the unknown.

Florence stood up and asked, "Would you like to take a tour of the farm?"

John was excited to see her world. He stood up with her and said, "Yes, please, show me your home."

Florence got up from the table and removed the plates of food and used dishes. She set them into the sink, preparing to wash them up.

Mamm Sara spoke up. "I'll take care of those dishes, girl. Go ahead and show your bruder around."

"Thank you, Mamm." She turned to John, motioning for him to follow her out toward the back room. She paused to pull out her boots and find an old pair for John to wear. They went out onto the porch and sat on the long wooden bench to put on the boots.

Florence wasted no time and headed to her favorite place of all, her garden. There wasn't much left to show him aside from the clean rows that earlier in the year produced tomatoes, squash, green beans and leafy greens. At the far end there were still large green clumps of herbs.

Florence pointed them out to John. "These herbs taste so good in soups, stews and roasts. I clip them all season long, letting them dry out, and then save them in jars to use all year."

"Will they come back next year, or do you have to replant them?"

"Most of them come back unless we have a freezing cold snap when they are trying to come back in the Spring. I love saving seeds to share and to replant if needed. I wish you could see my beautiful flowers that I plant around the garden in spring and summer. They're supposed to keep hungry insects away. Come along, I want to show you the barn."

John was getting a glimpse into his sister's world and could see how hard she worked. He imagined that she must have been kept so busy over the last twelve years that the pain he had felt missing her may have spared her. How wrong he was in thinking that way. They did not speak of that day she was taken away. Both seemed to want to focus their attention on the immediate time together and on rediscovering each other.

Florence led John to the wooden table beneath the tall oak tree. Its leaves had begun to turn, shimmering in shades of gold with hints of reddish orange, fluttering gently in the breeze. A few had already fallen, dotting the grass in a quiet welcome. She gestured for him to sit, and the two settled side by side, gazing out across the wide stretch of farmland. In the distance, John could see more of the teepee-shaped towers of corn shocks he'd passed on his way to the house.

Though Florence had already shared much of her life with John while showing him around the farm, she was eager, almost urgent, to know more about the family she had lost.

"Please, John," she said softly. "Tell me about Mamm and Frances."

John hesitated for a moment, unsure where to begin. His voice was low, thoughtful.

"Mom found work," he began, "and was able to get a home for all of us. It wasn't easy, she struggled, but she never gave up. She tried everything to find you. No one would help. Even the kind man she works for... he tried, too."

"What kind of work does she do?"

"She works at a bank near our house. The man she works for has looked after her and has been like a father to me and Frances. I think you would really like him."

Florence smiled and thought about what he must be like, but was more interested in hearing about her big sister and asked, "What about Frances, what is she doing?"

John went on to tell her all about Frances, her job and carefully took his time to tell her about Frances' husband. He wasn't sure how she might handle the thought of Frances being grown up and married.

John said, "Jeff is the reason I'm here today. He's an attorney in Philadelphia and is a good friend of Frances' boss. He heard our story and wanted to help. It wasn't easy and he risked a lot to find the paper trail that was locked up and sealed away. You must keep that to yourself, but I wanted you to know how we finally found you."

Florence was absorbed in what John had just shared with her and hardly heard the three strikes of the bell her Mamm was ringing, signaling the mid-day meal.

John asked, "What were the three rings of the bell that just sounded?"

Florence sat up straighter and said, "We must go in now for the mid-day meal, come along."

Both brother and sister walked across the leaf scattered lawn and over to the back steps. John followed her lead and removed his boots when she took hers off and left them on the porch. He in his stocking feet and her with bare feet, walked through the squeaky door and washed their hands at the small sink. She smoothed a lock of her hair and tucked it tidily under her prayer cap. When she came into the room, she was surprised that the table was completely set with a place for her brother to eat with them. Amos and Sara were already seated and welcomed them to the table to share the meal.

Mamm Sara had prepared a lovely roast with all her usual side dishes: warm roasted potatoes, fresh green beans and carrots. Every meal was served with her fresh warm bread. Amos gave a brief prayer of thanks. The meal was served family style and John was asked to begin. He was appreciative of their gracious offering and filled his plate with the delicious foods. He waited for his hosts to fill their plates before he took a bite of food.

They ate mostly in silence, but toward the end of the meal John said, "Ma'am and sir, thank you very much for allowing me to visit my sister today. She's been missed very much by me.

Actually, by her entire family. I'm thankful for how you've taken care of her and for you sharing your home with me today."

Amos spoke quietly. "We have been honored with caring for her as our own. Children are a blessing."

Mamm Sara then spoke. "She has brought us great joy and has learned our ways."

Mamm Sara and Florence got up from the table and began to clear away the dishes. No meal would be complete without one of her Mamm's pies. Florence had smelled the warm molasses when she first walked through the door. Shoofly pie was one of her long-time favorites. She couldn't wait for her brother to try it. Mamm sliced into the pie. It was still a bit warm as she placed a piece on each plate. Florence took her brother and Daed the first two slices. Mamm Sara came to the table with the other two pieces.

Florence watched John as he took his first bite. He looked pleasantly surprised. Florence couldn't wait to hear and asked, "So what do you think, isn't it the best?"

He smiled. "Absolutely the best pie I've ever had!"

Amos and John continued to talk while the ladies got up from the table to wash the dishes and put the food up after the meal. Amos was curious about what John's job entailed working for the railroad as an electrical man. They talked shop and current events. John probed Amos about the Amish community, country living, what it was like living alongside the modern world. After learning more, he came away with more questions, wondering what the last few years must have been like for the Amish, coming through the war and Spanish flu pandemic. But he chose to save some of these questions for another time.

He stood up and thanked his kind hosts for allowing him to visit. He said, "I'd like to visit again, and perhaps you wouldn't mind if my mother and sister came along too."

There was a silent and uncomfortable pause until Florence broke the silence. "I'd really like for them to visit. Could we see about that?" and looked over to her Mamm and Daed.

Amos spoke. "We will see."

As the afternoon light began to soften, Florence asked permission to walk John to the end of the drive for his return to the train station. Though saddened by how quickly their time had passed, she felt a quiet joy in having reconnected with her brother after so many lost years.

But before she could take a step, Amos abruptly tossed a basket toward her. "You've taken enough time away from your chores today," he said sharply. "You need to collect the eggs."

His tone was unusually harsh—cold, even—which startled both Florence and John. It was completely out of character, at least based on the warm reception from earlier in the day. For a moment, John wondered if he was seeing a crack in the image of the kind, tight-knit family Florence had described.

Was this just a performance? he thought. Was the affection I witnessed this morning only for show, while in truth they treat my sister like a second-class citizen?

Unable to remain silent, John stepped forward, his voice calm but firm. "Sir, would you mind terribly if Florence walked me back to the station? She mentioned a shortcut through the fields earlier, and I'd be grateful if she could show me the way."

Amos hesitated, clearly reluctant, but with little room to object in front of a guest, he relented.

"Go ahead, girl," he muttered. "But make sure you get back here and finish up your chores."

Florence nodded, holding back her emotion, and walked beside John toward the edge of the fields, grateful for the few more minutes together, and for someone who saw her with clear eyes.

John urged Florence to wear a pair of shoes for the walk to the station. They walked down the back steps and headed along the driveway, cutting off into the field before the end and walking by the towers of shocked corn. At the edge of the field, she stepped into the forest where there was a walking path, out of sight now from her house. She often watched the white-tailed deer take refuge onto this trail. She enjoyed watching and learning about the surrounding wildlife and often took to following the animals she came across when her chores were caught up. This is how she learned the shortcut to town.

John kept quiet much of the walk back to town with Florence. He was thinking about his visit and how it had ended on such a sour note when Amos seemed reluctant to allow Florence time with her family. He felt it was unfair for Florence not to be able to see them beyond this brief visit today.

Florence asked John as they got closer to town, "Will you please tell my mother and Frances about our visit and how much I'd like to have them come too?"

John answered, "I would be happy to share it all with them and rest assured they'd love to see you. Not only here on the farm, but at home in the city. Would you like to see them in Philadelphia?"

Not hesitating for a moment, she said, "Yes, very much."

He sensed it in her, the same deep sadness that had once lived inside him. That quiet ache of loss you can't quite name but feel deep in your bones. It had taken root in both of them the day Florence was taken from the orphanage, and though twelve years had passed, the wound hadn't fully healed. A single afternoon could never cover the distance that time had stretched between them. There was so much still to say, to learn, and to feel—not only for him, but for Florence. She deserved the chance to truly know her mother and sister, to reclaim the parts of her story that had been kept from her.

These thoughts swelled in John's chest as they approached the steps of the station.

"Come on up and wait with me," he said gently.

Florence nodded and followed him up to the platform. They took a seat on the bench beneath the station's awning, where the last golden light of day was just beginning to dim behind the trees. John slipped his railroad identification from his pocket and looped it around his neck, a familiar routine. It allowed him to ride free, and he was known to many of the conductors who ran this stretch of track.

Off in the distance, the train appeared. Its silhouette cutting cleanly through the clearing dusk.

Florence sat still, watching it approach. She had not been this close to the tracks in years. She hardly remembered the day she was brought to the farm, but now, in this place, a memory rose uninvited. She remembered pain—piercing and unrelenting—the kind that made breathing feel like a burden. She recalled hearing voices whispering above her while she lay feverish in bed. Someone had said it was heartbreak, the kind that strikes when a child is abruptly torn from everything she knows and loves.

The memory shook her. Her first instinct was to run, to put distance between herself and that rising tide of sorrow. But she stayed.

John, without a word, reached over and took her hand. His grip was firm, steady, protective.

And Florence didn't pull away.

He had always been her protector. Some bonds didn't need words. They simply held together.

KIDNAPPED
Florence | Philadelphia | Fall 1922

Brother and sister sat in silence as the train rumbled toward Paoli Station. They would need to disembark there and wait for the local line that stopped at every small station on its way to Overbrook. It would be a long, slow journey. John could have waited for a quicker route into Philadelphia, transferring at Thirtieth Street Station and then catching a commuter train—but he'd chosen this path deliberately. He felt it would be less overwhelming for Florence, easier to manage, and gentler in pace.

Passengers came and went at each stop. A few cast curious glances their way—an ordinary man traveling with a young Amish woman was a rare sight. Florence kept her gaze lowered, just as she had been taught. Among her people, the "English," as they called outsiders, were to be treated with polite distance, and in turn, rarely understood their way of life.

When the local train pulled into the station at Paoli, they boarded and found two open seats. John gestured for Florence to sit by the window while he took the aisle. As the doors closed and the train began its slow roll toward Overbrook, Florence peered out at the darkening world.

The lit windows of homes and quiet country estates flickered past. Pockets of forest blurred in the fading light, interrupted by the occasional flash of headlights from automobiles winding down distant roads. The rhythmic rocking of the train soothed her, and after a while, she gently rested her head on John's shoulder.

He didn't move, only shifted slightly to make her more comfortable. Outside, the night deepened. Inside, the space between them quietly disappeared, filled not with words, but with the comfort of presence and the slow stitching together of something long torn apart.

Bringing Florence home with him had not been the plan and he knew there could be big trouble waiting for him when he came back with his sister. He knew the entire family would be awaiting his return to Estella's house in Overbrook. They would want to know every single detail of the day.

As the train pulled away from Bryn Mawr Station, John glanced out the window and counted the remaining stops. He knew them by heart: Haverford, Ardmore, Wynnewood, Narberth, Merion... and finally, Overbrook.

He turned slightly toward Florence, sensing the weight of the moment. He wanted to ease her into what lay ahead.

"Florence," he began gently, "I didn't plan this, at least, not exactly. But something told me it was the right thing to do. I want you to know that when we step off this train, it's only a short walk to Mom's home. I'm certain she'll be there—Frances too, along with Jeff and Stephen. They're all waiting for me to return, and they'll be ecstatic to see that you're with me."

Florence gave a small nod, then spoke in a quiet voice. "I wanted to come... but a part of me is afraid."

John nodded, understanding more than she knew. "I get it. You're not sure what to expect... and maybe you're worried you've upset your foster family, too."

She looked down and whispered, "They will be worried."

"We'll figure something out," he said gently.

He didn't press her further, letting the gentle clatter of the tracks speak for a while. The train rolled on, each stop drawing them closer, not just to a place, but to something long lost, and now beginning to be found.

"We'll send a telegram or note letting them know you are safe with your family."

The train finally came to a stop at Overbrook Station. John stood up and took Florence's hand to help her down the tall steps of the train. They walked along the brick sidewalk leading to a set of stairs that took them beneath the roadway and through a tunnel to the other side of the street they had just crossed over in the train. They walked up a short hill and would soon be passing by Lafferty's market. It was well lit, and many passersby stopped in after working in the city to pick up groceries or other goods before returning home. No doubt his mother and Stephen would have gone there earlier in anticipation of him returning tonight.

They walked along the sidewalk that led them home. He stood with Florence looking up at the house and asked, "Are you ready to see mom?"

Florence couldn't speak. She simply nodded, eyes brimming with tears. John gave her a gentle motion to go ahead, and he followed closely behind.

He reached for the doorknob. He knew it would be unlocked and slowly opened the door. Inside, the family was gathered in the front room, every pair of eyes turned toward the entrance, waiting for John to appear.

But it was Florence who stepped in first.

She paused just inside the doorway, wide-eyed, momentarily stunned by the sight of so many faces, familiar and unfamiliar, all turned toward her. The room fell into a hush.

Estella leapt from her chair without hesitation and ran across the room. She wrapped her arms around Florence and pulled her in tightly clinging to her daughter for the first time since she had been taken all those years ago.

They held each other with desperate affection, as if trying to make up for every moment lost. Florence closed her eyes and breathed in deeply—there it was: her mother's scent, soft and familiar, like roses in bloom. The smell awakened a part of her memory she hadn't even known she'd kept.

Tears flowed freely—tears of joy, of grief, of time lost and love found again.

Estella's voice trembled through her smile. "Welcome home, young lady. You've no idea how long I've waited to say those words."

Florence stepped back just enough to look into her mother's eyes.

"Mother," she whispered, her voice thick with emotion, "I'm so happy to be here."

Estella motioned to her. "Come, sit with me here."

Frances smiled at her sister. "I've thought of you every single day and night especially when I looked up at the stars. You've been in my everyday prayers. I knew we'd see you again. I couldn't stop believing. This is my husband, Jeff. He is the one who found where you were."

Florence looked over toward Jeff and said, "Thank you for marrying my sister and finding me."

Jeff was thrilled to help reunite them and said, "It was my pleasure and I'm looking forward to knowing you."

Estella interjected. "And this is Stephen, the man who gave me a second chance and opportunity to work and buy this home. He has been a good father to both Frances and John and I'm so happy for you to know him also."

Stephen smiled warmly at Florence as she settled into the sitting room. He offered her something to drink—water, orange juice, or coffee. She gratefully accepted a tall glass of orange juice, sipping slowly as she spoke with her mother and sister. The juice gave her a small but welcome lift; it had been a long and emotionally charged day.

Meanwhile, Stephen, John, and Jeff quietly slipped into the kitchen to speak in private. As John recounted the details of the day's events, the weight of what he had done settled more heavily on the others.

Jeff's brow furrowed with concern. "John, I wish you hadn't acted so hastily," he said quietly. "You've essentially kidnapped Florence."

John took a breath, shoulders stiff. "I know. I couldn't help myself. But I'll fix this. You won't be involved. I take full responsibility." He paused, then added, "And I don't regret it. We lost her once. I wasn't going to let that happen again."

He motioned toward the doorway, where the soft sounds of laughter and conversation drifted in.

"Just listen to them. They're talking, laughing, finally together again. It's been so hard on the four of us, for so many years."

Stephen, ever the diplomat, stepped in to ease the tension. "Let's not lose sight of what's most important tonight. Florence is here. She's safe. Let's enjoy this moment while we have it."

He glanced at the others. "It's late. Estella's prepared a lovely meal. Tomorrow, I'll open the office early and send a courier to notify the Blanks. They deserve to know she's well and not in any danger. We'll figure out the rest—together."

The men nodded in agreement, and returned to the sitting room, where interrupting the women's conversation proved nearly impossible. The room was alive with stories and overlapping laughter, like years of silence had finally broken.

Stephen cleared his throat gently. "Ladies, shall we have dinner together?"

With smiling faces and a few last words exchanged mid-laughter, they all rose and made their way to the dining room, a space usually reserved for holidays or gift-wrapping, now transformed into a setting for reunion and celebration.

Estella's heart swelled as she watched her family gather around the table. It had been over a decade since all her children sat under one roof, let alone at the same table, sharing a meal. She and Stephen went into the kitchen to retrieve the food: a spiced baked ham, warm baked beans, and a simple fresh salad, hearty dishes she hoped would please Florence's palate and make her feel at home.

Tonight, more than just food would be shared. It was a long-awaited taste of belonging.

They carried the dishes into the dining room, setting them down at the center of the table. The familiar scent of spiced ham and baked beans filled the room, adding to the warmth already present in the laughter and voices.

The dinner table was lively, buzzing with conversation. Frances shared stories from her day at the courthouse, particularly the fast pace of her work under Judge Mulhorn. Jeff, with a grin, chimed in, "At this rate, I have to make an appointment with William just to get a lunch date with my wife."

Everyone laughed, including Florence, though she needed a moment to piece together that "the Judge" and "William" were the same person—Frances' boss.

Estella then turned to John. "Tell us, John, what's next for you along the Pennsy?"

John leaned back slightly, his voice calm but proud. "I'm being pulled from my current assignment in town. They want me working with the team in Harrisburg. There's a major push to modernize the electrical components along the line, and they're sending more experienced techs to support the newer crews."

Estella nodded, clearly proud. "They're lucky to have you."

As the meal continued, Florence found herself slowly settling in. The food was comforting, but it was the rhythm of conversation—the easy teasing, the genuine interest in one another—that helped her begin to relax. For so long, she had imagined this moment, but now, surrounded by the very people she had dreamed of, it felt at once surreal and right.

Estella looked around the table, her eyes resting on each of her children, here, under one roof, after so many years. She raised her glass slightly and spoke with gentle emotion.

"Florence, I speak for all of us when I say—you have been deeply missed. Not a day has gone by when we haven't thought of you, prayed for you, and hoped for this moment. And to have everyone here, tonight, for your homecoming... it's more than I could've ever hoped for."

She smiled warmly. "But I do believe you've had a long, emotional day. Maybe it's time to rest soon."

Florence returned the smile, eyes glistening. "Thank you, Mother. This has all meant more to me than I can put into words."

Stephen and Jeff stood up, taking the cue from Estella that it was time to say goodbye and allow Florence some winding down time with Estella. Jeff escorted Frances from the table, always the gentleman, pulling out the chair for her to stand. They wished Estella, John and Florence a good night.

Stephen told Estella, "I'll take care of the office. Take as much time as you need. You know where to find me. And Estella, I love you and am so happy for you and the family. Good night, my dear."

Kindly John told his mother and Florence, "Go, I'll take care of the dishes. You'll need to show Florence her room and lay out some clothing for her to wear tonight. I'll be out the door early tomorrow and will be on assignment for a week or more. I love you both."

Estella appreciated what John offered. He had already done so much that day, but she accepted his offer to clean up the dinner dishes.

She turned to Florence, "Would you like to see your room, young lady?"

Florence nodded her head vigorously and followed her mother up the stairs. As they walked down the hall, Estella pointed at a door and said, "This is my room, and you can come in anytime you need me. Come, let me get you some night clothes to wear until we can go shopping for some of your own."

Estella led the way, Florence following quietly behind. In the corner of the guest room, Estella opened the tall chifforobe and slid out a drawer lined with rose-scented paper. The delicate fragrance drifted into the air as she pulled out a soft, quilted nightgown—warm and welcoming, though slightly oversized for Florence's slender frame.

"This should do for tonight," Estella said gently. "We'll sort through some more clothing options tomorrow."

Florence nodded, cradling the nightgown in her arms as they stepped back into the hallway.

Estella paused next door, then opened it with care. "This room has always been yours," she said softly.

Florence stepped inside, her eyes slowly scanning the space. Though it had been over a decade, the room still carried echoes of her childhood. A small bookshelf held some of her favorite storybooks. On a nearby table lay paper dolls she had once played with for hours. The soft pink comforter on the bed looked freshly made, its silky trim smooth and glistening in the low light.

Faint memories stirred—bedtime stories read aloud, whispered conversations with Frances under the covers, the sound of John's voice lulling her to sleep. It all felt impossibly far away, like fragments from a dream she was just starting to remember.

Estella quietly closed the bedroom door behind them. On the back of the door hung a tall mirror.

Florence froze.

Her eyes met her reflection, and she looked quickly away.

In her Amish home, mirrors were strictly limited. A small one, tucked away in the back room, was used only to adjust prayer caps or hats. Looking into a mirror, especially with any focus on appearance, was considered a vanity, a distraction from the values of humility and simple living.

"I never expected..." Florence began, then stopped.

Estella turned toward her gently. "I understand," she said. "There will be many things that feel strange at first."

Florence nodded. She knew it too. There would be adjustments—small and large, visible and invisible. Questions long held inside her rose to the surface—questions about things she'd wondered but never dared to ask her foster family. Here, though, she sensed she would be free to speak them.

But not tonight.

Tonight, she simply stepped forward and placed the nightgown at the foot of the bed, then sat quietly on its edge, absorbing the quiet hush of the room and the comfort of being seen... truly seen.

In the corner of the room stood a small writing desk with a neat stack of paper and a cup filled with freshly sharpened pencils, waiting, it seemed, for a child who had grown in the years since she'd last sat there.

As Florence stood quietly, Estella moved about the room, gently pulling down the bedcovers and smoothing the pink comforter. The room carried the faint scent of lavender and old books—familiar, comforting.

Florence began to remove her plain clothes, folding each piece with quiet care. As she slipped off her blouse and skirt, Estella turned—and froze.

Her daughter's torso was wrapped tightly in thick cotton bindings, wound around her bust and midsection in stiff, restrictive layers. Florence began to unwind them slowly, and Estella could barely suppress the gasp that rose in her throat.

It was clearly a gesture of modesty, ingrained by her Amish upbringing. But seeing her daughter so swaddled—physically constrained even after returning home—filled Estella with a mix of sorrow and resolve.

She masked her emotions with a soft voice. "We'll get you some new things tomorrow, sweetheart."

She already knew whom she would call. First thing in the morning, she'd ring Stephen's sister Ruth and ask for a favor, access to Wanamaker's department store before hours. Florence deserved clothing that fit her growing identity, not the restrictions of another world.

Florence sighed as she stepped into the quilted nightgown, the fabric soft against her skin. She looked visibly relieved, no longer bound, her shoulders finally free to rest.

"Come, love," Estella said gently, opening the bedroom door once more.

They stepped into the hallway. From downstairs, the faint sound of dishes clinking told them John was cleaning up. Estella led Florence to the next room over.

"This is the bathroom," she said quietly.

Florence stopped at the threshold. She glanced inside, uncertain.

The tiled floor, porcelain tub, indoor toilet, and gleaming fixtures—all of it was foreign. In the world she had known, water was hand-pumped from a well, then carried in pails and warmed for bathing. Even the small white switch by the door, which Estella flicked to illuminate the room, was something she'd never used before.

Electric lights. Indoor plumbing. Modern comforts she'd only vaguely remembered from early childhood, if at all.

There was so much to discover in this English world.

Florence stood still for a moment, absorbing it all. The light. The mirror. The gentle hum of electricity.

She turned to her mother with wide eyes—equal parts awe and uncertainty.

Estella reached for her hand and gave it a gentle squeeze.

"We'll take it slow," she whispered. "You don't have to know everything at once."

Florence nodded. And for the first time in years, she felt what she hadn't dared hope for: safe, seen... and home.

Wanting to get Florence tucked in bed she took her back to her room. Pointing to the end of the hall she said, "That's John's room at the end and Frances' room is next door. I keep it all like it was, most especially your room."

Florence climbed beneath the covers, the pink comforter soft and warm against her tired body. Estella sat at the edge of the bed, gently tucking her in like she used to long ago. She smoothed the quilt near Florence's shoulder and leaned down, brushing a kiss across her forehead.

"Don't forget your prayers, sweetheart," she whispered.

Florence nodded, her eyes already heavy.

Estella rose and quietly crossed the room, pulling the door mostly closed but leaving it slightly ajar, just enough, in case Florence needed her during the night.

Darkness settled in like a hush, wrapping the room in stillness. Florence folded her hands beneath the covers and said her prayers in a soft, trembling voice. The words came slowly—familiar, but now burdened with longing.

Tears slipped down her cheeks as she wept quietly into the pillow.

She was exhausted—mentally, emotionally, spiritually. Though everything she had ever prayed for had come true—reunion, home, family. It had all happened so quickly, she could barely hold it.

And she missed them.

She missed her Mamm Sara and her Daed Amos. Whatever had been said or done, they had raised her with love. Her life had been simple, devout, orderly. Now, she was caught between two worlds, each holding a part of her heart. And she didn't yet know how to live in both or choose between them.

But sleep came, soft and insistent, drawing her gently away from her confusion and into its healing embrace. It would restore what the day had taken, giving her the strength to meet the new season ahead with all its unknowns.

And just beyond the cracked door, Estella sat quietly in her own room, listening to the silence, knowing that for the first time in over a decade her daughter was home, and under her roof once again.

THE BIG CITY
Florence | Philadelphia | Fall 1922

Estella was surprised to see John and Florence sitting at the kitchen table sipping hot coffee together. She hadn't overslept and coming into this nice surprise she said, "Good morning, you two early birds. I trust you both slept well. Nothing like a good night's rest to begin the new day."

They both wished their mother a good morning.

"Thanks, John for getting the coffee started. I could get used to your early departure days," Estella joked with him.

She walked over to the table and sat down with the two of them sipping the hot dark coffee she hoped would get her mind flowing better.

John asked, "So what do you two ladies of leisure have planned for the day?"

Estella looked at Florence and said, "We have some shopping to do in town and will most certainly find a place to have lunch together." She looked closely for a reaction from Florence and was pleased to see her in agreement with the plan.

John smiled. "I'm glad to be heading out of town for work and leaving you two to the shopping. Maybe Ruth will take part in your little luncheon."

"Yes, and thanks for the reminder," Estella said, rising from her chair. "I need to dash to the bank. Stephen's coming in early to send a telegram to the Blanks—just to let them know Florence is safe with us." She paused, then added carefully, "And I need to get a message to Ruth to arrange an early shopping visit at Wanamaker's—before the store opens to a sea of customers."

She moved quickly toward the door, grabbing her handbag on the way. "I'll be back soon," she called over her shoulder, her voice trailing off. "Help yourselves to anything!"

She reminded John of a locomotive on a mission, and nothing could stop his mother until she achieved her final goal. He had no doubt that Florence would have a whirlwind sort of day with little time to think about what was happening.

The two of them sat and chattered away about John's schooling. He shared stories about the nearby school that both he and Frances had attended.

Florence shared her school experience and the single classroom where they all learned together with the same teacher. Mostly basic math and English were taught. A lot of time off was allowed by the school so the children could work during the large growing seasons. Everyone helped one another in her community until all were caught up. Although the work was hard, she had fond memories to share.

John waited with Florence while his mother stepped away. She hadn't asked him to, but he thought it might feel awkward for her to be on her own in a strange place. He knew Estella would take care of the necessary things and return as quickly as possible. Not even an hour later, she came through the door again.

She announced, "All is taken care of, and Stephen was already a step ahead, as was his norm. He's sending his driver over so we must be quick about dressing. John, thanks for staying. I wish you well in your week and you shall be missed here. Be safe and I love you."

They never parted ways without those last three words. Estella reminded them always that those were the words she wanted to carry close to her heart, the last ones she had spoken to her children on that fateful day twelve years ago when the children were taken away from her. It was blazed into her soul, and it carried her through many dark days knowing those would always be the last words they heard from their mother. She hurried to dress for the day. She did her best to outfit Florence in one of her dresses, having to pin a few areas, taking up the extra fabric, then both she and Florence descended the stairs, ready for a busy day.

Stephen's driver waited patiently by the curb. Estella offered him a warm "Good morning" as she and Florence stepped into the back of the automobile. Once seated, she gently placed her hand over her daughter's, a silent gesture of reassurance. Today would bring a flood of new experiences, some thrilling, others perhaps daunting. But it was the beginning they both needed.

As they pulled away, Estella watched Florence closely. Her eyes were wide with wonder as they passed the bustling train station, the very one she had arrived at only the night before. Now, in the full light of morning, the city was alive with motion. Crowds of people rushed to work, delivery wagons rattled along the cobblestone streets, and streetcars clanged as they passed. Tall buildings stretched toward the sky, dwarfing the small houses Florence had known in Amish country.

Florence said nothing, but her gaze moved from one scene to the next, absorbing everything. She noticed women in stylish dresses—some showing bare calves, which was startling to her—and others with elaborate hats tilted just so atop their heads. It was another world, vibrant and strange.

The driver turned down a narrow alley, one he had taken Estella and Ruth through many times before. It led to the employee entrance of John Wanamaker's, the grand department store in the heart of the city. Ruth had called ahead, arranging special early access before the doors opened to the public.

Security, familiar with the arrangement, waved them through. A personal attendant was waiting inside to escort Estella and Florence to a private fitting area, where a wardrobe of clothing was already being prepared for Florence to try on.

It was more than just a shopping trip. It was the start of her new life—in the world she had been born into and was now returning to. A world she had been kept from, yet one that still quietly waited for her.

For Estella, one thing was of utmost importance: to have her daughter properly fitted for several brassieres. That would come first. She wanted Florence to feel supported, both physically and emotionally. With the right foundation, everything else—dresses, blouses, shoes—would follow. And perhaps, piece by piece, Florence would begin to feel at home in her own skin again.

Before long, the morning whizzed by quickly. The store had opened to their regular clientele, and it was getting busy with patrons shopping throughout the store. She could see that Florence was growing weary and needed a break. Estella asked one of the personal attendants to take their purchases to the side entrance where they would collect them after they had shared a meal together. She had arranged with Ruth earlier for the three of them to meet at The Crystal Tea Room in the same building. She and Florence walked to the elevators. The doors opened and a man dressed in a suit stepped out of the lift and ushered them in. After closing the cage-like gate and doors, he pressed number "9." Mother and daughter held hands as they rode to the ninth floor together.

When the elevator came to a gentle stop, the attendant stepped forward and opened the doors. Estella and Florence stepped out, and as they rounded the corner, Florence came to a halt—her mouth slightly open in awe.

Before her stretched the grand tearoom—an elegant expanse beneath glittering crystal chandeliers. The air buzzed with conversation and the clatter of dishes and silverware. Waitstaff in crisp uniforms weaved between tables, serving delicate lunches on fine china. The entire room glowed beneath the natural light streaming through the towering windows along the far wall.

Estella scanned the room, and with a knowing smile, spotted Ruth at her usual table near the windows. Taking Florence by the arm, she led her across the parquet floor toward the sunlit corner.

Ruth stood and turned as they approached, her face breaking into a warm smile.

"Ruth," Estella said brightly, "thank you for arranging this morning—and for joining us for lunch. I'd like you to meet my daughter... little Florence."

Ruth's expression softened with genuine affection. "It's my pleasure," she said, reaching out to take Florence's hand. "I'm honored to finally meet you, young lady. I've heard so much about you over the years."

She gave Florence an appraising but kind glance. "I trust you're enjoying your outing. I imagine you've worked up quite an appetite."

"Yes, ma'am," Florence replied, her voice shy but sincere.

Ruth gestured to the table. "Well then, let's not keep the tea waiting."

They took their seats, the linen napkins already folded neatly beside delicate china plates. A silver teapot and three cups rested at the center of the table, gently steaming.

To break the ice, Ruth offered a bit of history. "This tearoom opened in 1911," she began with a smile. "It's one of the largest dining rooms in Philadelphia—perhaps even in the world—serving up one thousand four hundred people at a time. It was modeled after the tearoom in Robert Morris' mansion, just down the way."

She paused, expecting some intrigue, but Florence simply nodded, her gaze already shifting to the menus placed before them. The grandeur of the architecture, the lineage of design—none of it truly registered. Not yet. Her world was still adjusting, moment by moment.

The weight of the linen menu in her hands felt unfamiliar, and the elegant script inside listed items she had never tasted or even heard of. But she focused, determined to take it all in—if not with excitement, then with quiet courage.

Estella glanced across the table at her daughter and smiled gently, knowing this was just the beginning of many firsts.

Once they had placed their orders, Ruth wanted to hear all about the morning shopping spree. "I can see you've already found a gorgeous dress and can't wait to see the rest of the attire on more outings we'll have together."

The chatter was endless, and the ladies laughed and shared some good stories together. Ruth was good at putting people at ease and asking them about themselves, always leaning in with interest. After the meal the ladies rode the elevator to the street level together. The three of them exited the lift and Ruth left them, returning to the bank. Estella and Florence walked over to the employees' side entrance, which was hidden from the main shopping area. Stephen's driver had already loaded the packages into the automobile and awaited the ladies to settle in the backseat before pulling away.

The city center was always filled with automobiles, wagons, and a lot of pedestrians. As much as Estella enjoyed coming to town to shop or do other business, she appreciated the return to her quiet home on the edge of the city. She always looked down toward the old mill house and thought of Nora, whom she kept in touch with every year by sending a Christmas card. She thought to herself how nice it would be to pay her a visit with Florence. She knew Nora would be happy for the family to be together again. The last time she'd seen Nora was at Frances and Jeff's wedding and then at her home in the old neighborhood.

Some weeks after the ceremony, Nora sent a letter to Estella, requesting to see her in private.

When Estella arrived at Nora's home, the afternoon light was low and slanting through the curtains. Nora met her at the door with a familiar gentleness but an unfamiliar tightness around the eyes.

"I didn't want to send this in a letter," she said, ushering Estella inside. "There's something you ought to know."

They sat at the kitchen table, the kettle already warm. Nora folded her hands, hesitating just long enough for Estella to feel the air shift.

"My nephew," she began. "Sergeant Murphy. He asked around. Did some looking on your behalf. And... he found him."

Estella's breath caught.

"Aaron," Nora said softly. "He's alive. Still in Philadelphia, not far from Kensington. He's been living in a boarding house for some time now."

Estella stared ahead, unmoving.

"He's not alone," Nora added. "He's living with a woman there. Works in the house, helps keep it clean. They're calling themselves husband and wife."

Silence settled in like dust. Estella's hands lay folded in her lap, motionless, except for the tightening of her knuckles.

"So he never left," she said finally, her voice quiet. "Only left us."

Nora reached out and placed her hand gently over Estella's. "I thought you should hear it from someone who cares about you."

Estella nodded once, slowly. The ache that had lived nameless in her chest for years had a shape now. A name. An address. And it was just down the trolley line.

Estella had long released her anger, forgiving Aaron for what he had done to the family, having long ago surmised he had met his demise. This new information felt like betrayal reawakened—sharp, fresh, and cold. It was not death that had taken him from her and the children, but choice. Deliberate, daily choice. He had not been lost—he had simply walked away and never turned back.

All those years she had grieved, had prayed for peace, had built a life from the ashes with nothing but grit and borrowed strength—she had done so under the illusion that he was gone. But now she knew: he had not disappeared. He had replaced her. Replaced them all.

And yet, as the wave of shock receded, what remained was not rage. It was sorrow. Sorrow for the children who had gone without, sorrow for the love she had wasted on a man who never looked back, and sorrow for herself—for the silence she had mistaken for death.

The driver pulled alongside the curb at Estella's home. Stephen was walking inside the house with a man in a service uniform. She wondered what was happening but was more focused on helping Florence with the cumbersome packages.

"Welcome home!" Stephen called from the hallway as the front door opened. "I see you both had a successful outing today."

Estella smiled, brushing a few stray strands of hair from her forehead. "We did and even had the privilege of joining Ruth for lunch in the tearoom."

Stephen raised an eyebrow playfully. "The tearoom? Quite the affair."

Estella set a parcel on the hallway table. "So tell me, what have you been up to here?"

Stephen hesitated, hands behind his back like a child caught sneaking sweets. "Well... it was meant to be a surprise, but it seems you've caught me red-handed. I've been wanting you to have a phone of your own. It's not right for you to have to run to the bank every time you need to reach me or anyone else. I just thought it might make life a little easier."

Estella sighed dramatically, putting her hands on her hips in mock exasperation. "You're impossible, Mr. Masters. Did you know that?"

Stephen laughed, unfazed. "If you say so, Madam."

Florence stood quietly, observing the exchange with quiet appreciation. Their warmth and teasing affection were so natural, so easy. She couldn't remember ever seeing her foster parents interact that way. Theirs had been a home of duty and reverence, not laughter and soft glances.

Outside, Stephen helped retrieve the remaining parcels from the car. He turned to his driver and said, "Head to the tavern and grab a meal. Put it on my tab."

"Thank you, sir," the man replied, tipping his hat before climbing in and driving off.

Together, they carried the parcels inside. The telephone installer met them at the door, holding it open as they entered. His work complete, he gave a quick nod and departed with a purposeful stride, vanishing down the walk.

They climbed the stairs to Florence's room and set the shopping bags neatly beside her wardrobe. Stephen turned in the hallway, offering a reassuring smile.

"I'll be in the kitchen. Take your time—no rush. I've got dinner under control."

Estella glanced at him with a softened expression. "Thank you... for everything."

Inside the bedroom, the late afternoon light spilled through the curtains as Estella and Florence began to unwrap the packages together. Dresses, blouses, underthings, stockings, a modest new hat—it was a fresh beginning, carefully folded into tissue paper.

Estella opened the tall chifforobe, and as the doors creaked open, she paused.

Inside, still hanging, were several of Florence's old outfits—faded, tiny, untouched. For a moment, it felt as if time had collapsed inward. Estella stood still, the air thick with memory. She pictured her little girl running barefoot through the grass, swinging with John and Frances, dancing around the room in the very dresses now hanging limp before her.

"I had forgotten these were still here," Estella murmured, more to herself than to Florence. "I suppose they won't fit you anymore."

Florence stepped closer, brushing her fingers over the soft, worn fabric of a pinafore.

Estella smiled and turned to her. "I know a lady who would be thrilled to have these for her grandchildren. We can wrap them up and bring them to her sometime."

She was thinking of Nora, of course, and her lively household of little ones. It was the perfect reason to stop by—not that she ever needed one.

Once all the new dresses were hung neatly in the chifforobe and the accessories folded and tucked away in the drawers, Estella and Florence made their way downstairs to the kitchen. The familiar smell of freshly brewed coffee greeted them, mingling with the comforting scent of warm biscuits.

Stephen looked up and smiled as they entered. "There you are," he said cheerfully. "Have a seat. I've just made a fresh pot."

He set two steaming cups in front of them and placed a plate of buttery biscuits at the center of the table. Then, gesturing toward the far corner behind the kitchen table, he added, "And while we're at it, I'd love to hear all about your day but first, let me show you how to use the candlestick phone."

Florence turned her head to look. The device stood tall and black, with its mouthpiece fixed at the top and a separate earpiece resting in its cradle. She had seen telephones before—but only briefly, and never up close.

Stephen continued with a chuckle. "I know Estella's not fond of the things. Thinks they're monstrous time robbers." He glanced at her with a playful smirk. "Some of her best clients talk about party lines—how they can listen in on half the neighborhood without ever leaving their chairs."

Estella rolled her eyes with a faint smile. "It's a terrible habit. People should mind their own conversations."

Stephen nodded knowingly. "That's why I had it installed on the outer kitchen wall, tucked back, close to the wiring, but far enough out of your path. And it has an extra-long cord, see? Coiled up neatly so you can sit while using it. Or not use it at all, if you prefer."

He said it all lightly, but there was care in his design—thoughtfulness in every decision.

Florence sipped her coffee quietly, watching the exchange between her mother and Stephen. Again, the ease of their interaction, their gentle humor—it felt new and familiar all at once. It was nothing like what she had known in the Blank household.

And as she reached for a biscuit, warm and crumbly in her hand, she thought for the first time that this place—this house, this table—might one day truly feel like home.

Estella laughed. "That would've come in handy this morning, I suppose. I do appreciate you always taking good care of us."

Stephen smiled warmly and then turned his attention to Florence. "I'm so happy you were able to find some new clothes and also get to meet my sister, Ruth."

Florence remained mostly quiet, though she was attentive and polite, answering when spoken to and listening carefully to the conversation around her. This way of being—sitting at a table with warm coffee, gentle talk, and no urgent tasks waiting—was unlike anything she had known.

Back in her Amish home, days were filled with purposeful labor from the moment the sun rose. Chores, mending, cooking, and tending to the land filled every hour. There was little time for leisure let alone shopping, reading, or sitting with others simply to talk. The quiet stillness of the afternoon felt indulgent, foreign... and a little unsettling.

Yet, beneath her unease, there was a stirring curiosity. The conveniences of the home—the electric lighting, the indoor plumbing, the way meals could be prepared without stoking a fire or pumping water—had not gone unnoticed. These things gave time back to the people who lived here. What they did with that time, Florence wasn't yet sure.

After their tea and conversation, Stephen stood and brushed his hands together. "Let me finish preparing the evening meal," he said with a smile. "You two ladies should relax in the sitting room—read a little, perhaps."

Florence hesitated. Her instinct was to clear the table, wash the dishes, earn her place. Rising without helping felt... improper.

But Stephen gave her a gentle look. "Truly, Florence—it's all right."

She gave a small nod, still unsure, and followed Estella to the front of the house—the same room where, just the night before, her world had quietly begun to change.

The sitting room was calm and cozy, its shelves lined with books—some brought home by Stephen, others gifted from clients who knew Estella's love of reading. On a side table sat a neat stack of magazines.

Florence's eye caught a bright, colorful cover: a beautifully illustrated woman in a flowing, fashionable dress, carrying a delicate parasol. The word *Vogue* was written across the top in elegant lettering.

She reached for it instinctively; drawn to something she didn't yet understand. She'd never seen anything like it.

Turning the pages slowly, she stared at the glamorous images of women with bold eyes and confident postures, their clothes light years from the starched simplicity she had known. It felt like a glimpse into another universe.

Estella watched her quietly from across the room, recognizing the look in her daughter's eyes—not vanity, not rebellion, but wonder.

And for the first time, Florence allowed herself to wonder too.

Estella sat in her favorite corner and picked up her book, *Main Street* by Sinclair Lewis. Florence noticed the cover depicting a row of houses and a dark silhouette of a woman in the foreground. She returned to her *Vogue* and got lost in the pages of fashion. She wondered how fun it would be to create some of these outfits. She was quite talented with needles and thread.

***

The weeks passed, and Florence began to establish new routines. Ones that allowed her to explore parts of herself she'd never fully known. With each passing day, she grew more at ease in her new surroundings, slowly turning her attention to the curiosities and comforts of suburban and city life.

She discovered, to her own surprise, that she had an eye for fashion and an ear for music. Estella often found her quietly sketching dresses she'd seen in shop windows or humming melodies from the radio or theater. Florence adored every opportunity to attend a show downtown, where she was mesmerized by the grandeur of the live orchestra, the deep resonance of the pipe organ, or sometimes, both, setting the tone for the moving images on the silver screen. These outings stirred something in her, a joy that felt both brand new and deeply familiar.

Estella encouraged her youngest daughter to follow her interests wherever they led. Part of her carried a quiet ache, a guilt she couldn't entirely name. Florence had missed so much. While John and Frances had been shaped by the rhythm of life with their mother, Florence had lived an entirely different story. There was no way to erase that loss, no way to rewrite those years.

But now, at last, Florence had the freedom to explore, to discover, to grow. And it brought Estella a profound joy to witness it.

What she hadn't expected, however, was the quiet strength and steady depth her daughter had brought with her from Amish life.

Florence had been shaped by more than hardship—she had been formed by purpose. The long hours of work, the discipline of daily life, had not made her hard or bitter. They had shaped her character.

She worked with quiet diligence, not from obligation, but from love—love for God, for family, for order and care. Her labor had not been in vain.

Florence carried a deep respect for family and a work ethic that served not just herself, but those around her. Her talents—practical, creative, and spiritual—wove together to form a different kind of completeness. She was not like Frances. She was not like John. She was wholly herself—strong, kind, curious, and full of possibility.

And Estella, watching her bloom, understood more clearly than ever that despite all they had lost, something beautiful had still taken root.

Estella often thought of the Blank family. She didn't know their daily rhythms or what kind of life Florence had truly lived in their care, but she imagined a tidy farmhouse, a braided rug by the hearth, the warmth of soup in winter and the hush of hymns on Sunday mornings. She believed they had loved her daughter in their own quiet way—had taught her kindness, hard work, and reverence. It gave her comfort, even as it stung.

Amos and Sara Blank missed Florence deeply, though they spoke of her only in hushed tones—when the fields were still or the lantern had just been blown out for the night. Out of respect for the Ordnung and under the guidance of their bishop, they kept a respectable distance. No letters. No visits. No questions. Their heartache was tucked inside, buried beneath layers of obedience and faith. They had given Florence back to the world when called to do so, but not without grief.

Unspoken but understood, there remained a thread between them all—Estella's aching hope, and the Blanks' quiet yearning. Each waited in their own way.

One day, that thread would pull taut. A letter would arrive. A door would open. And what had once been severed would begin, slowly, to mend.

EMPLOYMENT
Florence | Philadelphia | Winter 1924

The winter months stretched on, long and heavy, draped in darkness and snow. Florence, now more familiar with the city's rhythms, still found it challenging to navigate the icy streets and the chaos of crowded corners and slushy curbs. The sky often hung low and gray, making the days feel even shorter. She missed the sun. She missed the warmth. And yet, she pressed forward.

One morning, as she hurried toward the trolley station, bundled tightly against the cold, something caught her eye—a small burst of color breaking through the edge of a dirty snowbank. A single purple crocus, delicate yet determined, had pushed its way up through the frozen crust.

Florence stopped for a moment, stunned by the contrast. That brave little flower, blooming despite the weight of winter, stirred something inside her. It willed itself forward, she thought, just as I have.

It felt like a sign, an omen of better days ahead. Encouraged, she stepped more briskly toward her destination.

Today wasn't just another outing. She was headed to The Aldine, a grand new movie palace built by the respected William Steele and Sons Company. Set along the edge of the distinguished Rittenhouse-Fitler neighborhood, The Aldine was a marvel of modern design, elegance, and artistry. Florence had visited before as a guest, captivated by the gilded ceilings, velvet seats, and the magic of music and motion on screen.

But this time, she wasn't there for entertainment.

Florence had dressed with care, choosing a simple yet smart outfit and pulling her hair back neatly. She clutched her gloves in one hand and smoothed her coat with the other as she walked. She wasn't going to see a movie—she was returning to the theater to ask about employment opportunities.

A bold step. A hopeful one.

And like the crocus pushing through the snow, it marked a quiet breakthrough—Florence, too, reaching for the light.

When she arrived there was a "help wanted" sign posted in the window of the box office. She walked around to a side entrance and was able to get inside. She worked her way around to the front of the building and was met by the manager, whom she had seen many times before.

"May I help you, ma'am?"

"I saw a sign in the box window and am interested in working here."

The manager introduced himself. "I'm Charlie Millard. Do you have any work experience?"

A bit flustered, she said, "I'm Florence Fitler. I'm hard working and learn quickly."

"So I'm taking it you don't have work experience then?" he asked.

She started to speak, but he put his hand up to silence her. "Look, how 'bout we start you out in the ticket office upfront, working with one of the experienced box office workers and see how fast you learn. When can you start?"

She wasn't prepared for that response, but blurted out, "Today!"

Charlie smiled and gave a nod. "The job's yours," he said, matter-of-factly. "You'll just need to come into the office and fill out some paperwork—name, address, that sorta thing. The new labor laws make it all official now. We'll start you off with the matinee shift. It's a good place to learn the ropes."

Florence beamed, her heart leaping with excitement. She could hardly believe it—she was being offered a job in the very place she loved to spend her free time. And now, she'd not only be part of the magic, but she'd earn a bit of money too.

One of the unexpected perks she learned about was being able to see all the latest films that came through town. That alone felt like a dream come true. She didn't even think to ask what the pay would be. The experience, the chance to be part of something she loved, was reward enough.

After completing the necessary paperwork—just the basics—Charlie led her through a narrow hallway and into the box office.

Florence paused at the threshold, taking it all in. She had only ever seen it from the sidewalk, behind the glass, where she and her family had once stood in line for tickets. Now, she was on the other side. Inside.

The space was small but tidy, filled with neatly stacked ticket rolls, a stool, a narrow countertop, and the curved pane of glass that separated the seller from the street. She touched the polished surface of the desk lightly, a smile spreading across her face.

It was more than a job, it was a small, shining step into a world she was learning to claim as her own.

A plump, middle aged woman with red hair that curled around her round cheeks was setting up a drawer of coins when she walked inside. Charlie quickly introduced the two women and disappeared. He was needed in the projection room.

Bridie was her name, and she reminded Florence of the older Mrs. Murphy whom she had visited with her mother not long ago.

Bridie said, "Come over here Flo, and I'll show you how to set up your cash drawer before the movie goers arrive."

A tall, lean man wearing a dark suit and jacket with a hat passed by the window smiling and wished Bridie a good morning. She pressed a bell that signaled the doorman to let the man in. She leaned over toward Florence, "That's the music man and he comes in early to play the sounds for the motion picture." He caught Florence's eye, and she watched him disappear. He seemed like a kind, gentle man.

The flurry of activity came all at once.

Florence kept her composure, carefully watching Bridie and mimicking every move. For a solid thirty minutes, patrons streamed to the window in a rush to purchase tickets. The Aldine seated one thousand three hundred people, and by the end of the surge, Florence felt as though she'd seen every one of them at her window.

Bridie gave her an approving nod. "You're picking this up quickly," she said, pleased. "I'm going to excuse myself for just a moment—think you can hold down the fort?"

Florence nodded confidently, a small thrill rising in her chest. Alone in the box office, she felt capable and trusted. A late-arriving patron approached the window, purchased a single ticket, and hurried inside. Florence briefly wondered why anyone would want to miss the beginning of a film but reminded herself that wasn't hers to worry about.

Bridie soon returned, and together they closed the ticket window. There were end-of-shift accounting steps still to be completed, and Florence followed Bridie into the back office, both carefully carrying their cash drawers.

By the time everything was logged and secured, Florence felt tired—but satisfied. It had been a good first day.

As she made her way to the trolley station, the last light of day softened the edges of the city. Just ahead, near the platform, she noticed the music man—the one from the theater—waiting quietly for the same trolley. He stood alone, hat in hand, and she recognized him immediately.

Florence didn't approach, just observed from a distance. When the trolley arrived, she stepped on and took her favorite seat by the window on the far-right side, where she could watch the green spaces pass on the ride home. The music man sat a few rows ahead, opening his folded newspaper with quiet precision.

She was intrigued by him. There was something about the way he carried himself—his calm, his kindness. When the trolley filled with passengers, she watched as he stood to offer his seat to an elderly woman with a cane. Her admiration grew.

As the trolley reached Overbrook Station, he stepped off. Florence followed a few paces behind, her gaze lowered, wondering where he lived and whether their paths had crossed before.

Maybe it didn't matter, she told herself. *He works at The Aldine. I'll see him again.*

Still, she walked the rest of the way home with a lightness in her step. She couldn't wait to tell her mother about her new job—and maybe, just maybe, mention the music man too.

Estella immediately sensed her daughter's excitement the moment she stepped through the door. She set down her sewing and looked up with a curious smile. "What have you been up to today?"

Florence beamed, unable to hold it in a moment longer. "I got a job today!"

Estella's eyes lit up. "That's wonderful, dear! Where—and when do you start?"

"I've already started," Florence said, barely able to contain her enthusiasm. "You know that big, new movie palace—The Aldine? I went by this morning and saw a 'Help Wanted' sign in the ticket window. I decided to ask about it, and the manager hired me right on the spot. I worked the matinee selling tickets!"

Estella stood and came closer, pride in her eyes. "I'm so proud of you—for finding something on your own, and especially something you love. I know how much the movies mean to you."

Florence's words tumbled out in a rush. "That's the best part of the job! I get to watch all the new movies—not all at once, of course—but eventually we get to see them. And the music... oh, the music is beautiful. I could sit there and listen to it all day."

Estella smiled and gently touched her daughter's arm. "It sounds like the perfect place for you right now."

And in that moment, both women felt it—a shared sense of pride and possibility, and the quiet joy of a new beginning unfolding just as it should.

Estella said, "I'd like for you to come by the bank tomorrow. I will set up your first bank account for you. You'll have a safe place to save your money. I can teach you some of the basics."

CHANGE, FASHION, FLAPPERS
Florence | Philadelphia | Spring 1924

The April edition of *Vogue* lay carefully placed on the kitchen table, a deliberate gesture from Estella. She had brought it home from the office, knowing full well her daughter would be the first to spot it when she came downstairs for breakfast.

The cover was a burst of spring elegance: sweeping skirts, impossibly tiny waists, and the latest Parisian fashions rendered in rich illustration. Estella always found herself chuckling at the extravagance of it all. Who wears these things? she often wondered. Certainly not the clients at the bank—none of whom had ever come in wearing embroidered gloves or feathered hats like the ones splashed across those glossy pages.

Still, she was glad to bring the magazines home to Florence. There was no sense in tossing them when new editions arrived. Besides, *Vogue* offered more than just fashion—it was sprinkled with society news, film gossip, and articles with far lighter fare than the headlines crowding the newspapers.

She'd noticed how eagerly Florence devoured every detail—the fabrics, the colors, the silhouettes. It wasn't just passing curiosity. Her daughter had an eye, a true appreciation for beauty, for artistry, for the stories clothing could tell. Estella was quietly proud. Florence had a hunger to learn, and she wasn't just learning about style. She was discovering herself.

***

Florence slept later that morning as she was working the evening shift at the box office. This was an honor and her first opportunity because one of the other employees was away due to a family illness and didn't have anyone to cover. She came into the kitchen and welcomed the coffee and leftover bowl of oatmeal her mother left behind for her. She heated milk on the stovetop to pour over her cereal and diced up a small apple to put on top. Walking over to the table she spotted the *Vogue*. Sipping her coffee, she flipped through the pages intently, studying the new and fresh designs.

She was glad to be making her own money so she could buy materials to create some outfits and accessories similar to the ones she saw in the magazines.

Florence had an air of simplicity and modesty from being raised in the Amish ways. She was intrigued by the flapper attire yet didn't fully embrace all of it. She thought of flappers as young women, much like herself, enjoying an exuberant freedom and liberated lifestyle and moving away from the traditional Victorian values. Many viewed this new generation of independent women as outrageous, immoral and dangerous to society. Florence just saw them as beautiful creations blossoming, just like she had witnessed the flowers in her garden. Her entire perspective and influence came out of the natural world.

Multiple changes, political, cultural and technological, led to the rise of these flappers. Florence was mostly unaware of the events that paved the way for this development as she was sheltered from the news and happenings in the Amish countryside. During The Great War, women joined the workforce in large numbers, earning higher wages that they were not willing to give up once the war ended. She began to learn and understand some of the history she hadn't been exposed to, piecing it together as tidbits of information came her way. Perhaps she would never fully understand all of it but her quest for learning was unending. She felt much like one of her little seeds that she had tucked away for planting at just the right time.

Women's independence took a monumental step forward with the ratification of the 19th Amendment in August 1920, granting women the long-awaited right to vote. Not long after, social reformers like Margaret Sanger stirred public discourse even further by championing women's access to contraception—an issue that sparked significant controversy in this rapidly changing era.

Florence came to learn that while Estella didn't always agree with the more radical shifts in society, she firmly believed that women needed to have a voice. For Estella, it wasn't theoretical—it was personal. Her own dependence on an incapable man had cost her dearly. She had lost two children temporarily and nearly lost a third permanently. The scars of that experience never fully faded, and she recognized how rare her eventual reunion had been.

Many women in similar circumstances were not so fortunate.

Through conversations with her sister and quiet observation, Florence was beginning to understand the complexity of the world she'd reentered. A world where progress often came in messy, imperfect strides.

Florence was more intrigued by the designs and fabrics worn by the fashionable flappers that some considered rakish attire. She adored Coco Chanel and Elsa Schiaparelli for the no-nonsense lines they created in women's apparel. The shorter, calf-revealing dresses and lower necklines created a streamlined silhouette. The flappers wore high heel shoes and tossed their strangling corsets aside in favor of bras and lingerie. Heavy use of rouge, lipstick and mascara was a classic feature of the new young woman who also enjoyed shorter hairstyles.

Florence's appearance changed drastically from when she had first arrived in Philadelphia. She adored her entire transformation, most especially the short new bob haircut that framed her face beautifully. It allowed her naturally thick and wavy curls to come to life in a flattering way. She wore her necklines high, but she did reveal her shapely ankles and lower calves and wore a slight heel. Her feminine side was being expressed modestly, in a way that suited her tastes and comfort level. She dabbled a bit with cosmetics, but she preferred to only wear a touch of lipstick to enhance her full lips. She preferred a more natural appearance. Of course, every young lady needed a strand or two of long pearls to finish off the complete look.

After poring over the latest pages of *Vogue* and letting her imagination drift into the world of silk gloves, Parisian gowns, and elegant silhouettes, Florence glanced at the clock—and leapt to her feet. She rushed to get ready for work.

She always made a point to dress well for her job at The Aldine. As the face behind the ticket window, she understood that she offered the first impression of the grand movie palace to its patrons. A smart blouse, a neat skirt, polished shoes, these things mattered. Presentation was part of the experience.

Mr. Millard, the manager, often complimented her appearance. Too often, in fact. While he never crossed any clear line, something in his tone occasionally made Florence uncomfortable. She was always cautious, though never alone with him, and learned to smile politely while keeping her distance.

Still, she wouldn't have minded being noticed by one person in particular—the music man.

She didn't even know his name, but she had come to recognize his quick stride, the way he carried his case, and the slight lift of his brow when he passed her station. There were times—just brief flickers—when she thought he might be glancing her way. But before she could be sure, he'd vanish behind the velvet curtain and down into the orchestra pit.

He seemed to follow his own rhythm, appearing unpredictably—there one day, absent the next. Florence imagined theater work wasn't suited to routine. Still, she couldn't help but hope their paths might one day align—clearly, unmistakably.

Until then, she smoothed her skirt, pinned her hair just right, and gave herself one last glance in the mirror before heading out. Maybe today would be different.

Florence stepped out the front door and onto the bright sidewalk, her purse tucked under one arm and a familiar sense of anticipation in her step. She always preferred leaving early for work. It gave her time to move at her own pace, without the pressure of rushing, and allowed her to take in the gentle beauty of the season.

Spring was beginning to show itself in earnest. The leaves on the trees were that bright green, the kind that only comes after a long winter, fresh and full of promise. Soon, their shade would be a welcome refuge from the heat of summer.

Tucked inside her purse was a small book, one she often carried in hopes of finding her favorite bench unoccupied in Rittenhouse Square. The park was just a short detour from her route to work, and when time allowed, she'd linger there for a few minutes, soaking in the sights and sounds of the city.

She especially loved watching the people, many of them among the wealthiest Philadelphians, strolling through the square with an ease that fascinated her. Their clothing was tailored, their conversations practiced, their posture confident. It wasn't just wealth that set them apart, it was a whole way of being.

Florence rarely saw these people at The Aldine, even though the theater wasn't far from the park. They seemed to orbit a different part of city life. She watched without judgment, only curiosity. She wasn't envious, only intrigued. There was something about the way they moved through the world that she wanted to understand—not to mimic, necessarily, but to study. To learn how city life worked. How people connected, how they chose to be seen.

With a little time before her job started, she took a seat beneath a budding tree and opened her book, letting the rustle of leaves and the hum of footsteps become the backdrop to another quiet moment of discovery. She read for a short time enjoying the story.

Keeping an eye on time, Florence closed her book and stood up from the bench. She brushed off her skirt and began walking toward The Aldine, the theater now just a few short blocks away. The tall trees lining the path were bursting with new spring leaves, their bright green canopy dancing lightly in the breeze. She walked with a quiet purpose, enjoying the rhythm of her footsteps and the fresh air that carried the scent of earth and flowers.

Just ahead, she spotted a lone figure seated on a bench beneath the trees—a tall, slender young man in a dark suit and hat, his head bowed intently over a book. Her heart gave a sudden flutter. Was it him? Could it be the music man?

As she drew nearer, she slowed her pace slightly, stealing a better glance. From the angle of his profile and the curve of his jaw, she was almost certain. It's him.

In that moment, as if sensing her gaze, he looked up.

Their eyes met—only for a second—but it was long enough to set her cheeks ablaze. She instantly turned her face away, pretending to study the sidewalk ahead. The heat flushed up her neck and into her cheeks, and she knew her face must be bright crimson.

Oh, how could I be so obvious? she silently scolded herself, biting the inside of her lip. She dared not look back.

But after a few paces, she couldn't help herself. She risked a glance over her shoulder.

He was still there, head down again, absorbed in his book as if nothing had happened.

Florence exhaled, her heart still fluttering. She pressed her hand lightly against her chest and smiled to herself. She wasn't sure if it was embarrassment or something else entirely that made her feel so alive just then.

As Florence neared The Aldine, she sensed something unusual. A crowd had gathered on the sidewalk just outside the grand entrance—restless and loud, their voices rising in animated conversation. A few pointed upward while others stood with arms crossed, shaking their heads in disapproval.

Curious, she followed their gaze and stopped short, astonished.

The soaring window bays of the movie palace had been completely covered by a massive eight-by-ten-foot advertisement for the upcoming premiere of *Beau Brummell*. The entire front of the building had been transformed into a striking visual spectacle, a bold, theatrical frame for the portrait of the film's dashing star, cloaked in regency finery. The effect was breathtaking, if a little overwhelming.

So that's what all the fuss is about, she thought.

She stood silently for a moment, taking it all in. It was a clever tactic, really, turning the building itself into a billboard to draw in the evening crowds. And judging by the buzz around her, it was certainly working. But the reaction wasn't all admiration.

The voices she overheard weren't those of delighted moviegoers. They were critical, even hostile. She caught snippets of complaint: "It's a disgrace to the Square..." "...ruining the architectural integrity..." "...just another assault on good taste..."

Florence was taken aback. She had assumed that everyone must feel as she did—that the magic of the theater, the music, the costumes, the lights—was a kind of gift. But it seemed The Aldine's opulence and popularity had earned it some vocal detractors, particularly among the well-heeled residents of Rittenhouse Square.

There's more to this city than meets the eye, she thought, sensing another layer of social complexity beginning to unfold.

Still, there was no time to dwell on it. She straightened her blouse and stepped carefully through the edge of the crowd, making her way toward the side entrance reserved for staff. Inside, there would be final preparations, a flurry of tasks, and then—curtains up.

The premiere of *Beau Brummell* awaited, and Florence was ready for the night ahead.

THE ALDINE'S MUSIC MAN
William & Florence | Philadelphia | Spring 1924

The Aldine's exterior architectural design resembled an Italian Renaissance palazzo. The layout of the building was necessary to accommodate the large picture screen and orchestra pit. It led movie patrons into a large, grand foyer, giving them a feeling of entering a royal palace. The foyer ascended to a higher level which looked down over the mezzanine. It was all about the experience and spectacle to entertain and captivate the audience. In essence, the movie palace concept had changed how theater was perceived by its patrons, replacing the negativity that earlier Vaudeville theaters had unwittingly caused.

Florence approached the grand building and was allowed to enter the theater as the security guard recognized her, unlocking and opening the door for her to enter. She went into the main office behind the foyer and collected her cash drawer. On top of it was a folder with the word, "RESERVED" marked across it in bold letters. She had heard about this new procedure which made it easier for a theater patron to come in, give their name and walk to their seats so they wouldn't have to wait on the street in long lines. The management felt that the practice might have a better chance of attracting the groups of people who still looked at the movie palace as just another form of Vaudeville. Reserved seats could encourage people to come visit and learn to enjoy the entertainment.

She set up her space while another woman named Helen, who she had worked with a short time ago, set up in the other window.

She turned to Helen and said, "This should be an exciting show from the looks of it. I do hope we get to see some of it."

Helen wasn't much for chatter and just simply said, "Yah, wouldn't that be a nice change."

It was nearly showtime, and Florence and Helen pulled up the roller shades of the ticket booth, revealing the eager crowd outside. They exchanged wide-eyed glances—the line stretched far down the sidewalk and spilled into the street, buzzing with anticipation. The premiere of *Beau Brummell* had drawn a massive crowd, just as expected.

Thankfully, many patrons had purchased reserved seats in advance and flowed swiftly through the front doors with tickets in hand. The rest formed a steady stream at the booth, inching forward to secure whatever seats remained. For about forty-five minutes, the pace was relentless—a flurry of voices, coins, bills, and the rhythmic clicking of the ticket machine.

Time blurred.

Florence barely noticed the minutes ticking by as she handed out tickets with practiced ease, her excitement building with each transaction. She loved this part—the energy, the chatter, the subtle elegance of opening night.

When the final stragglers rushed through the entrance and the street finally began to quiet, Helen turned to her with a grin. "Go on—get your cash box counted and turned in. I'll stay and cover the booth so you can catch the opening of the show. We'll switch at intermission and trade places. Next time, you'll do the same for me."

Florence hesitated for a moment, grateful but surprised.

"Now hurry!" Helen added with a playful shove. "You don't want to miss the best part."

Florence hurried to the back office, her cash box heavy with the evening's receipts, the largest she'd handled since starting. Her heart thudded with excitement, not just from the rush of a successful night, but from the anticipation of seeing the film that had drawn such a crowd. After turning in her numbers, she made her way quickly but quietly up the narrow back stairs that led to the upper viewing gallery reserved for staff.

She entered the grand hall just as the final notes of the orchestral prelude echoed off the theater's ornate walls. The soft glow of the music stand lamps illuminated the backs of heads in the orchestra pit below. Then the conductor's baton lowered, the ensemble faded into silence, and one solitary light remained—the warm halo shining down on the organist.

Florence leaned forward, her breath catching in her throat. It was him. The music man.

He adjusted his fingers on the keys and began the film's musical introduction. A rich, sweeping melody filled the air, punctuated with subtle harmonies that made the theater feel enchanted. As the first frames of *Beau Brummel* flickered to life on the screen above, Florence was torn between watching the cinematic grandeur unfold and studying the young man who brought it to life with sound.

John Barrymore's striking features appeared in close-up, followed by Mary Astor's ethereal beauty. The romance and regality of the Regency period unfolded in flickering black and white. But Florence found herself glancing back toward the pit, mesmerized by the way the organist's hands moved—fluid, graceful, expressive. She wondered: was he following sheet music? Or was this all his own?

She didn't realize how quickly the time passed. The lights rose slightly for intermission, and she knew it was time to return to her post and relieve Helen.

Navigating the narrow hallways that snaked behind the stage, Florence rounded a corner and stopped abruptly.

He was there.

The music man.

They both paused, surprised to find someone else in the usually quiet employee passageway.

He was close enough now that she could see his face clearly for the first time—sharp eyes, a strong brow, and a shy sort of smile that flickered the moment he noticed her uniform.

He tipped his hat. "You work the box office, don't you?"

Florence nodded, suddenly speechless.

He extended a hand. "I'm William. William Adams. Organist, at least for tonight." His voice had a low, melodic rhythm to it, like the music he played.

Florence hesitated just a moment, then took his hand. "Florence," she said softly. "I've... seen you play. You're very good."

William smiled, his gaze kind. "Thanks. You must've had a busy night."

She nodded again, warmth rising to her cheeks. "It was... a full house."

"Well then, I guess we both had good performances," he said with a grin.

They stood in the quiet hallway, the hum of the crowd returning to their seats just beginning to echo through the walls. Florence wished she didn't have to leave so soon.

"I'd better get back," she said reluctantly.

"Me too," William replied. "But... maybe I'll see you again? After the next show?"

Florence gave the smallest of smiles. "Maybe."

And then, just like in the movies, they each turned in opposite directions, hearts slightly lighter, uncertain where the next scene would lead but hoping, somehow, that they'd share another.

She dashed back to the box office. Her main job now was to answer questions from patrons and make reservations for future shows. She could barely contain her joy for having finally met the music man, William. She hardly heard Helen wishing her good luck with the patrons.

She thought Helen had done her a favor earlier, giving her the second shift in the box office. Little did she know that street life took on a completely different character after dark. Although prohibition had put a stop to alcohol sales there were no fewer drunks stumbling about and getting themselves into trouble. She had to contend with a few of these intoxicated men when they came up to her window. They were unintelligible. Florence had been told to ring a buzzer that got the attention of the guard at the front entrance. She rang it now and he stepped out to handle the unfolding scene.

It was important for the theater to maintain a clean reputation so as not to be considered a bad neighbor to those who already didn't approve. It was becoming obvious why this theater could present a problem to the crowd she'd seen earlier that was disturbed by the big colorful advertisements on the side of the theater.

Florence finished her duties in the box office. As she left for home, William was waiting for her to come out. She was happily surprised when he said, "There's a Horn & Hardart Automat close by. We could get coffee and pie. That is, if you'd like to join me."

She had only passed by one of those places but was eager to know more about William and said, "Yes, I'd like that very much."

William led Florence toward a small table near the tall front windows, the noise of clinking dishes and quiet chatter surrounding them. Florence took a moment to soak in the atmosphere, the gleaming chrome fixtures, the glass-fronted compartments lining the walls, each holding an array of tempting desserts and light fare. It felt modern, alive, and very different from anything she'd known.

"I've never been to an automat before," she admitted, glancing around.

"They're sort of a miracle of efficiency," William said with a half-smile. "Pick what you like, drop a few nickels in, and it's yours. No waiter needed."

She followed him to the wall of food. "It's like a vending pantry," she said with wonder.

He chuckled, inserting a coin and retrieving a slice of cherry pie. "Only better. The pies here are famous."

She selected a lemon meringue, intrigued by its tall cloud of golden-tipped fluff. With pies in hand and hot coffee retrieved from a central urn, they returned to the table and settled in across from one another.

"I've been meaning to ask," she began, her voice a little unsure but eager, "the music you played tonight... was it written for the film, or do you make it up as you go?"

William's expression brightened. "Some is pre-scored, but honestly, I improvise quite a bit. Especially when I've seen the film a few times. I like to match the mood of the moment. Each audience is different, and that changes how I play."

Florence's eyes lit up. "That's incredible. I could never do that."

"I bet you could," he replied gently. "Music's just another language. You've got a keen ear. I could tell from the way you watched. You hear more than most."

She looked down at her coffee, a smile playing on her lips.

Florence looked up, surprised. "You noticed me?"

He smiled. "Hard not to."

The moment lingered between them, sweet and uncertain. Florence felt the warm stirring of something new, something she hadn't allowed herself to imagine before.

She picked up her fork. "Well then," she said softly, "here's to noticing."

William raised his coffee cup. "To noticing."

The automat was beginning to grow quiet as the crowds of people dispersed and faded away. They too decided it was time to make their way home. In conversation they discovered they lived near one another and would take the same trolley to and from the city for work. Florence hadn't let on that she had seen him the week before riding it home to the same station.

They made their way to the trolley station. William brushed his hand against Florence's and took hold of it to cross the street together. His hand was warm in her cooler grip, and it felt comforting. She felt safe with him walking her at this late hour toward the station. It was a good thing they left when they did as they caught the final trolley of the day. Perhaps he was aware of this as she had not been out this late before.

They talked the whole way. When they arrived at Florence's stop, William insisted on walking Florence home through the darkened streets. He took her hand in his again and they made their way to her house. The two of them turned and looked into each other's eyes to say goodnight. Florence felt something for the first time ever, and she was drawn to lean up to him. But she stopped herself. He too felt the same urge and paused, taking a deep breath to take in the heady feeling. William asked, "I'd like to see you again, perhaps you would like that too?"

Florence immediately responded, "I would like that very much." She dashed around the side of her house to the back door while William watched her disappear.

She couldn't wait to share with her mother the wonderful news of the day. She wondered what she might think of it all. The hour was late, and she would not disturb her mother, tiptoeing in the door. She planned to wake up early to have breakfast with Estella and fill her in on the evening at work and afterwards with William. She had to work an early shift, which would be difficult after this late night.

William made his way back toward the trolley station and on toward home. He was renting a room from his uncle and aunt while attending the Philadelphia Conservatory of Music—a dream he was determined to make his own. Mornings were spent at the conservatory; afternoons and evenings, he worked to cover his expenses.

His Uncle Luther, who owned a nearby grocery store, was generous and often away tending to the business. It was his Aunt Mae, who had first encouraged him to pursue music. A teacher herself, she taught piano lessons in the city and had a deep appreciation for the arts. Though they had no children of their own, they had opened their home—and their hearts—to William.

William had grown up near the state capital, in the quiet river town of Marysville, nestled along the Susquehanna. His musical training was rooted in classical piano, following a rigorous curriculum modeled after European traditions—one that gave him a strong foundation to perform nearly any piece with ease and expression.

At the conservatory, his studies extended beyond the piano to include instruction in voice, theory, harmony, and musical literature, as well as various instruments. This broad and immersive education had made him an ideal fit for the movie palace where he now worked. There, he had mastered the pipe organ, embracing its complexities with the same passion that had guided him since childhood. His ability to improvise on the spot—an art in itself—set him apart.

He thrived in symphonic ensembles, his playing both disciplined and alive. Music wasn't just a part of his life—it was the very shape of it.

He still remembered the first time he sat at a real piano. He was seven, visiting his Aunt Mae—the one who would later become his greatest champion. She had invited him to press a few keys on the upright in her sitting room, a honey-colored instrument bathed in sunlight from the tall window beside it. When his small fingers stumbled through a scale, she didn't laugh—she smiled, pulled up a second stool, and played the same scale beside him, slow and steady.

From that afternoon on, Mae never let his curiosity go to waste. She found sheet music at church rummage sales, tucked away coins for lessons when his parents couldn't afford them, and eventually invited him to live with her and Uncle Luther in the city so he could attend the conservatory.

Without Mae, none of it would have happened. She didn't just open her home to him—she opened a future.

He couldn't imagine a world without music. It had always been the truest part of him.

WILLIAM AND FLORENCE
Courtship | Philadelphia | Summer 1924

The hot, steamy days of summer stirred Florence's longing for the flower gardens she once tended on the farm. She shared her love of plants with William, just as he shared his world of music with her. Together, they visited many of the city's public gardens, often spending hours or entire days strolling the grounds and enjoying picnic lunches. William's uncle, ever generous, allowed him to fill a basket with special treats from his grocery store—delicacies not easily found elsewhere in Philadelphia.

Lately, Florence had been reading a *Better Homes & Gardens* magazine and was especially curious about one place in particular: Bartram's Garden. Founded by John Bartram in 1728, it was the oldest surviving botanical garden in the United States, celebrated for its diverse collection of North American plant species. After years of changing ownership and neglect, the Fairmount Park Commission had taken control of the property. News of its restoration thrilled Florence, especially the announcement that the gardens and historic buildings were now open for public enjoyment. More than once, she had told William she dreamed of spending a day there with him.

On his next day off, William arranged to go into the city early to help his uncle with a faulty cooler in the store. They rode the trolley together, and during the ride, William asked, "I'm planning an outing with Florence and wanted to pick up a few things for a picnic..."

His uncle, Luther, waved off the question mid-sentence. "Of course. You don't ever need to ask, but I appreciate you doing so. Just help yourself and I'll tally it later."

William thanked him, knowing the bill would be modest. He often helped around the store with repairs—he had a knack for figuring things out—and Uncle Luther had come to depend on him. It saved money on outside labor, and William never asked for more than what was fair. He had long since earned his uncle's trust.

After unlocking the storefront, Uncle Luther headed to the register while William walked straight through to the back of the store, into the storage area, and out to the alley where the cooler sat humming unevenly. It didn't take long to pinpoint the issue and make the necessary adjustments. When he returned to the front, he let his uncle know the cooler was up and running.

"Thanks a lot," Luther said, clearly relieved. "I knew you'd get it sorted. Now go on—fill your bags for that picnic with Florence."

William got to work selecting the perfect items. He picked out fresh fruit, a few tempting sweets, a bundle of celery, and a section of roasted chicken. He grabbed a small bag of pretzels too—Florence's favorite. He wrapped up day-old bread that would still be delicious once toasted. Then, with a smile, he remembered her fondness for the new club sandwich trend and made a mental note to replicate it for their outing.

He wrote up his items on a scrap of paper, leaving a makeshift "IOU" beside the register for his uncle to sort out later. Then, eager to get home and start preparations, he stepped back out into the summer air.

On his way to the trolley stop, a young mother caught his attention.

She looked weary, her brow furrowed, with two small children clinging to her skirts. "Any spare change?" she asked softly.

William instinctively reached into his pockets but came up with only a few pennies. "I'm sorry," he said as he handed them over. Then, almost without thinking, he reached into one of the bags and pulled out the sweet treats he had chosen for the picnic. He handed them to her without a word, just a gentle smile.

She looked up at him, her eyes wide with gratitude. She said nothing, but her expression said everything. William tipped his hat and hurried on. Her face stayed with him as he walked. Since hearing Florence's story, and Estella's struggle to keep her children, moments like this carried deeper meaning.

Back home, William wasted no time assembling the picnic basket. He toasted the bread, trimmed off the crusts, saving them for the birds and koi fish, and layered bacon, tomato, sliced chicken breast, and lettuce. A light spread of butter and a dollop of mayonnaise brought it all together. He cut the sandwiches into tidy triangles and arranged everything neatly in the basket.

Then, from his nightstand, he retrieved a small, carefully wrapped package and slipped it into his jacket pocket. Everything was ready. With the basket in hand, he stepped out into the fresh, sunlit day and made his way to the trolley station. Rounding the corner, he spotted Florence approaching from the other direction—graceful and stylish as ever. He waved, and she smiled back, their excitement for the day already written on their faces.

Florence had looked forward to this day for weeks. Now, standing with William at the entrance of the historic treasure that was Bartram's Garden, she could hardly contain her excitement. She began to share with him some of the fascinating facts she'd recently read.

"In 1765," she told him, "John Bartram was appointed by King George III as the 'King's Botanist' for North America. He identified and introduced more than two hundred native plants into cultivation and supplied seeds and specimens to horticultural enthusiasts across England and Europe. Even George Washington ordered seeds from him for Mount Vernon."

William listened as she spoke with genuine admiration for the self-taught botanist. Once left in disrepair, the gardens had recently been restored by an organization determined to preserve Bartram's legacy and open the grounds for the public to enjoy again.

They passed through the gate on Lindbergh Boulevard and followed a winding path that led them into an open meadow. A stunning palette of wildflowers stretched before them, reaching eagerly toward the afternoon sun. Florence imagined how the meadow must have looked earlier that morning, still cloaked in mist.

William slowed his pace and asked, "Would you like to spread our picnic here?"

"Yes," Florence replied, "this is perfect. Let me help."

She unfurled the blanket into the breeze, letting it float gently to the grass. Together, they unpacked the basket. When Florence spotted the neatly cut triangle sandwiches, she smiled in delight—he had remembered her fondness for the club sandwich she'd once described.

They ate quietly, savoring the meal and the moment. Birds flitted among the wildflowers, and a lone wood thrush appeared from the tree line, observing them cautiously from the edge of the forest.

William grew thoughtful, and Florence noticed the change. "Are you feeling well?" she asked.

He nodded and replied, "Yes, just thinking about school starting up again next month."

"This will be your final term at the conservatory, right? Do you think they'll offer you a position?"

William paused, considering. "It's hard to say. The theater keeps me busy, and they've hinted at a projectionist position. It pays more, but I'd miss being at the center of the music."

They finished the last bites of their lunch, and William glanced toward the woods. "Shall we take a walk down the path to the river?"

Florence's face lit up. "Yes, let's do that. Please."

They crossed the meadow of wildflowers, following the edge of the woods where they had earlier spotted the light brown wood thrush. Now there were two—likely a pair guarding a hidden nest nearby. As they stepped onto the forest path, another bird flitted anxiously along the tree line, stirred by their presence. The winding trail led them deeper into the trees until it opened at last to a quiet bend in the Schuylkill River.

There, set into the bedrock at the river's edge, was a large, circular stone carving—weathered, mysterious, and slightly tilted toward the water. It resembled a massive stone wheel with an opening at one end and a hollowed-out center. Curious, they stepped up onto it together, the stone warm beneath their feet from the midday sun.

William gently took Florence's hand and looked out across the river. With his free hand, he reached into his jacket pocket and pulled out the small package he had hidden there. Turning to face her, his eyes steady, he said softly, "Florence, will you be my wife?"

She stared at him in wide-eyed wonder, her heart bursting. "I'd love to be your wife, William!" she beamed.

They embraced and shared a long, tender kiss—one so deep and still it seemed the whole world had fallen away. For that brief, perfect moment, time stopped. It was just the two of them, standing together on that ancient stone by the water, suspended in joy.

William opened the small box and revealed a posy ring: a slender band of gold engraved on the inside with the words "You have my heart."

He had planned this moment for weeks, even asking Estella for her blessing beforehand. Everyone had known he intended to propose—everyone except Florence. They just hadn't known when, where, or how he would do it. He had wanted the moment to be hers to discover.

Overwhelmed with happiness, Florence barely heard his next words: "We will build a beautiful life and family together. I promise to protect and care for you, always. Shall we?"

He helped her step down from the carved stone, which still held their curiosity. As they walked back along the path through the woods, they speculated about its origin. They both guessed it had once been a cider press—and later that afternoon, a docent at Bartram's stone house confirmed it: the press had likely been carved by John Bartram himself, measuring an impressive twenty-five feet in circumference.

Still caught in their private world, Florence and William wandered the garden paths, hand in hand, dreaming aloud of the life they would build. William hadn't been sure exactly how the moment would unfold—but when they stepped onto that ancient stone, he knew. It felt like the foundation of something lasting. A quiet monument to love, hidden in the green heart of the city, just waiting to bear witness to their promise.

EPILOGUE

The autumn of 1924 marked a new chapter for Florence and William, who were married in September. They moved into a small, rented apartment owned by William's uncle, eager to begin their life together. Just two years earlier, Florence had spent many nights wondering about her future—who she might marry, whether she would ever reconnect with her true family. Now, all she had once longed for had come to pass. It was almost too much to process at times. When it overwhelmed her, she would busy herself with work or some new task to steady her thoughts.

She missed the farm and gardens of Lancaster County. That life, so steeped in rhythm and quiet beauty, had shaped her in deep and lasting ways. It would always be a part of her.

Florence had written several letters to Mamm and Daed Blank, hoping to keep a connection with the family who had raised her with love and devotion. Only one letter came back, from Mamm Sara. Florence had hoped for more. The Blanks had left an indelible mark on her values and beliefs, so different from her Philadelphia relatives in many ways, yet similar in their dedication to family and in their quiet generosity. Still, Florence understood they would likely not approve of the choices she had made as a young woman living in a bustling, modern city. She was growing fluent in a new way of life—the one she had been born into, then lost, and was now learning to embrace.

One afternoon, a package arrived in the mail: a small, handwritten recipe book from Mamm Sara. Its pages were smudged and stained, familiar in the most comforting way. These were the recipes she and her Mamm had used together countless times. As she turned the pages, Florence felt a pang of sorrow and gratitude rise in her chest. She held the book in her lap like a sacred artifact, her hands trembling slightly.

A folded note slipped from between the pages. In it, Mamm Sara had written to wish Florence a good and joyful marriage, and a home filled with many children—God's most treasured gifts, she had once said, and the only things we can take with us to heaven. Florence pressed the letter gently back into the book and let her fingers trail across the aged pages. There were her favorites: pickled eggs, Sunday meatloaf, shoofly pie, peach pie, berry muffins topped with brown sugar streusel, and the daily bread Mamm had made every morning of her life.

It was more than a book, it was a bridge between two worlds, and a reminder that love, once given, never truly leaves us.

Amid the roar of the 1920s, a woman unlike any other emerged, shaped by upheaval, uncertainty, and the enduring love of two very different families. Florence developed a taste for the fashions and freedoms of the modern flapper, yet it was tempered by the quiet humility and grace instilled in her from childhood. It was as though she lived between two worlds—distinct and often in conflict—yet she moved through both with astonishing poise. She did not reject either; instead, she wove them together, carefully, to create a life of her own design.

At her side was William, steadfast and encouraging, never judgmental, never critical. He championed her curiosity, inspiring her to pursue music, literature, and all the things she had once been denied. Together they cultivated a life of discovery—a garden neither of them could have dreamed alone. Out of the ashes of Florence's fractured past, William became her anchor. From that unlikely ground, something rare and exquisite began to bloom.

Florence immersed herself in the era's literature and shared it with William. Their curiosity led them beyond the page of Fitzgerald's "The Great Gatsby", and into the speakeasies and jazz clubs that whispered of rebellion and glamor. There, tucked behind hidden doors and velvet curtains, they tasted the intoxicating spirit of the age—both literal and figurative. It was a world far removed from Florence's upbringing, one that startled her, challenged her, and made her even more grateful for her roots.

In these shared joys and new experiences, Florence and William uncovered layers of themselves they had yet to understand. Like forest paths winding through uncharted terrain, they followed each one with wonder. Through books, music, art, and each other, they built a life rooted in mutual respect, exploration, and enduring love.

Florence was not the only one forging a new beginning.

Estella and Stephen were finally married in the spring of 1925, in a quiet ceremony attended by close friends and family. There were no fanfares, no announcements in the paper—just two people who had walked through fire and chosen, at last, to walk the rest of the way together. Estella had waited many years for her children to be safe, to be home, to be settled in lives of their own before allowing herself this new beginning.

Stephen had long been a presence in their world—a steady, kindhearted man who had quietly stepped into the spaces others had abandoned. To her children, he had already been like a father. And to Estella, he had been a companion in grief and in rebuilding, a man who never pushed, but always remained.

Their marriage was less a turning point than a gentle continuation of something already deeply rooted. Together, they shared a home filled with hard-won peace and the kind of love that asks for nothing but gives everything in return.

John, Florence's older brother, found his rhythm and purpose working for the Pennsylvania Railroad. His quiet nature made him dependable, and over time he earned the respect of his peers and supervisors alike. He remained loyal to his family and kept in regular contact with Florence, whose return had knitted their long-fractured family closer together.

As for Jeff and Frances, their love, which had first blossomed in the quiet corridors of the courthouse and over shared files and whispered hopes, grew into a partnership both personal and profound. After their wedding in August 1922, the couple began working toward a cause born out of their own painful family histories. Together, they established *The Florence Foundation*, named not for vanity but for victory—for every child separated from their kin, for every mother left unheard. The organization offered legal support to families fractured by well-meaning but misguided systems, advocating for reform, reunification, and above all, dignity.

What began as a personal search became a public mission, and the work Jeff and Frances pioneered would go on to help hundreds of families find their way back to one another.

Though the world around them roared with change—from war to jazz to the humming energy of a new age—it was these quiet triumphs that mattered most: a mother reunited with her daughter, a sister rediscovered, a family rebuilt not in its old image, but in a new, hard-won shape.

In the years to come, Florence would often return to that little recipe book from Mamm Sara, and to the memory of Estella humming at the stove, of Frances's steady hand, and of the garden she and William would one day grow.

Because no matter how far she traveled from where she began, she was never far from the roots that held her.

And from those roots, a legacy bloomed. A legacy of a woman her family would come to know—nearly a century later—as *The Philadelphia Matriarch*.

***

A tribute expressed in poetry through the eyes and heart of her granddaughter:

My Nana

by Beth Brubaker

Beloved lady whose presence is never so far away,
Often we catch a glimpse of you each passing day.
Whether in the beautiful garden where the flowers thrive,
Or high above gliding upon butterfly wings thou strive.
Her ethereal fragrance lingers beyond the rose bouquet,
Brought back to life in the glimmer of a morning sun ray.
Her endless love goes beyond sheer magnificence,
And for a moment we see her true significance.
Beloved and cherished for her tender loving heart,
You gave joyously the treasures that shall never part.
A kind encourager filled with a beacon of streaming light,
Shone warmth and love in abundance before she took flight.
Vulnerable no more she rests in the arms of all eternity,
Awaiting patiently in the realm of all earthly modernity.
Kind lady shall always be in our hearts and near,
Still loved, still missed for all she held dear.

***

What was taken from Florence could never be undone—but what she gave in return became her legacy. And the best is yet to come. *The Matriarch's Legacy*.

About the Author

Beth Brubaker is a former educator and figure skating coach who now turns her attention to the written word, where memory and imagination meet. *The Philadelphia Matriarch* is her debut historical novel, drawn from the quiet courage and untold stories within her own family's past. She is also the author of *A Leap of Faith*, a reflective memoir on perseverance, purpose, and the bonds that shape us. With a heart for stories steeped in resilience and hope, Beth writes from her home in Fernandina Beach, Florida, where she lives with her husband, Scott. They have two grown children. When not writing, she finds joy in book club conversations, ocean breezes, and the loyal companionship of their dogs. She is currently at work on the sequel to *The Philadelphia Matriarch*.

Read more at https://www.bethbrubaker.net/.

www.ingramcontent.com/pod-product-compliance
Lightning Source LLC
Chambersburg PA
CBHW020537020726
47494CB00006B/1801